SHW

Making It Up

Also by Penelope Lively
in Large Print:

Judgment Day
The Road to Lichfield
Moon Tiger
Perfect Happiness

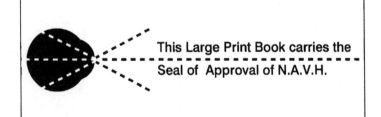

Making It Up

Penelope
Lively

Published in 2006 by arrangement with Viking Penguin, a member of Penguin Group (USA) Inc.

Wheeler Large Print Hardcover.

The text of this Large Print edition is unabridged.
Other aspects of the book may vary from the original edition.

Set in 16 pt. Plantin.

Printed in the United States on permanent paper.

Library of Congress Cataloging-in-Publication Data

Lively, Penelope, 1933–
    Making it up / by Penelope Lively.
        p. cm.
    ISBN 1-59722-140-6 (lg. print : hc : alk. paper)
    1. Girls — Fiction. 2. Egypt — Fiction. 3. British —
Egypt — Fiction. 4. World War, 1939–1945 — Egypt —
Fiction. 5. Large type books. I. Title.
PR6062.I89M34 2005b
    823′.914—dc22   2005025940

To Lawrence and Helen

As the Founder/CEO of NAVH, the only national health agency solely devoted to those who, although not totally blind, have an eye disease which could lead to serious visual impairment, I am pleased to recognize Thorndike Press* as one of the leading publishers in the large print field.

Founded in 1954 in San Francisco to prepare large print textbooks for partially seeing children, NAVH became the pioneer and standard setting agency in the preparation of large type.

Today, those publishers who meet our standards carry the prestigious "Seal of Approval" indicating high quality large print. We are delighted that Thorndike Press is one of the publishers whose titles meet these standards. We are also pleased to recognize the significant contribution Thorndike Press is making in this important and growing field.

Lorraine H. Marchi, L.H.D.
Founder/CEO
NAVH

* Thorndike Press encompasses the following imprints: Thorndike, Wheeler, Walker and Large Print Press.

Contents

Preface   9

The Mozambique Channel   13

The Albert Hall   73

The Temple of Mithras   111

The Battle of the Imjin River   167

Transatlantic   197

Comet   239

Number Twelve Sheep Street   296

Penelope   335

Preface

When I was very young I made up stories — the refuge of an isolated and frequently bored child. These were fables that I told to myself — long satisfying narratives that passed the time and spiced up otherwise uneventful days. For this was how life seemed to me, growing up in Egypt in the early 1940s — the Libyan campaign ebbing and flowing across the desert, the Middle East seething with its nascent conflicts. With the wisdoms of today, I see that I was living in interesting times, but a seven-, eight-, or nine-year-old has strictly personal horizons, and my idea of a spot of drama came from my reading — from Greek mythology, from *The Arabian Nights*. My internal narratives featured gods and goddesses, heroes, mythical figures, magicians and princesses. And, of course, myself — out there in the thick of it, with a starring role. And now, at the other end of life, storytelling is an ingrained habit; I wouldn't know what else to do. But the mythology that is intriguing today is that of

9

imagined alternatives. Somehow, choice and contingency have landed you where you are, as the person that you are, and the whole process seems so precarious that you look back at those climactic moments when things might have gone entirely differently, when life might have spun off in some other direction, and wonder at this apparently arbitrary outcome.

Novelists have absolute control over their material — what to put in, what to leave out, how people are to behave, what is to happen. That, of course, is also the problem with writing fiction, and accounts for much, from writer's block (which means simply that you don't know where to go next) to individual shortcomings. But the writer is able to impose order upon chaos, to impose a pattern. Real life is quite out of control; you have been a straw in the current, it seems, snagged up against a rock, hurtling down a rapid, not quite sucked into a whirlpool.

This book is fiction. If anything, it is an anti-memoir. My own life serves as the prompt; I have homed in upon the rocks, the rapids, the whirlpools, and written the alternative stories. It is a form of con-fabulation. That word has a precise meaning: in psychiatric terminology, it refers to the creation of imaginary remembered experiences which replace the gaps left by disorders of the memory. My memory is not yet disordered; this exercise in confabulation is a piece of fictional license.

The Mozambique Channel

My childhood was spent in a garden. This garden was in Egypt, a few miles outside Cairo, but its furnishings were English — ponds and pergolas and rose beds. There were majestic eucalyptus trees, with which I communed — children are natural animists. Beyond the garden were fields of sugar-cane, mud villages, palm trees, donkeys, and camels — the familiar trappings of my world. I had been born in Egypt and knew nowhere else; England was a vague memory of a cold, damp place visited when I was very young. And on the outer rim of this known landscape was the desert, to which we went for picnics, though not just now because it was out of bounds. It was full of soldiers, and battles were being fought there. I accepted this distant unrest as a normal procedure and in any case it was nothing to do with me, busy with my fantasy life beneath the eucalyptus trees. Except that it was, of course.

In the spring of 1941 the German

*advance across Libya brought Rommel's
army to Sollum, on the western edge of
Egypt. The British garrison at Tobruk was
encircled. A British offensive at the end of
the year had Rommel in retreat, but in
June 1942 his Panzer divisions came
surging on again. Tobruk was taken. The
Eighth Army fell back, and the Germans
entered Egypt. They halted at El Alamein,
a mere seventy miles from Alexandria.*

*Everything pointed to a German assault
on Cairo. An aerial invasion was anticipated, along with widespread bombing of
the city. These were the days of "the
Flap," when the burning of the files at the
British Embassy and GHQ sent charred
paper raining down onto the streets, the
banks were besieged, and the railway station was packed with those seeking flight.
The wives and children of military personnel had been evacuated the previous
year, but British residents had stayed put,
for the most part. Now, there was a serious
exodus. Family parties headed in different
directions — the civilian expatriate families
whose men worked for Shell and the other
oil companies, the appendages of the
engineers, the bureaucrats, the government
administrators, the Embassy and Consulate
staff, the bankers like my father, who*

*worked for the National Bank of Egypt.
Many went to Palestine, as it then was;
others to Kenya, Tanganyika, Aden. And
those who could get a passage boarded
ships bound for South Africa. Cape Town
was said to be delightful.*

She stood on the promenade deck, up
against the rails, looking down at the water
and quayside, keeping a careful hold on
Jean. The rails had streaks of orange rust
and she didn't want Jean's frock stained,
clean on today, so she wouldn't let her hang
over the top rung like some of the children
were doing. There were native boys lined
up on the quayside who would dive for
piastres — they gesticulated and pointed
and someone on the ship would throw a
ten-piastre piece up in the air, and down it
would go, flicking the water, and the boy
would already have flung himself after it
and time and again they'd surface,
clutching the money.

There were people still coming on board.
She could see the Stannards making their
way up the gangplank, with that Irish
nanny holding the baby who was yelling
his head off, and Mrs. Stannard shouting
at the porters. One of them had just
dropped a hat box. Thank goodness for

15

having got on board early; she had already unpacked their things and Mrs. Leech was off at the Purser's office trying to get them changed from second sitting to first for lunch.

Suez. She'd never been to Suez before. Port Said, lots of times. Ismailia. Qantara. Never Suez.

She was Shirley Manners, of Pinner, but no one called her Shirley now. She was Nanny. Or she was Film Star; that was what the other nannies called her because she was pretty. She wished they wouldn't; it embarrassed her, but they meant it kindly, just a joke. It didn't suit her, either, as a nickname; she wasn't that type. On her afternoons off she wore lipstick, never at other times. And she saved her only pair of silk stockings for then, and her two good frocks that she'd made herself — seersucker from Cicurel. Ordinary days she always wore the same — gray or navy shirtwaists with a gray or navy cardigan in winter. The gray serge suit for Sundays if they went to the cathedral. And a hat, gray or navy felt with a matching petersham ribbon.

One thing was already clear, this wasn't going to be like P&O or Bibby Line before the war. There weren't the white-jacketed stewards, and the ranks of deck chairs with rugs, and the nice cabins. This was a troop ship. She had brought soldiers and military supplies out from England, right round by the Cape, weeks at sea, and now she was going back for more, and dropping several hundred women and children off at Durban and Cape Town on the way. So the men in white jackets weren't stewards but naval officers, who were running the ship, and Mrs. Leech was already saying they were absolutely sweet. And there were no deck chairs but notices everywhere about Lifeboat Stations, and the cabins were very basic and not enough room. Four bunks, and they'd got a retired teacher from the English School in with them, a bit of an old prune-face, to be honest. Mrs. Leech didn't reckon much with that; she was going to have a quiet word with the Purser and see if there couldn't be some other arrangement for her.

They were saying there'd be a big battle soon, in the desert. They were saying Rommel would push through to Alex. It wouldn't happen, she was sure of that. So was Mrs. Leech, so were most people. It was all just a flap; in a few weeks or months they'd be back, and all this up-heaval for nothing, except that actually she didn't half mind seeing South Africa, they said it was so different from Egypt, and Cape Town quite English really. Mrs. Leech didn't mind either, though she kept going on about how beastly it was having to leave Reggie behind. The Consulate staff were staying, of course, and the Embassy, and the other men, come to that — the government advisers and the Shell people and the Bank people. It was just women and children being shipped off. Lots of families had preferred to go to Palestine, but Mrs. Leech had been there several times, and never to the Cape.

The deck was packed. There were people who'd come to say goodbye — the loudspeakers were calling for them to go ashore now — and natives selling oranges and mangoes and peanuts and pistachio nuts and everyone milling around meeting up with friends. That was what Mrs. Leech would be doing too, down at the Purser's office. She was already fussing about who they'd get on their table.

Shirley didn't really like Mrs. Leech. Mr. Leech was all right, but she didn't see so much of him, so that was neither here nor there. Jean was a dear little girl, good as gold, which was why Shirley stayed: she loved Jean. Oh, she could have got another job with a snap of her fingers, anytime she liked, and Mrs. Leech knew that. People were crying out for English nannies; the rich foreign families would pay the earth, and some girls took advantage. But it wouldn't be her cup of tea, no thank you; she'd rather an English family frankly. Not that she couldn't have taken her pick there too. Lady Clayton had come over and talked to her for ages at Billy Clayton's birthday party, too nice and friendly for words, and Shirley had a pretty good idea what that was all about. So Mrs. Leech knew that if she overstepped the mark, Shirley would be liable to pack her bags, which was the last thing Mrs. Leech wanted. She would be seeing to Jean herself until she could find someone else, and then probably she'd have to settle for one of those Armenian girls who let the children run wild and hadn't a clue about table manners.

This meant Mrs. Leech had to be as nice as she possibly could, which was quite an effort for her. And she couldn't criticize, because she didn't know the first thing about children and didn't want to. Shirley had once heard her say to a friend that it took a particular mentality to look after children; you knew exactly what was implied by that.

All right, Shirley had thought, but if you're so jolly superior then you can leave me in peace to get on with what I do. No interference in the nursery — that was the rule, and Mrs. Leech knew it all right.

Shirley had had Jean from six months. From birth is best, of course; before Shirley there had been a Swiss nurse, and Shirley sometimes felt that she'd left some faint, unwelcome imprint. But Jean was her creation, through and through — obedient, lovely manners, and of course always beautifully turned out. Shirley made most of Jean's clothes herself: cotton frocks with ric-rac round the sleeves and hems, and silk smocks for parties. She was a good needlewoman, and that made her smugly pleased; some of the other nannies were hopeless. From time to time Mrs. Leech would come humbly with a hem to be taken up, or a zip to be replaced; she couldn't sew for toffee.

Jean loved Shirley more than she loved her mother. If she hurt herself, it was to Shirley that she ran; on Shirley's evening out, she cried herself to sleep. Mrs. Leech must have been aware that things were so, but there was no indication that this bothered her. Presumably she saw it as the price you pay, which of course it was. Personally,

Shirley couldn't imagine handing your child over to someone else like that, but then she couldn't actually imagine having a child of her own anyway. She couldn't imagine getting married, not that there weren't men who showed an interest, now and then.

The Buchan nanny had up and married a Lebanese last year. Goodness knows how she met him — you didn't get Lebanese coming to the YWCA, for heaven's sake. They said it was probably on the beach in Alex, Sidi Bishr, he must have come up and talked and one thing led to another. She'd always been a bit of an odd girl, and none of them saw her anymore now. Apparently she'd had a little boy, and of course he'd be half Lebanese. Shirley knew she couldn't take that, personally, but each to his own.

There was a naval officer coming round now, chivvying the orange sellers off the ship and asking visitors to go ashore. He gave Shirley a smile and said Suez was quite a place, wasn't it? So she smiled back and agreed.

Actually, she wouldn't be sorry to see the back of Suez. It was jam-packed with the Army, trucks and stuff everywhere, the gharries could hardly get through, they'd

21

had a fine old time trying to get the luggage down to the quayside. The gharry driver had wanted some ridiculous price, and when the porters turned up there was a trunk missing and Mrs. Leech was getting in a proper state until they discovered it had been left at the guest house. They'd had to spend last night somewhere after the train journey from Cairo, and all the good pensions were booked up, so Mrs. Leech was forced to take a room at this tatty place, Greek-run, horrible food, and the sheets were none too clean. There'd been no hot water for baths, and Shirley didn't dare let Jean touch the milk. There was a prewar poster for Thomas Cook stuck up in the entrance hall: "Going Home? Save Time, Money and Worry by booking at Cook's. They will ship, forward or insure all baggage, furniture . . . even Polo Ponies, at the best rates. . . ." Well, nobody was going home now, that was for sure, not for the duration anyway.

Shirley couldn't remember England very well. At least, it wasn't so much that she couldn't remember it as that she could no longer imagine being there. The place was in her head still, a series of sharp images: a blowy Cornish beach, the brown moquette suite in her parents' front room, children sailing toy boats on the Round Pond, chestnut trees in flower, glinting wet streets. It was in her bones, too, of course — one was English, and that was that. But somehow a shutter had dropped down between that time and this, so that the norm was now heat, dust, the raucous street life of Cairo, and all those routine accompaniments to living out here. The insistent daily perils of dirt, disease, sun: these dictated a routine that was now second nature, she knew no other way to be.

Everyone out here got ill at some point — malaria, dysentery, typhoid, sandfly fever — and lesser afflictions waited to pounce on a daily basis. You never went anywhere without the iodine and the mercurochrome — every cut or graze or insect bite was likely to turn nasty, surging into a ripe infected wound within hours. Children were forever being daubed with yellow iodine and scarlet blotches of mercurochrome. You couldn't trust the water, let alone the milk. Shirley saw to it that Jean never drank anything that hadn't been boiled. She had her own little meths stove in the nursery and insisted that the milk was sent straight up to her. And of course you slept under a mosquito net and were strict about hand washing and no fingers in mouths. Even so, Jean had had scarlet fever and a bout of impetigo, and of course endless tummy upsets and styes and boils. Shirley was good with boils. She could do hot poultices, draw the thing gradually day by day until it was ready to burst, and then you squeezed firmly and the pus came oozing out, a yellow worm. Mrs. Leech had had to come to her once when she had one on her behind. Sometimes when Shirley saw her done up to the nines to go out to some do, all lipstick and scent and low-cut frock, she would get a picture of Mrs. Leech facedown on the bed, with her bare white bottom and the angry red hillock of the boil.

And then there was the sun, the remorseless battery of the heat. Sun hats, Nivea cream, trying to keep children in the shade. They all got sunburn and prickly heat. But that too had become normal, the way of the world; she could not now conjure up cool English weather, or rain. It was as though all that had slipped away, an unreal and unreachable place, much like the time that was equally unattainable: before the war.

Before the war, they went to England every summer. Long summers of rented houses in Cornwall or Devon, and spells in London, and visits to the Leeches' relatives. Shirley saw her parents quite a bit, and her sisters. But even then she had begun to feel a bit strange with her family. Distanced. She no longer talked like them, she knew that. Her parents and her sisters had the voice of suburban London, they had what Mrs. Leech called "an accent." Shirley's had gone, all but. She spoke like her employers and their friends. Her family's speech sounded unfamiliar now, and bothered her in some disturbing way, as did the speech of servicemen she met on her days off, at the YWCA, at whist drives there and tea dances. She was no longer used to that speech, she had been for years among those other voices, those of the Leeches and before them the Arlingtons, who were grander, actually, titled, and who had a huge house in Belgravia, and all the children's clothes from Harrods, dozens of smocked dresses and little tweed coats. Shirley had been the nursery maid then, and Nanny Collins was a dragon, which was partly why she had left, but also she had thought it would be exciting to travel, so when she saw Mrs. Leech's advertisement in *The Lady* she had written off at once: "Cairo. Summers in England. Large house and garden in best residential district. One six-month-old baby girl."

The parameters of her life were now the house in Zamalek, the Gezira Sporting Club to which she walked with Jean most afternoons, and the YWCA on her afternoon off. In the summers now they went to Alex, except for this year — this year was different, the Germans had put the kibosh on Alex for this year. And she hadn't had her afternoon off for the last three weeks, what with the packing up and Mrs. Leech running round like a scalded cat getting the train reservation and visas and stocking up with all the things they'd need on the ship.

Well, Shirley would make up for it in Cape Town, by all accounts. There was a YW there, people said, and lovely cinemas, better than the Cairo ones. She often went to the Kasr el Aini cinema with a bunch of other nannies; they'd seen all the Deanna Durbin films and *Gone With the Wind* and they never missed a Bob Hope, but it was a bit of a flea pit; you always felt you might pick something up. In Cape Town they didn't let the natives in, apparently.

Everyone was on board now who should be, and everyone off who shouldn't, and the gangplank was being taken up, so there wasn't anything much to watch on deck. She took Jean down below for a wash and found Mrs. Leech fussing that there wasn't anywhere to hang her frocks. She was moving out of their cabin. She'd got round the Purser and wangled a two-berth cabin that she was going to share with Mrs. Clavering. The Clavering nanny and Jamie were going to come in with Shirley and Jean, which would be much better, according to Mrs. Leech, because the nannies could then take it in turns to stay with the children in the evenings, after they were in bed. And of course Mrs. Leech and Mrs. Clavering wouldn't be woken up first thing or in the night, but that was passed over. The Purser was going to find somewhere else for the retired teacher; he was really terribly sweet and helpful, Mrs. Leech said.

Sometime in the night they sailed. Jean woke up early and said, "Everything's moving outside, Nanny," and yes, there was blue water sliding past and you could feel the thump-thump of the ship's engines. Shirley felt a little rush of excitement just as she used to before the war when they sailed from Port Said for home, and you saw the statue of the man who built the Canal, and then the Mediterranean beyond. Actually, the Red Sea looked much the same, except at the moment it was flatter, she could remember the Med tipping up horribly. Up on deck, she could see a long gold-brown line of land, but during the day that disappeared and there was just sea. A great bowl of sea and sky, with them in the middle.

It was funny how quickly you settled down to being on board, as though there'd never been any other kind of life. There was a routine, right from the start. Mealtimes ruled — the bell for eight o'clock breakfast, and then later first- and second-sitting lunches and in the evening children's high tea at six, which included nannies, and dinner for everyone else at seven. After dinner, there was always a bit of a party going on in the bar, and Mrs. Leech was in on that right away, of course, done up in one of her best frocks — oh, she was having a high old time, she'd always loved the trips home and back, prewar, and this might not be P&O but she was making the most of it, all the same. Shirley was much in demand with the mothers who hadn't got nannies, she and Nanny Clavering, to keep an ear out for their children while they were up in the bar, or in the lounge where people played bridge: "Oh Nanny, *would* you be an angel — she's fast asleep, but if you could just have a peep at her every now and then . . ."

So she and Nanny Clavering played box and cox, one staying down with the children while the other had a bit of time off — joining a whist game with some of the NCOs or just sitting on deck where it got nice and cool after dark. Pretty dark, too, what with the blackout so there couldn't be any lights on and you kept falling over things and you weren't supposed to smoke, not that Shirley was a smoker anyway. But it was lovely up there, in the night, with just the sound of the engines and the sea, and when there was a moon you got these great paths of light over the water, rippling away into the distance. There were always quite a few people up there, leaning over the rail — smoking, unless one of the ship's officers was around. Shirley liked to find a place on her own where she could just watch the sea and listen to it and feel the wind on her face. But she never stayed that long; Jean might wake, and while Nanny Clavering was there, of course, it would be Shirley she'd want, and no one else.

The families were all together, at one end of the main deck, in cabins at either side of the long passage. There were bath-rooms in the middle, and you had to queue up, and then it was a saltwater bath you got, so not much joy there. Shirley preferred to stick with the hand basin in the cabin, and give Jean an all-over wash out of that. A terrible run on the toilets, all the time.

At the far end of the accommodation deck there were people who were going home, right the way round the Cape and into the Atlantic — six weeks it would take and they said it would get really rough once you were round the Cape, and there were lots of U-boats in the Atlantic. There was a chance of them off the east coast of Africa, apparently, on the way to Cape Town, which was why there had to be lifeboat drill, and life jackets, and blackout, just in case, but it wasn't nearly as bad as the Atlantic, they said, and nothing like the Mediterranean, which the convoys hadn't been able to use since 1940. Thank goodness they'd be getting off at the Cape; two weeks of this would be quite enough, thank you very much. The ship was jam-packed, you were cheek by jowl all the time, which made the heat even worse, and the food left much to be desired. Powdered milk, and the tea wasn't made with boiling water, you got the leaves floating on top. No, she wouldn't want to be going home, to be honest. And anyway it was pretty wretched there by all accounts, what with rationing and shortages and the Blitz. Shirley's letters from her parents and her sisters were just one long moan.

There was a handful of families who were going home, and some military personnel — a few officers who were being retired or sent back for some reason, and very popular they were with Mrs. Leech and her friends, seeing as how this was such an all-women party. Of course there were the naval officers too — Mrs. Leech and Mrs. Clavering were always having a drink in the bar with one or another of them. And on the lower decks there were the other ranks, who of course didn't count so far as Mrs. Leech was concerned. Actually, there was a medical orderly who was ever so nice; Shirley had got talking to him when he was helping with the organized games they had on deck for the children every morning. He was in charge of some soldiers who were being invalided down to hospitals in the Cape, men who'd lost arms or legs in the desert battles, or been blinded, poor things — horrible, you didn't like to think about it. They were brought up on deck and you saw them lying around and some of the children would go and talk to them — the men seemed to like that. That was how Shirley had met the orderly. He had asked Jean to come over and say hello to this soldier who'd had his foot blown off, and then they chatted a bit, Shirley and the orderly. He'd been in Egypt since 1940, at the military hospital in Cairo, he was an ambulance driver in civilian life, he came from Devon. He had a country sort of voice, but actually Shirley rather liked that. It made her think of holidays by the sea when she was a little girl. He gave Jean a Cadbury's chocolate bar from the NAAFI, which was a real treat, and he told them there'd been flying fish that landed on the deck yesterday, which they'd missed, so he promised to come and find them next time it happened.

Of course, Jean was all eyes, staring at the men with amputated limbs, though goodness knows she was used enough to that sort of thing — plenty of the Cairo street beggars had bits missing, and there were blind people all over the place. It was these being English, and like that. What had happened? Did it hurt? Shirley had had to go a bit carefully. Jean knew about the war, of course, they had a little pray about it every night before she was put to bed: "Please, God, make the war end soon. Amen." But she didn't know about death. A child can't take that in, at six, in Shirley's opinion. So when Mrs. Leech's spaniel died, Jean was just told that it had gone to sleep because it was very old and tired, and the same with Mr. Leech's father, and squashed dogs by the side of the road, and Jean's tortoise when the ants got it. A child that age isn't ready for death.

Goodness, it was hot. She should be used enough to heat by now, for heaven's sake, but the Red Sea was in a class of its own. All around was this glassy smooth water, and the heat seemed to whack back from it, and mostly there wasn't a breath of wind, except in the evenings when this hot breeze would get up. But the cabins were stifling; you lay there dripping all night, you didn't want even a sheet over you, indeed stark naked would have been best, but Shirley didn't fancy that with Nanny Clavering and the children there. Jean had a nasty bout of prickly heat, all red and raw, poor little soul. And up on deck you had to keep slapping on Nivea cream, but even so some of the children were getting dreadfully sunburnt. The crew had rigged up a sort of canvas swimming pool for them to splash around in, and there were endless deck games — quoits and skittles and so forth — so they didn't get too bored and bolshie, on the whole, though some of the bigger boys were starting to run wild a bit. Shirley blamed the mothers, frankly. If she'd had anything to do with it, they'd soon have been under control, she'd always been able to deal with badly behaved children.

In fact, one day she did step in. There were these ten-year-olds pestering one of the lascars. A lot of the crew were lascars — small wiry brown men who did all the donkey work, scrubbing the decks and that — and this one was climbing up the side of the ship doing something to the lifeboats that were slung above the promenade deck. The boys were yelling "Monkey! Monkey!" — the Garrick twins and a couple of others. "Look at the chimp!" they were saying, and Shirley felt herself flare up. I mean, all right, maybe he did look a bit monkey-like, climbing hand over hand, very athletic actually, but that was just plain rude, you don't talk like that to anyone. So she moved in and gave the boys a telling off. She'd thought they might answer back — the Garricks had that Greek girl for a nanny who let them get away with anything — but they just shuffled around and wouldn't look at her and then wandered away.

When she first came to Egypt she'd been shocked by the beggars and the droves of children asking for money — "Baksheesh! Baksheesh!" — and the sheer startling difference from anything she'd ever known. Men hawking and spitting in the street; women up to their elbows in cow muck and straw, making fuel; the babies with flies crawling all over their eyes. How could people live like this? But they did, and after a while you got used to it. You seemed to be shut away on the other side of a glass screen, where things were done in the way that you knew, and out there was their world, in which everything was otherwise, but it was none of your business.

And then she'd been differently shocked by the way people treated the natives. Especially since the troops arrived, at the beginning of the war. Some of them made her feel quite ashamed, the way they'd bawl them out, or take the mickey. You'd see a bunch of drunk tommies in Cairo snatching off a man's red fez, and throwing it under a gharry, or mobbing a woman, trying to get her to take her veil off. That was disgusting. All right, their ways weren't our ways, out here, but that didn't mean you had any right to interfere. She'd always made sure that Jean spoke politely to the servants, and had told her never to stare at them when they were saying their prayers, knees down on a mat in the garden. Not that Mr. and Mrs. Leech wouldn't be particular about that too, Mr. Leech especially; for the Consulate people there were all sorts of dos and don'ts and what Mr. Leech called a code of conduct.

The Garricks were Shell, which might account for the twins' behavior. Shell and the other businesspeople were definitely a peg or two down from the Consulate. Just as the Consulate was a step down from the Embassy. Embassy nannies tended to pull rank; that didn't bother Shirley, but she knew Mrs. Leech felt it when it came to Embassy wives. Still, Consulate meant you were on all the lists, for parties at the Embassy and so forth, and Mrs. Leech could usually get a cabin on Sidi Bishr for the summer, when they went to Alex, and she and Mr. Leech could join the Yacht Club, and got asked to everything, which frankly for Mrs. Leech was the be-all and end-all.

They would be calling in at Aden soon, and that would be the end of the Red Sea, thank goodness; people said it wouldn't be so hot once you were out on the Indian Ocean. Back in Cairo, in the Zamalek house, there was a big map of the world on the wall in Mr. Leech's study; Shirley had sometimes looked at this, pinpointing Cairo up at the top of Africa, with the fan of the Delta reaching up to the Mediterranean. So she had the shape of Africa in her head now, and could see the funnel of the Red Sea, and then the bit called the Horn of Africa sticking out and up, round which they had to go, and then it would be down and down past Africa until at last they got to Cape Town. Quite exciting, really, to think you were going all that way, crawling across the world.

They would be allowed to go ashore while the ship was berthed at Aden. Everyone was looking forward to that. There would be hotels where they could have a decent meal, Mrs. Leech said, and a chance to stock up with the sort of things they would soon run out of — toilet paper, and Nivea, and cigarettes and gin. Oh, and of course they would have to see the mermaid; she and Mrs. Clavering went into fits of laughter about this.

Apparently there was a mermaid in a glass case in one of the Aden hotels. It was famous.

In fact, Aden was a bit of a letdown, Shirley thought, when at last they were tied up at Steamer Point. A scruffy sort of place — the shops nothing to write home about, the hotels not a patch on Cairo or Alex, the streets awash with men selling Turkish delight or dirty postcards. They disembarked with the Claverings, and had to fight their way through the scrum on the quayside — Arabs who were mostly half-naked, and some of them with knives tucked into their waists, pi dogs, beggars, mangy camels that looked like they were about to mow you down. Mrs. Leech had found out which was the hotel with the mermaid and they were going to have lunch there.

Jean was so thrilled with the mermaid. She knew about mermaids; one of her books had a picture of a mermaid sitting on a rock and looking at herself in a mirror. Shirley knew what she was imagining — this beautiful girl with long yellow hair and a delicate green fishy tail. She guessed the child was going to be let down; whatever it was that they'd got in a glass case here, she couldn't think that it was going to be quite like that. But Mrs. Leech kept on getting Jean more and more worked up: "Isn't it exciting, darling — we're going to see a *mermaid*. Do you

think the mermaid will be singing a song?"
Shirley felt like hitting her.

When they found the hotel, it turned out
that you had to pay to see the mermaid,
even if you were coming in to have lunch.
There was this case with a cloth on it in
the passage outside the dining room, and
the proprietor wasn't going to take the
cloth off unless you paid, and he was
asking what Mrs. Leech and Mrs.
Clavering thought was an exorbitant
amount, so there was the usual haggling.
All the time, Jean just stood there, stiff and
tense, her fist clenched to her mouth,
staring at the case with enormous eyes.

At last the cloth came off, and there in
the case was this brown leathery-looking
thing, like the mummies in the Cairo Museum. It was obviously some kind of animal, or had been, though it did have what
you could imagine as a sort of bosom. Mrs.
Leech and Mrs. Clavering started laughing
hysterically; Shirley could hear the stories
they'd be telling in the ship's bar that
evening: "My dear, it was just too ridiculous
for words . . ."

And Jean just gazed. Then she turned
and looked up at Shirley with this awful
disappointment in her face. Really, it's too
bad what children have to go through, and

there's nothing you can do about it.

They had lunch, which was roast lamb with all the trimmings, just like being back in England, and afterward treacle pudding, one of Jean's favorites, but even that didn't help. She stayed very quiet all through, and honestly, Shirley's heart bled for her. Mermaid, indeed.

So what with that, and the heat, she wasn't sorry when they left Aden. And yes, once they were out of sight of land it did begin to get cooler, and the sea had a lift to it, with even little choppy waves. On the first afternoon out she got talking to the medical orderly again, or rather, he came over while she was watching Jean, who was playing in the canvas pool. His name was Alan. Alan Baker. He had a brother serving in the Far East, and a sister in a munitions factory, he played the mouth organ, what he missed most out here were cricket and Saturday night in the village pub and his dog Trigger. He was due a week's leave in Cape Town and he couldn't wait. You find out quite a bit about a person in just a short chat, it's surprising.

She'd been feeling rather on her own, actually, ever since they came on board. She had some good friends in Cairo among the Cairo nannies, but none of them were here. Nanny Clavering was much older and always laying down the law about this and that, Shirley couldn't abide the Stannards' Irish girl, and Nanny Peterson was slapdash to a degree, in her opinion. There were the Greek and Lebanese girls, who were nice enough, but you didn't have all that much in common, did you? Oh, they all sat around together on deck during the day, keeping an eye on the children, but Shirley didn't really feel what you might call at home.

But who could feel at home anyway, perched there on a ship that was just a dot on hundreds of miles of water? Day after day, now, that was all they saw — just the sea. And you thought about the depth of it — a mile down to the bottom, she'd heard someone say. Sometimes there were porpoises — sleek black shapes dashing along beside the ship — and everyone rushed to the rails to watch. And flying fish, skimming along the surface. They said there were sharks, plenty of those. And once one of the ship's officers spotted a great turtle, and people took it in turns to have a look through his binoculars.

The second night out they ran into a storm. The ship was pitching about, everything slid off the washstand, Jean was starting to feel sick and so was Jamie Clavering, Nanny Clavering was yammering away about how what you had to do was lie absolutely flat and look at the ceiling, or drink Epsom salts, or suck barley sugar. Or shut up, thought Shirley. Then Jamie was sick all over his bunk and after that there was no sleep for anyone until at last around dawn it began to calm down and by breakfast there was just a bit of a heave still, not that many wanted anything to eat — the dining room was half empty. In fact, Shirley felt fine; she'd always had good sea legs. Mrs. Leech was prostrated, of course, laid up in her cabin with the Purser bringing her lime juice.

It was cooler that day, after the storm, really nice up on deck. People were talking about how there would be a crossing-the-line ceremony when they got to the equator — not a full-scale do, the officers said, seeing as it's wartime, just a bit of fun for the children. One of them would dress up as Neptune, apparently. They would need a costume. "You'll have to get Film Star on to that," someone said. "She's the dressmaker."

He must have heard. Alan. Alan Baker. Later, he came over to her again, made a paper airplane for Jean, asked how they'd been in the storm. Then he said, "Why do they call you that? Film Star?"

She felt herself blushing. A great rich red blush. Thank goodness she was leaning over the rail, and no one else very near. "Well . . ."

He laughed. "I can guess. Quite right, too. Except that a Hollywood type would be all covered with makeup, and you're not, so you're prettier by far."

She didn't know where to look. Was he being cheeky? Should she make an excuse and move away? You met soldiers some-times in the YW who tried it on, and she knew how to give them the brush-off when they were getting a bit too fresh, she didn't stand any nonsense. But he wasn't that sort. She knew he wasn't. And what he'd said was said perfectly nicely — straight-forward, an opinion, and that was that.

She said, "Well, thank you."

And then Jean came running up, wanting him to make another airplane, which he did, and now the other children were wanting them too, so he was kept busy. He was good with children — one of those people who are naturally at ease with them.

Shirley had been that way too, right from when she was not much more than a child

43

herself. She used to be asked in to mind the little ones while their mums went shopping, up and down their street. So when she left school, it seemed the obvious thing to train as a nursery nurse. Her mother was all for it; a nicer sort of job than working in a shop, or office work, even if it did mean living in other people's houses, but if you had good qualifications you could pick and choose, by all accounts. Some of Shirley's schoolfriends weren't so enthusiastic: "Like a servant," they said. "Catch me . . ." Which really made Shirley see red. She'd never thought of it like that; the whole point was working with children, doing what you were good at.

Nowadays, she wasn't so sure, sometimes. It wasn't that she'd gone off children — goodness no. She loved Jean, and she was proud of her. But there was a sense in which she had come to feel that she belonged nowhere now. She lived in the world of the Leeches and their friends, but it wasn't really her world; when she visited her parents, before the war, she walked down their familiar street like a stranger, seeing and hearing things she had never noticed back when she was younger. The milk bottles on the doorsteps, the net curtains at the windows, chiming doorbells, wireless music spilling from kitchen windows. She thought of the way Mrs. Leech said "suburban," which made it a different word from the one she had always known, that was simply to do with railways: London and Suburban. She was conscious of her parents' speech, of the way they pronounced words; what had been entirely known and usual had become discomforting.

Sure enough, she got dragged into this crossing-the-line business. Apparently it involved a silly ceremony in which people who hadn't crossed the equator before had to appear before the court of Neptune, and were made to drink some horrible mixture, and were shaved with wooden razors, and then ducked in water. So there would be someone done up as Neptune and someone else as his daughter, and heralds and trumpeters, and some bears to do the ducking in the children's canvas pool. They would need various costumes, so it was "*Please,* Nanny, you're said to be such a genius with a needle. . . ." It all sounded too daft for words, but she wasn't going to be a spoilsport, so she set to and managed to rustle up some old sheets, and sacking, and rope, and this and that. Helpers were to hand, everyone had sug-gestions, and one way and another there was some pretty successful costume making. Neptune's long flowing hair and beard were made of frayed rope, the crowns were done with silver foil from cigarette packets, with jujubes for jewels, the bears wore sacking suits and navy socks on their heads. Mrs. Clavering was Neptune's daughter, wearing her bathing suit and a crown and a lot of crêpe paper as seaweed. There'd been a bit of friction between her and Mrs. Leech about who was going to get the part; Mrs. Clavering won because her bathing suit was a sort of shimmery green and would look right. They weren't quite so pally for a while after that.

On the day, most people were up on deck. This was supposed to be a bit of fun for the children, but the grown-ups weren't holding back. One of the ship's officers was Neptune — the good-looking one who was always life and soul of the party in the bar — and some of the others were the bears, crouched down by the pool ready to duck people, and of course *that* was going to be an excuse for lots of jiggery-pokery. The younger children were a bit scared, and even more so once things got going and the Purser was made to be the first victim, and had to drink something out of a jug (just rum punch, apparently), and got flour and water slapped all over his face as shaving cream, and then was pushed into the pool for the bears to shove him under. Screams of laughter. Only the bigger boys wanted to join in; the younger children wouldn't have anything to do with it, so in the end it was mostly grown-ups getting ducked. Mrs. Leech had her bathing suit on; she wasn't going to let herself be outdone entirely by Mrs. Clavering, and when it was her turn there was plenty of giggling and shrieking when the bears got her.

Jean didn't like it. At first, she had thought it was all quite funny, but when she saw her mother up there in front of Neptune and then being bundled about in the pool she got hysterical: "What are they doing to my mummy?" Well, nothing that Mrs. Leech wasn't thoroughly enjoying, as it happened, but the child saw it differently: "Why are the grown-ups being like this? Why?"

She might well ask. It was all too silly for words, in Shirley's view, and some people were making fools of themselves. She was glad to see that Alan Baker hadn't joined in, though she caught sight of him watching, with some of the hospital case soldiers. Later, when it was over and the lascars were scrubbing down the deck, which was in a right mess with all the flour and water that had been thrown around, he came up and congratulated Shirley on the costumes. Jean was still very down in the mouth, and Shirley told him she hadn't reckoned much with it — grown-ups fooling around like that.

He smiled. "She's got a point, hasn't she?" He bent down and said to Jean, "It's something that's always been done, the sailors told me. Because the sea's a dangerous place and you've got to keep it sweet. You've got to give a person to Neptune so he'll leave you alone."

When Jean had gone off to play with the other children, he turned to Shirley: "Fancy a turn on the upper deck this evening, after dinner?"

She had to look away; she could feel herself getting all hot and bothered. But pleased — oh, yes, pleased.

"All right," she said. And then Mrs. Leech appeared, and Alan Baker went off to see to his soldiers, and that was that, but all day she hugged to herself this sensation of surprise, of interest. And she kept seeing his face.

At first, she couldn't spot him, up on deck. Hardly surprising, in the dark. She wandered about, and nearly fell over a pile of rope and suddenly there he was — laughing and putting a hand under her arm to steady her. They went to the stern, where there was no one else around, and leaned over the rail. It was a lovely night, not hot, the sea almost still, with a shimmer of silvery phosphorescence. She said that she didn't understand how that happened, and Alan Baker said that neither did he, and he'd find out from the sailors.

They talked about before the war. He described the village he came from where his dad was a postman and his mum worked in the shop; his work, driving an ambulance around Exeter, and some of the dramas — he'd delivered babies a couple of times, and once he'd help fish some lads out of a reservoir. "Silly little beggars went fishing and couldn't swim — oh yes, they were fine." She told him about her family and her home — her once-home.

"Town and country, you and me," he said. "Opposites." He smiled — a close, direct smile that made her feel quite odd. "I hope not," he added.

They were side by side, almost touching, the rail cool against her arms, the water rushing by below and foaming away behind, the deck throbbing under their feet. It occurred to her that she'd seen something like this in a film once, only the people were in evening dress, the man and the woman, and it was all romantic, with smoochy music in the background.

He asked her how she'd got into nannying. She talked about that and he was quiet for a few moments. He offered her a cigarette; she shook her head and he lit up.

"You should have kids of your own."

She was startled, didn't know how to take this. She said, "Why do you think that?"

"Well, you're a natural mother, aren't you? Sticks out a mile."

That threw her. She was silent.

"I like that in a girl," he said, after a moment. "I'd like kids myself, come to that. One day. When all this is over."

She'd never had a conversation like this before. Not with a man. Part of her was embarrassed; another part was excited, all keyed up. It was as though she'd stepped aside from her ordinary, everyday self and become someone else.

He said he was probably getting a transfer, when he got back to Cairo. He'd be leaving the big base hospital and moving up to one of the frontline field hospitals, in the desert, with a driving job. He wanted that; you felt out of the action, stuck in the Delta. And there was going to be action, no question about that. Rommel was on the move; he'd got to be stopped.

"The Germans aren't going to get to Cairo, are they?" Almost for the first time, it came to her that this might happen. She thought of Mr. Leech, of the other fathers, of the big house in Zamalek with all their things in it — and Sambo the dog and the nursery canary in its cage.

He said, "Probably not. But we'll have to clobber them. It'll be rough."

And then he did this thing. He put his hand over hers. He wrapped it round hers, so that she felt the warm size of it, and her own fist curled beneath. The warmth seemed to rush through her whole body; she'd never felt anything like this, she didn't know what it was that she was feeling. It was as though she had discovered another sense, one of which she had known nothing. She saw the hairs on his wrist, dark against the brown skin, she saw the shape of his knuckles; the sight was somehow so intimate that she was amazed.

Afterward, she had no idea how long they had stood like that, not speaking, looking out at the sea. At last she had said that she ought to get down to the cabin, and check on Jean. He lifted his hand, and trailed his fingers for an instant along her arm.

"I'll be seeing you, won't I?" he said.

They were out in the Indian Ocean now, heading for Mombasa, where the ship would berth for a day or two and passengers would be allowed ashore again. It was much cooler, and quite rough sometimes. The routine was to get the children up on deck soon after breakfast; Shirley found that all the time she was watching to see if Alan Baker came. Sometimes another orderly would bring up the invalid soldiers, and then she would feel a dull creep of disappointment. When she did see him, she quickened with pleasure. And then, at some point, he would come over, play with the children, have a few words. She was wary now of being seen talking to him for too long — the other nannies would soon start making remarks. Maybe he also had thought of this; he just chatted for a minute or two, and moved away, but she felt his eyes on her. Then, a day or two on, he said quietly, "That phosphorescence — it's because of little creatures in the sea. Plankton."

"Oh . . ."

"Be nice to take another look at it, now that we know. Tonight?"

"Yes," she said.

There was that night, and then another. As she waited for those times, for the moment of going up alone to the dark deck, she knew that she had never known anticipation of this kind in all her life. He seemed no longer a stranger, but someone who was urgently her concern — some intense and startling connection that she could neither understand nor challenge. Her feelings amazed and embarrassed her; she knew about being in love, but if that was what was going on, then she had had no idea that it was like this. That you felt it — well, in your body. At times she scolded herself: you're being daft — stop it.

He talked mostly about England, about his life before the war. Listening, she experienced a nostalgia, but it was a yearning for a world that she hadn't known since she was a schoolgirl — the comfortable community of Pinner, which was not like his village but nevertheless bore some eerie likeness. A place in which everyone knew their neighbors, in which people did not talk up or down to anyone else. She had for so long been a subordinate, an accessory to families not her own, that she had forgotten the easy equality elsewhere. There floated into her mind the notion that she would not want to go on like this for always, perhaps only until Jean no longer needed her. After the war, perhaps she would think about some other kind of work.

Once, they saw a school of porpoises — swift shapes breaking up the silvery sheen of the water. She cried out in delight, and he put his arm round her.

"Listen," he said. "In Cape Town there's wonderful beaches, the lads say. You'll get some days off, won't you? I'll take you swimming."

That was when he kissed her. At the time, she could barely believe that this was happening. Only later, reliving it, did she realize that she had not known at all what a kiss was like — that it was warm and wet, that you felt his tongue push between your lips, that you opened your mouth, that a thrill rushed down your body. What you saw people doing in films bore no resemblance.

She felt these days as though she were two people; there was this new self, who lived differently, for whom each morning was a rich, fresh realization, and there was the old Shirley, who knew nothing of this, who walked in a kind of innocence. She knew too that, whatever came of all this, nothing would be the same again. She could not go back to that former self.

They arrived at Mombasa. There was a long quayside with ships tied up; they disembarked in the afternoon and went to the old town, where there were little narrow streets with verandas that jutted out from the houses, and markets with toppling heaps of fruit, and stalls selling colored baskets, and others with bales of bright materials. Mrs. Leech bought a length for a dress — "There's bound to be some wonderful little dressmaker when we get to Cape Town" — and another for Jean, and piled a basket high with fruit to take on board. Then they walked around the harbor and looked at the dhows until it was time to go back to the ship. There were crowds of people — Arabs, Africans, lascar seamen — and Shirley had to keep a tight hold of Jean. They kept running into others from the ship; one of Mrs. Leech's officer friends joined up with them. Shirley looked for Alan Baker, but probably he had stayed on board with the soldiers. Just thinking of him made her buoyant; she seemed to float through this place with its vibrant people, the exotic smells and sounds. Soon, she would see him again.

They sailed the next morning; now there would be the long plunge down past the rest of Africa, through the Mozambique Channel and on to the next stop, Cape Town. The last stop. Back at the start, she had thought that two weeks on this ship would be unbearable; now, she wanted this time to go on and on.

The days were long; the sun swung slowly across the sky and the hours crept toward evening. They could not always meet. Once there was a concert arranged for the soldiers and another day Jean was running a temperature and Shirley didn't like to leave her. But each time she was with him seemed to mark some unstated confirmation of what was between them. When she had left him, she would catch the now familiar smell of him on her own skin — that male smell of sweat and cigarettes. It was intimate and disturbing.

He was by way of talking a lot to the sailors and so knew about the ship's course. He told her that they had now entered the Mozambique Channel; there was land on either side, but miles and miles away so you'd never know it, with nothing but sea to be seen, as always. And it was not that long now till they would reach

Cape Town. Once there, he had to get the soldiers to their hospitals and convalescent homes, and then he could start his leave: "Where will you be? How will I find you?"

She wasn't sure. Mrs. Leech had talked about this pension she had heard of that sounded perfect — "Marvelous food, and run by an English couple." Shirley would try to get the name of it tomorrow.

"That's good." His arm was round her. There were people not far away along the deck, but it was so dark you couldn't tell who anyone was until you were close up. And anyway, even if Mrs. Leech appeared — so what? I'm doing nothing wrong, she thought, I've a perfect right. It surprised her that she could think like this.

The feel of him was all over her, later on, when she got into her bunk. His voice was still in her head, so that she hardly heard Nanny Clavering nattering away about the state the toilets were in. He said, "Good night," again and again, as she lay there on the brink of sleep. "Good night. Take care. Tomorrow — yes?"

She dreamed. She dreamed of porpoises, slicing through the dark water, and of a mermaid on a rock, like in Jean's book, and of Alan Baker. And then something invaded the dreams — a crash, a great distant

57

rumbling noise, she was being shaken around, her body was juddering.

The alarm bell pitched her wide awake. She seemed to have slept for no time at all, but her watch said half past three. The bell was loud, penetrating; Nanny Clavering was sitting up in her bunk saying it was perfectly disgraceful having a lifeboat drill in the middle of the night.

As soon as Shirley was standing she felt that there was something not right; the throb of the ship's engine felt urgent, erratic, and the slant of the floor was odd.

She said, "It's not a drill. Get dressed. Get Jamie dressed."

They had had lifeboat drills several times. You knew what to do. You knew where your lifeboat station was; you knew that you had to dress in warm clothing, put on life jackets, take only essentials with you. You knew that you had to move quickly and calmly to the correct station. She dressed Jean first, then herself, putting on their thick jerseys. Then she got their life jackets on, properly tied. She had to help Nanny Clavering, who was getting in a state. She took Jean's little seed-pearl necklace, which she wore to parties, and her own charm bracelet and her silver filigree brooch from the Mouski, and her passport, and put them in her bag along with the Nivea cream and the bottle of Milk of Magnesia and the iodine and the mercurochrome and some handkerchiefs and a box of plasters. When the others were ready she opened the cabin door and got them all out into the corridor.

It was filling up with people, everyone trying to get to the stairways. Some people had suitcases. Mrs. Leech's cabin was back toward the end, and to get to it they would have to push against the crowd, so Shirley decided they must go straight to the boat station on the promenade deck and meet up with Mrs. Leech and Mrs. Clavering there.

They were on the stairs when there was a tremendous thump. The ship lurched and all the lights went out. There was a series of muffled bangs, and now this pungent, acrid smell. People fell against each other; there were screams and shouting. There was a great crush on the stairs, with people barging and shoving; an officer at the top was calling out to stay calm, not to push, to take it easy. He was telling the people with suitcases that they must leave them, they couldn't take them on the boats. Shirley was jammed against the people in front of her, she was clutching hold of

Jean, and someone behind had a case knocking against her legs. Just ahead, one of the Armenian girls was weeping and wailing, the Hamilton baby propped over her shoulder.

They got to the upper deck, but then there were more stairs up to the promenade deck, and more people. She kept looking back to see if she could see Mrs. Leech, but no sign, and anyway it was too dark to make out faces. Everyone was shouting out names, trying to find each other. Jean was terribly confused: "What's happening? Where are we going? Why aren't there any lights?" The officers were flashing torches to help people find the way, and when at last they were up on the top deck it was easier to see, with some moonlight. But the deck wasn't level, it was sloping, so that there was a pull up toward lifeboat station number six, by the rail, which was theirs — and then she realized that the whole ship was listing over to one side.

They were lowering the lifeboats from the boat deck — lascars swarming around on ropes, sailors hurrying to and fro. As more people came out of the stairway onto the deck, she spotted Mrs. Leech and Mrs. Clavering — Mrs. Leech with her dressing case, which she must have got past the officers somehow, and her silver fox fur cape.

Mrs. Leech was hysterical. Mrs. Clavering wasn't much better. They were relieved to find the children, but it made Jean even more upset, seeing her mother like that. Shirley tried to distract her, getting her to look at the lifeboats coming alongside the rail. The next station was already getting into their boat — about thirty people, with an officer in charge and several lascars. There was a lot of shouting from the seamen and the boat was lowered, but not gradually, it went in fits and starts, something kept getting stuck it seemed, and the people in the boat were being thrown around. She heard screams. Because of the ship's list, the side was like a great cliff and the sea far below, dark as anything, glinting here and there in the moonlight. Shirley didn't want to look. It would be them next.

Each lifeboat station was alongside one of those stretches of rail that were made to be opened, as though the ship had always been waiting for this. She had stood with Alan Baker against one of them, only hours before.

Now it was their turn to get into the lowered boat, the officer helping them on one by one, telling them to go to the end quickly, make room for the next person. Mrs. Leech was saying, "Oh, no — no, no," again and again. Shirley had to man-handle her into the boat and onto a seat. She said, "Shut your eyes now," and Mrs. Leech did, obedient, like a child.

When they started to lower the boat, Shirley took Jean on her lap and held her tightly — she'd seen how those other people had been pitched about. And it was horrible. They hung there rocking, in midair, and then the boat began to go down, slowly at first, and then it dropped, and they hit the sea with a wallop, water surging over the sides, people falling off the seats.

At once, the lascars were rowing. She saw why. They had to get away from the ship. Another lifeboat was banging up against the soaring hull, sucked in by the current, desperately trying to get clear. And up above more boats were coming down — there was a confusion of ropes and flashing torches and shouting and children crying. Shirley had to watch, she couldn't take her eyes off the sight of it — the great leaning ship, with smoke billowing up now from somewhere, and the little boats coming down into the heaving sea. And so it was that she saw one boat tip up at one end and hang there crookedly with people falling out, dark shapes pitching into the water. And another smashed into the side of the ship — planks flew apart and dropped, people were falling again, and then down in the water there were heads bobbing, and someone trying to get into the broken boat. She sat rigid, watching; suddenly there were lights — the emergency lights on the decks must have come on — and you could clearly see figures moving about, and piling into the boats that still hung up there.

The lascars were struggling to get the boat away from the side of the ship, pulling frantically on the oars. They managed to open up quite a gap, and then there was a surge that washed them back toward the hull. Up above, another boat was just starting the descent, packed with people. It swung, lurched, and then crashed hard into the side. Someone fell — Shirley saw the tumbling body, only yards away. There were other things falling — ropes, bits of wood — and then an oar came crashing down into their boat.

It knocked several people off their seats. There was screaming. The officer was shouting to the lascars to pull harder.

Jean was sitting close up against Shirley.

The oar caught her on the side of the head; she fell across Shirley's lap like a little rag doll.

Shirley clung on to the child. She lifted her up on her knees and cradled her head in the crook of her arm. She couldn't see or feel blood, but she knew that Jean was unconscious. The people who had been knocked into the well of the boat were trying to get back onto their seats; someone was moaning "My arm — oh, my arm."

The lascars had opened up a gap at last. There was clear water between the boat and the side of the ship, but it was water littered with debris, with people in life jackets, with bobbing heads. A lifeboat had capsized, Shirley now saw; everyone in it had been thrown into the water. There were flares going up from the ship — amber, red, and white distress flares that threw a momentary lurid light on the sea, and lit up the blackness of the sky.

She held Jean. She ran her fingers around her head and could feel a bump now, and the stickiness of blood, but there didn't seem to be much. It hadn't been so very hard a bang — surely she would be all right? A woman on the bench behind was saying that she thought her arm was broken. Shirley could see Mrs. Leech, leaning up against Mrs. Clavering, looking dazed; she wanted to tell her about Jean, but could only have done so by shouting across the people in between.

They were getting farther from the ship all the time. The shapes of other lifeboats were dotted about on the sea, all trying to pull away from the ship. The seamen were flashing torches, to keep in contact. There were figures still visible on the ship, moving about on the deck, and a lifeboat coming down; Shirley thought she could make out the shapes of two or three more, hanging there waiting to go. What was happening seemed to have been going on for hours, but she realized that in fact it had only been minutes — half an hour, perhaps — since they left the cabin, since they made their way up to the deck, since the torpedo hit them. The second torpedo — because she now knew that the first one must have been when they were still asleep, when her dream had seemed to roar and heave.

Where was he? Where was Alan Baker? She stared at the listing ship, and she knew that he was still there, still on board, because he would have been helping the soldiers to get up on deck, those men without a foot or a leg, or unable to see, and he would not leave until the very last one of them was on a lifeboat.

She looked down at Jean. Her eyelids seemed to flutter, which must be a good sign, and Shirley could feel her breathing. They were well away from the ship now, and the lascars were resting on their oars; the young officer was calling out, was everyone okay?

Well, no. There was the woman with the broken arm, and someone else who had a badly gashed leg. And Mrs. Leech wasn't making sense anymore, apparently. Mrs. Stannard, who had had VAD training, had a look at her and said she was in deep shock. She looked at Jean too and thought that she was probably concussed, and that there was nothing to be done but just to keep her warm and still and she should come round in time.

People were quiet and calm now, on the whole. Scared — you could feel the fear running from person to person like a current. And then suddenly there was something else — gasps, someone saying "Oh, my God . . ."; they were all seeing what was happening, that the ship was going, the bow tilting up, the whole great shape sliding away, in slow motion it seemed, upending into the sea.

It was there, and then it was not. In darkness and in silence, it went. They sat watching, twenty-five people in the rocking boat; someone was crying, someone else prayed out loud: "Our Father, which art in Heaven . . ." One of the lascars made a kind of wailing noise, and then fell silent.

Just the sky and the sea now, a vast surrounding space with nothing visible but here and there the flashing light from another of the boats. The officer was counting heads and checking names, calling out from a list. He was trying to keep people's spirits up: they'd be picked up, no question, the signals would have been heard, the flares seen, there was water on the boat, and rations. Shirley knew him well by sight; he had been one of those life-and-soul-of-the-party chaps from the bar, of an evening, and he had dressed up as Neptune for the crossing-the-line ceremony. She had helped to arrange his frayed rope wig and beard, and had made his robe out of an old sheet. Now, he was somberly brisk and controlled, but he looked younger, somehow; he was probably her own age, she saw, around twenty-four. Two of the lascars were just boys, another was almost an old man. The rest of them were . . . women and children.

As daylight came you could see faces. The Stannards were all there, and the teacher from the English School, and Mrs. Hope with that tiny baby. It was the teacher who had a broken arm. She sat, white-faced; Mrs. Stannard was trying to fix up a splint.

First of all there were streaks of light to one side, and then the whole sky gradually lightened and you could see the rim of the horizon all around, and then other life-boats — some quite far away, others near enough for the officer to shout across to them. They were trying to stay together, but the wind had picked up now and the sea was choppy, so that the lascars had to row to keep within the ring of boats. They were being flung about by the waves; people were starting to be sick.

Later, it became calm again. But now the sun was right up, and inescapable. No shade, the heat beating down, the light hitting back up off the water. Shirley had one of the Armenian girls next to her on the seat, and they laid Jean out on both their laps with her head on Shirley's arm and Shirley's jersey arranged so as to keep as much sun off her as possible. She was moving a little, occasionally; at one point her eyes opened, and then closed again.

Measures of water were given out, and biscuits. Shirley tried to trickle water into Jean's mouth, but she wouldn't swallow. They had now been hours and hours on those hard wooden seats, sitting bolt upright, with only each other to lean against — you ached all over. People had made handkerchiefs into hats — anything to keep the sun off; the children were getting frantic. Mrs. Stannard tried to get up a sing-song, but that soon petered out; nobody had the heart for it.

The hours inched by. In the middle of the day, the sea was like molten metal. Shirley's head was pounding; her mouth was dry and parched. There would be another handout of water later, they said. How much water was there? No good thinking about that. She tried to think about nothing at all, to focus on sounds — the creaking of the boat, the slap of water against the side — or just to stare at the back of the person in front of her, the paisley pattern of a blouse, the texture of the material. Now and again she changed Jean's position a little; sometimes the little girl would whimper, which seemed promising.

Occasionally she heard Mrs. Leech talking incoherently. People said she was hallucinating — didn't understand where she was or what was happening. Which could be a mercy. For the rest of them, who understood only too well, there was nothing but the grim passage of time. The officer was constantly watching the sky and the horizon, his eyes screwed up against the glare; you knew what he was searching for.

The sun crept down the sky. The water ration came round again. The teacher had been given some brandy; she was in a lot of pain from her arm. At one point, a girl passed out; they managed to lie her down for a bit in the well of the boat, but you couldn't do that for long — they were so tightly packed, there simply wasn't room.

In the early evening, Jean died. Shirley knew at once: the stillness, the sense that something vital was gone from the body across her lap.

She sat on, as the sun sank, as the light began to drain from the sky, as the moon's disk rose above the horizon. She was so tired that she felt numb; sometimes she drifted into a kind of floating state, and then would come to with a lurch, aware again of the people crowded around her, of Jean inert across her knees.

In the wastes of the night she must have slid deeply into this condition — some sort of mockery of sleep. And then people's voices came rooting in — she heard them but seemed unable to respond, to feel anything at all. They were saying that there was a destroyer, that it had seen them. It's over, they were saying, it's over, we're going to be picked up.

But it isn't over, she thought. It has only just begun. She knew that the sinking ship had taken with it a whole life that she would never live, a time that would never be. Jean's cold little body lay across her knees, and all she could think was that Jean hadn't known about death, she didn't even know what death was.

This never happened. Or rather, it did not happen to me — to us, to the triumvirate of my mother, my nanny, and myself, who did indeed flee Egypt during the run-up to the battle of El Alamein, but not to go to South Africa. We went to Palestine, and that is another story, part of the indestructible fabric of my life, of our lives. The fate of the sunken ship is confabulation, and so are all who sailed in her. Shirley Manners is not Lucy, my real-life nanny; but there was a girl in Cairo in the early 1940s whom the other nannies called Film Star, and by some perverse quirk of memory I know this still, though I don't remember her at all. I have given her a fictional reincarnation, for her to speak for a time, and a place, and a climate of opinion and of behavior.

There were Japanese U-boats active in the Mozambique Channel in June and July of 1942. Twenty Allied ships were sunk by these before they withdrew at the end of July. Shipping traffic was dense up and down the east coast of Africa, with most vessels sailing independently, since antisubmarine escorts were not available. One of those sunk ships could have been carrying British civilian passengers, along with military personnel. For some reason, my mother had decided to head for Palestine, rather than South Africa, thus twitching me away from that particular whirlpool, or rapid, or treacherous rock.

The Albert Hall

I came to England at the age of twelve, just before the end of the war, to an alien place of astonishing cold and a social system that was mysterious to me. I had spent my childhood in African sunshine, in the polyglot and cosmopolitan ambience of Cairo. The next few years were a time of grim adjustment, passed mainly at a boarding school on the south coast. I remember a fair amount about that stultifying institution, but for the most part those adolescent years are long periods of darkness, into which occasionally a light shines.

I am lying on the veranda at my grandmother's house in Somerset, trying to get a suntan. Doves coo, someone is mowing the grass; the day is stationary, time itself is at a halt. I am fifteen, and waiting to grow up.

And, after more impenetrable months and years, here I am in the Albert Hall, which is filled with music, dancing people, roving lights, streamers . . . I am wearing calf-length blue jeans, a green-and-white-checked shirt with its tails knotted so that my midriff is bare, a kerchief over my hair, vast hooped gold earrings, and I am carrying three herrings in a string bag. This is the Chelsea Arts Ball, and I am a fishergirl, I think. I am eighteen, so perhaps I am grown up. At any rate, I am in love. I am in love with the man who has brought me here, who is done up as a pirate. This man is thirty; I am besotted with his sophistication, his assurance, his flattering attention. Oh, this is the life. At midnight, a thousand balloons float down from the great domed roof. The floor is a mass of dancers; a singer is belting forth into a microphone:

> The years go by
> As quickly as a wink.
> Enjoy yourself, enjoy yourself . . .
> It's later than you think.

We dance and dance, and sometime in the small hours we leave for his flat. There is only one way in which this night can end.

I have had two children; they have been the light of my life. But what about the *children who never were, the shadow children never born who lurk in the wings? One such must hover there in the Albert Hall, a person who might have been the product of that night. In those pre-pill days, girls diced with death. The backstreet abortionists were busy, along with others trading behind a respectable Harley Street nameplate. The single mother was not a recognized social category then, accepted and inviting sympathy. In 1951, those who got "caught" were discreetly tucked away, or faced it out in defiance of the prevailing mores, depending on circumstances. For me, the night of the Chelsea Arts Ball was just a heady rite of passage — but suppose it had been otherwise?*

On Swanage Beach, when Chloe was twelve years old, she gave her mother a piece of her mind. "You're impossible," she said. Loudly. She stood there with arms akimbo; half the beach must have heard her. And Miranda laughed. That was another thing. Other people did not have mothers with a stupid name that you had to use instead of Mum. Other people called their mothers Mum or Mummy. Other people's mothers brought picnics to the beach — padded plastic bags full of sandwiches and apples

and drinks. Other people's mothers remembered swimming costumes; their children did not have to go into the sea in their
knickers. Other families had a father, not
someone called Mike with long hair who
sat there on the sand playing his guitar,
which was so embarrassing that Chloe
wanted to scream. Miranda had met him
last week.

Years later, Chloe would remember that
day. "I blame the zeitgeist," she told her
husband. "It was 1963. The sixties went to
her head entirely. After all, she had been
creating her own version of the sixties for
years."

Chloe's husband, a nice man who
worked in local government, indicated polite agreement. There was a familiar
agenda here, and one is not required to go
to the stake for one's mother-in-law. In any
case, he did not recall the sixties, except
for a vague impression of black leather and
loud music; he had been into bird-
watching and hiking as a teenager and
hence was out of step with the times.

John Bagnold, Chloe's husband, was
part of a life strategy and may have been
subliminally aware of this. By the time
Chloe was twenty she knew that she
wanted a job, a mortgage, a pension

scheme, and a husband — probably in that order. By the time she was thirty she had all of these.

At forty-five Chloe was a chief inspector of schools, a career destination that was perhaps inevitable, given the circumstances. She herself had been at four different schools by the age of ten. Consequently, she had got the hang of schools very early on; she had schools all sorted out. She knew how to interpret playground politics and make the right friends; she knew how to enlist the support and sympathy of teachers. When Miranda forgot to send any dinner money, or was half an hour late at the school gates, Chloe looked forlornly helpless, to good effect. She also shone at her work, and applied herself with enthusiasm. At the comprehensive, she was in the top stream for everything. The head teacher begged Miranda to stay put for long enough to allow Chloe to do A levels. By now, Chloe had perfected certain negotiating skills, where her mother was concerned; she had learned how to out-maneuver Miranda. She talked darkly of child support agencies and helplines. Miranda festered in one place for two solid years; Chloe got her two A's — and went to Warwick to read politics and economics.

After that, it was just a question of setting off to become the kind of person she had always meant to be.

As time went on, Chloe was less given to harping on her disadvantaged youth. Her reflections about her mother became less condemnatory and more analytical.

"She reinvented herself, basically. She turned herself into your original Bohemian, to use an old-fashioned term. She hung out with arty-crafty people. Everyone we knew when I was a child painted or potted or wrote poetry. None of them had a bean. Nobody had ever heard of them, either. This wasn't your Augustus John set."

Her husband wondered if perhaps Augustus John was dead by then, anyway. Chloe ignored this.

"Don't get me wrong. I've got plenty of time for art. I respect art. I admire art. I think that governments should subsidize art. It's the artistic attitude that I detest. I grew up with the artistic attitude. I grew up among people who traded in artistic pretension. Most of them weren't any more artists than you and me."

John said he believed that T. S. Eliot worked in a bank at one time.

"Quite so," said Chloe. "And Larkin was a librarian. That's the stuff. You can keep your Dylan Thomases."

In moments of irritation, she would pick on basics. "She even gave herself a new name. Said she'd always felt like a Miranda, and people should be allowed to choose their own names, rather than having them slapped on by parents. In which case I should have shed Chloe long ago. I'm a Jane or a Susan."

John had met Chloe during a conference at which he had delivered a keynote speech on the crisis in education; he had been flattered when she had come up to compliment him and had subsequently married her because it became clear that he was now a part of her long-term arrangements. An obliging man, this was all right by him so long as he was allowed to pursue his own career plans and also go fishing on Saturdays. Actually, the marriage worked out rather well. There were three meticulously planned children, and a series of calculated moves to better jobs and improved housing. Nothing was left to chance. Chloe had no time at all for the serendipitous approach. Needless to say, she ran a tight ship where the children were concerned; but she strongly favored nature over nurture. Her own experience was the perfect illustration, as she was quick to point out.

"If nurture rules, then I should be scraping a living out of handcrafted cushion covers, right now. I knew by the time I was eight that I'd been hatched in the wrong nest."

Her children, when older, were known to turn this argument to their advantage, requesting various freedoms on the grounds that they too needed to follow their own inclinations. Chloe was unimpressed.

"You don't know when you're well off, you lot. Try a home life in which anything goes and there's nothing for supper and no clean clothes and you'd soon be complaining."

Chloe's infancy was a blank, of course. In her childhood memories, she seemed to emerge fully fledged at about five. No, exactly five, because it is her birthday and she does not have a white cake with her name in pink icing but a victoria sponge made by Miranda which has sagged dreadfully in the middle and is adorned with sprinkles and some silver balls that have rolled into the central dent. They were supposed to be spelling out Chloe's name.

Miranda did not want to be called Mum or Mummy because she said she never really felt like a mother. She was too young herself. In no way did this mean that she did not love Chloe — absolutely not; she

80

adored Chloe, but she didn't see the point of setting up as some kind of maternal wonder. They could have much more fun together just being natural, as though Miranda were a big sister.

Miranda did not attend parent-teacher meetings, nor did she join in the mothers' race on school sports days. In her time, Chloe found herself at cozy village primary schools and inner-city jungle outfits, thus acquiring an insider view of the system, which could perhaps be seen later as a distinct career asset. At the time, this erratic progress merely served to hone a capacity for survival. She learned adaptation skills, and also how to turn circumstances to her advantage. At village primaries, she was a sweet-faced conformist; at cutthroat comprehensives, she was in there with sharp tongue and flailing fists. She always took care to stay on the right side of authority; Chloe's school reports were euphoric.

By the time she had got to O levels, she had long since realized that Miranda was no help when it came to homework. "She'd been to some crappy boarding school and had forgotten anything she learned there anyway. If she hadn't had me when she was eighteen she would have gone to Oxford.

At least, that was the story. Frankly, can you see her as a student? Buckling to and writing essays? No way!"

When this point cropped up, John would murmur that one supposes that student life is in itself a formative experience. Like so much.

Chloe was dismissive. "She wouldn't have lasted five minutes. She hadn't the temperament."

Chloe told her story frequently. She liked to tell her story, if only to demonstrate what can be done, if you are single-minded. Sometimes, the story was received in the wrong way. The new acquaintance would say, "But your mother does sound quite fun . . ." — or — "All the same, it must have been a wonderfully *varied* sort of childhood. . . ." Chloe would see that she had made a mistake here; the relationship would not be pursued.

The story that she told was circumstantial. It established the background from which Chloe had emerged and had launched herself into achievement and citizenship. It touched on illustrative detail — the peripatetic lifestyle, her mother's choice of associates, the absence of a role model. Told and retold, it had become a familiar mantra to her husband, who knew better than to do otherwise than provide the ritual prompts and endorsements. Their children went through several phases of response. When very young, they were entranced, for the wrong reasons: "She let you stay up as long as you liked! You had fish and chips nearly every evening! Oh, it's not *fair*. . . ." In time, they learned that this was a cautionary tale, not the account of some lost arcadia. They listened with cynical resignation, occasionally rolling their eyes at each other. They did not see a great deal of their grandmother, who was by now living with a Spanish woodcarver somewhere in Catalonia. When she visited, they found her delightful, though perhaps not quite what you expect a grandmother to be. She had a mane of graying hair down to her shoulders, wore rather low-cut tops, painted her fingernails, and smoked. In their household, this last was the ultimate depravity; their father would go around with an expression of patient endurance, Chloe flung open the windows, coughing violently. Miranda ground out her stubs in saucers, since no ashtray was on offer.

As the narrator of her story, Chloe of course controlled the supply of information. Occasionally, the listener would want to follow up certain themes, in which case Chloe was quite prepared to oblige, within reason.

"Oh yes, my father did the decent thing. He arranged for an allowance. Cash — regular payments. But he moved offstage. We hardly ever saw him. No, no — he wasn't an artistic type at all. He was a guy who owned espresso bars."

"Surely her parents . . . ?"

"Yes — they stumped up too. We certainly didn't starve. Truth to tell, most of the time she never worked. Well, she couldn't have done when I was an infant, but after that . . . Not that she was qualified for anything, was she? But it was all part of the reinvention process. A free spirit, her own woman. Answerable to no one. Doing her own thing. Huh — the zeitgeist again."

Chloe was impatient with fashionable stances. Her childhood had taught her to be resourceful, and to act expediently. At the same time, she had developed a tendency to query orthodox attitudes, along with a taste for the combative approach. She also believed strongly in self-sufficiency. When Mrs. Thatcher came along, Chloe found herself quite out of sympathy with the distaste inspired by the Prime Minister in most others of Chloe's generation. Here was a sensible woman doing sensible things, in Chloe's view. She maintained a lone defense, not popular in educational circles, and wondered what Mrs. Thatcher had been like as a mother.

She was quite astute enough to be aware of the orthodoxy of her own reaction. We all blame our parents; that is the universal self-justification. No, no — she would say, it's not a question of blaming, it's more a matter of inspection and analysis. One blames at the time — later on, for anyone with a degree of sense, the thing is to detach yourself and take stock. Good therapy, too.

She would never have had any truck with professional therapists, of course. No way; if you can't sort yourself out, it's unlikely that anyone else is going to be able to do it for you. She had been contemptuous of the counseling on offer in her student days: "If a person can't write an essay because they've bust up with their boyfriend, they should give up either higher education or sex."

Her own children understood from an early age that whingeing would get them nowhere. Domestic drill required them to get their school things ready the night before, put their pocket money into the post office, and account for their friends. Needless to say, they took pleasure in flouting these demands as often as possible and spent much time in skirmishes with their mother. Their father — a softer touch — would sometimes plead their case. This did not cut much ice with Chloe, who would listen with apparent impartiality and then explain why she was right. In time, John rather gave up, and told the children privately that their mother was a woman with high standards and that in any case they could hardly claim child abuse, could they?

"We all object to the parental regime," said Chloe. "Some with more reason than others, if I may say so."

She had spent her childhood deploring her own circumstances and equally those of her mother's friends, who on the whole lived as Miranda did, moving from one rented flat or cottage to another, with occasional interludes in such light-hearted accommodation as a canal narrowboat or a trailer. When Chloe began to visit school friends, she discovered home ownership, washing machines, and fitted carpets. As she grew up, she perceived that other people's parents were a part of the social fabric: they were policemen or postmen, or they ran a business or worked in offices or shops. They were not useless adjuncts. Their contributions were necessary; they did not drift or improvise. She became a figure of silent adolescent disapproval at raffish and jolly gatherings of Miranda's cronies, for whom hippie culture was tailor made.

Chloe had a favorite refrain: "It's a question of taking control of your own life, that's all."

When the children heard this said, they would get a picture of life as a dusty rug being given a brisk shake. The remark was usually made in connection with some acquaintance seen by Chloe as behaving in a feckless or ill-considered way: they were in arrears with their mortgage, or at odds with their partner, or in the wrong job. Chloe's views were expressed with detachment, but the particular instance would be used as an admonition: take note of what is to be avoided. The two boys, Philip and Paul, let this sort of thing wash over them, on the whole; they had perfected a strategy of morose apparent attention whereby they could not be accused of never listening to a word that their mother said but at the same time were doing more or less exactly that. Sophie, the eldest, was unable to do this because natural curiosity about people and what they got up to obliged her to listen. Chloe did not believe in concealing from the young the rash excesses of the adult world. It was only through awareness of what's out there waiting that they would learn to take evasive action. Accordingly, Sophie heard a lot about people who had dropped out of school or college or run up enormous debts and others who had fallen into drugs or drink or mere apathy. She and her brothers — who weren't really listening anyway — were presented with a vision of the good life which reflected the Whig interpretation of history: the idea was that everything got better and better as you ascended the ladder of the years. You moved from respectable A levels to a degree to satisfactory employment. You notched up salary increases and extensions of power and responsibility and eventually you reached the safe haven of your retirement from which you contemplated your successful progress.

By the time she was seventeen, Sophie was familiar with the general message, which she heard as the background noise of her home life, subsumed into the whole ambience and roughly on a par with the creaking floorboard on the landing and her father's habit of humming Mozart in the bath. There was a bit more to it than that, of course: she was aware that there was a cautionary element, but saw that as on a par with the other warnings with which she had grown up, to do with crossing roads and being circumspect about friendly strangers.

But Sophie was of course growing up in a culture resonant with warnings and advice. Fatherly police officers came to school, sat down in their shirtsleeves and told everyone about the perils of crack and coke and heroin. Brisk, approachable women dealt with sex and contraception: they drew diagrams of the reproductive system on the board and handed condoms around the class. If you had a problem you got counseled, and if you were at all flaky over your career intentions you were given a good talking-to about UCAS forms and job prospects.

Chloe approved. All this had been around in her youth, but in a more muted and amateurish way. As for Miranda's time . . . Chloe would sigh wearily: "It was the dark ages, wasn't it? The kids were left to fend for themselves. Of course, drugs weren't there yet, but there was everything else."

She did not blame Miranda for her untimely pregnancy or, indeed, her father for his role: "I mean, that would be a bit rich, given that I was the outcome." No, Miranda's failing had been her slide into what Chloe referred to as the alternative lifestyle, and moreover one which flouted every kind of aspiration or regularity.

"I'd take a more kindly view if something rich and rare had been the product. I've said it before and I'll say it again — I bow to none in my respect for art. But what her chums were into was the style alone. All you ever saw was batik and macramé. I grew up wearing tie-dyed shifts."

Chloe's refrain about taking control of her life was not just an exhortation: she felt strongly that this can and should be done — a belief that did not spring solely from her rejection of the laissez-faire circumstances of her upbringing. Her education had taught her that people are pitted against misfortune and ever have been: poverty, disease, and history itself with its malevolent strikes. Well, if you have a war flung at you, that is indeed a major setback, but even so a degree of manipulation is usually possible. You cannot sidestep the cancer cell, admittedly, but whereas market forces are the undoing of many, there again expedient action can keep you buoyant.

People are themselves the central problem, of course. Other people. Here, Chloe drew upon experience, starting off with the rich seam of her childhood and all those fly-by-night associates of Miranda's — the creators of batik and macramé and aromatic candles and herbal soaps, the families who lived in tumbledown outbuildings down muddy lanes, the craft market stallholders and the traveling theatrical groups. Plus the shifting cast of boyfriends, live-in and live-out. Here were people who operated according to whim, who seldom made plans, who lived in the moment. Which is all very fine provided that you do not have to deal with them if you yourself are of a different persuasion. Chloe had been able to break free of all this as soon as she had grown up and was her own woman, but then the people problem rears up again in different guises, she discovered. The trouble with them is that they are not always going to do what you want them to do; they will persist in their own opinions and intentions, they constantly obstruct your carefully designed route. Employers, colleagues, subordinates — none could be relied on for absolute cooperation. Friends must be judiciously selected.

People management was therefore a prime consideration, a central feature of this business of exercising control. Chloe considered that she had got pretty good at it. There were occasional failures of course — irreparable differences of opinion with workmates, unfortunate collisions with some teaching associate — but on the whole she usually managed to achieve her aims without running into altercation or causing offense. Perhaps it was a matter of personality as well.

That was working life. Private life was another matter. John was never a major obstacle; a naturally compliant man, he was usually prepared to come to an agreement so long as there was no interference with certain sacrosanct areas, mainly to do with Saturday-afternoon fishing and rugby matches on television.

Children were something else.

Confronted with her first baby, Chloe was stopped in her tracks — scuppered, floored. This was the most intransigent being she had encountered, bar none. She faced anarchy, on a daily basis. Nothing she had learned or experienced had prepared her for this — this collapse of all expectations of order. Sophie performed as babies do, and had her mother on the ropes, glassy-eyed.

Second time round, Chloe was grimly prepared. She knew the battle lines, she knew the limits of her endurance, she knew that even in this ultimate test of the human spirit there is a little room for maneuver, even for some travesty of negotiation. When the third baby arrived, Chloe was ready and waiting — trained, hardened, a combat veteran. She knew how to do babies, insofar as that is possible.

But this was only the beginning. Beyond the intransigence of infants there lies the guile of childhood — the awesome powers of manipulation, the tenacity, the volatility, the flight from anything approaching consistency or rationality. Chloe saw that a successful parent required the skills of an industrial arbitrator — the patience, the craft, the ability to identify and push forward a cohesive argument. Along with qualities of leadership and a taste for coercion. Well, she could supply all of that, given time and practice.

It is of course an uneven contest, in every way. Adults dictate, in the last resort, but children hold the insidious card of vulnerability. Chloe had normal maternal instincts: she beheld her offspring at their most appalling moments, and loved them, quite against her better judgment.

There thus ensued a precarious balance of power, with the upper hand swinging from one side to the other depending on the age and capacities of the child in question or on Chloe's stamina at that particular moment. And, indeed, as time went on, it seemed to Chloe that although she would sometimes have to concede an individual battle, the long-term offensive had on the whole been won. She did not like to think about parental life in those terms, but they seemed distressingly apt.

She came to see her own contests with Miranda in a different light. Except that "contest" was not the right word. Since Miranda had made no rules and set no behavioral parameters, there was nothing to fight about. And Chloe had not wanted to ride a bike on the main road, or consort with undesirable friends, or stay at a disco till after midnight. She wanted regularity, on a daily basis; she considered her mother's friends undesirable. There had been a sense in which the situation was reversed, with Chloe the sweet voice of reason and Miranda the force of anarchy.

Nevertheless, by the time the children were all into adolescence Chloe felt that it was possible to be fairly confident that home life would proceed on an even keel. The children might be occasionally mutinous, but by and large they did what was expected of them. Their school performances were entirely adequate; the boys were into sport but not to excess, Sophie played the violin rather well and was wondering about music college.

Miranda parted from the Spanish woodcarver and came back to England, where she set up in a tiny terraced cottage in a Cornish fishing village inhabited almost exclusively by painters and potters.

"Wouldn't you know?" said Chloe, on a visit. "Get me out of here! The sense of déjà vu . . . I feel as though I were ten again." John had been rather enjoying the local fish restaurants, but piled uncomplaining into the car and drove her back to normality. Miranda had given them a cheery though slightly abstracted welcome; she was much involved with the local community arts group and was learning how to weave. She asked tenderly after the children but had rather forgotten their ages. She was quite shocked when told. "I have grandchildren *that* old! Ssh . . ." She was in her late sixties and resented the fact.

By now, Chloe regarded her mother as simply a part of life's complexity. She could still be mildly irritated by Miranda but saw her as, essentially, the crucial directive element in her own struggle for fulfillment. "I mean, in a sense I should actually be *grateful* to her. If she hadn't been the way she was, would I be who I am? Look at it this way — maybe I needed that sort of kick-start. It's an old story, isn't it? Making good. I didn't exactly claw my way out of the gutter, but there's an analogy, don't you think?"

John, who knew what was expected of him, would say that indeed, yes, that might well be so. But since he did have views of his own he would tell his wife — fondly enough — that she was a born coper, in his opinion, and would have pursued much the same course, whatever.

"That's as may be," said Chloe. "Possibly. I'm a total believer in control over one's own destiny, to be grandiose. Well, you haven't lived with me for all this time without being aware of *that*."

John would agree, heartily.

"But, that said, I will allow that circumstances are formative. It may well be that my mum's deficiencies set me going, as it were."

The children, growing in articulacy, would put political interpretations upon their mother's attitudes: "Mum, you're just *so* right-wing."

"And you are being simplistic," she would tell them. "Politics don't enter into it. Though, as it happens, all politics are about control, anyway — whether it's the left or the right. My opinions aren't political, they're to do with how a person is to deal with life. And I vote pragmatically, I'll have you know."

The lives of children are mysterious, opaque even to those who know them best. Parents, existing cheek by jowl with their offspring, feel them to be almost an extension of themselves — their bodies, their habits, their speech and mannerisms so familiar that they seem to require no further consideration. This is not so, of course; much is going on there that would be startling and alarming if decoded. Mercifully, this alternative existence of children is also impenetrable.

Chloe had been aware of this problem, and so, in the early days of motherhood, she had boned up a bit on developmental psychology, which did not seem to get her very far. She learned about the limitations of spatial and temporal perception in infants, and that small children have difficulty in conceiving of a point of view other than their own, which perhaps accounts for some of the intransigence, but when it came to explaining the more baffling practices of nine- and ten-year-olds, let alone of adolescents, the experts were not much help. Like most mothers, Chloe came to accept that there is an uneasy duality with one's young: they are indeed those beings so intimately familiar to you, but these are shadowed by others who are away on business of their own which you would not understand even if you knew what it was. To dwell too much on this uneasy situation is to find your parental confidence corroded. Accordingly, Chloe did not, and got on with the practicalities of family life.

The boys were pretty unfathomable, as teenagers. Chloe decided that much of this otherness was to do with the gender divide, and did not get too concerned; after all, if you have never been a male adolescent yourself, there are going to be certain experiences that are a closed book. Sophie seemed considerably more transparent. Chloe knew — just — what it was like to be worried about your bust development or the shape of your legs; admittedly, she herself had been rather less focused on such matters than most girls, being principally concerned with the escape and advancement plan that she had already drawn up. Sophie was altogether dreamier, less applied and more susceptible to distractions. But nothing to get exercised about; she was doing fine.

Chloe's own career was in full swing, at this time. She was a busy woman, locked into a demanding schedule of meetings, school visits, desk work. It was a relief to feel that the children were nicely on course now, that they did not need the full beam of her attention, that you could allow the week to pass with only routine checks that all was what it should be. No need to be breathing down their necks; better, indeed, to allow them some space. The careful nurturing of the early years had paid off, she told John; they're motivated, they're as sensible as anyone can be at that age. Not much longer and they would be out on the open sea of adult life, for better or for worse. We'll have done our bit, she said, we've pointed them in the right direction, we just have to hang in there a while more, that's all.

Sophie's school reports suggested that she was perhaps underperforming, but she'd never been exactly a highflier, and looked set to get three A levels, if modest ones. Her eighteenth birthday was coming up, and Chloe planned an indulgent party, as encouragement. The boys, on the other hand, had become interestingly competitive — no bad thing, in Chloe's view. Trying to outdo one another would keep them on their toes.

Sophie announced her pregnancy over breakfast, one Sunday morning. "I'm going to have a baby," she said, and smiled modestly round the table.

It seemed to Chloe that the entire room swayed and heaved. She was unable to speak; she simply sat there staring at her daughter. The room swung around her; the faces of her husband and her sons lurched from side to side. Over the next couple of minutes Sophie spoke again, in a kindly way, and still Chloe could say nothing, and John was looking worriedly toward her, and the two boys had mumbled some excuse and left the room, taking their breakfasts with them.

At last Chloe found her voice — a low, shaky voice. "We can sort this out," she told Sophie.

And Sophie shook her head vaguely and said don't worry, Mum, I've been talking to people, everything's going to be fine.

"Fine?" cried Chloe. "Fine?"

Yes, Sophie had seen the doctor, and yes,

there had been discussion of abortion and the doctor was entirely sympathetic about Sophie not wanting that. Forget it. Not an option. The doctor had put her in touch with counseling people and clinics, everything was taken care of, Sophie knew where to go and what to do, she had diet sheets and an exercise program. And of course she would do her A levels, she could fit them in before the baby came. Sophie had talked to the Head and she had been really nice about everything.

No, she didn't want to talk about the father. He was someone she wasn't going out with anymore and she didn't want him in the picture.

Chloe was beginning to feel more stable. The room had ceased to swing. She could plan; her mind was racing — making arrangements, lining up possibilities.

"We can sort this out," she repeated. "We'll see what's the best way to go about it. We'll talk to people, find out about agencies, which are the best ones. . . ."

No way, said Sophie.

John cleared his throat and said that this needed thinking about, there was no need to do anything in a hurry, Sophie had to think this through, they must all take it calmly.

Chloe was silenced, poleaxed. For moments she just sat, staring at Sophie. Then she went into overdrive. "People are crying out for babies these days," she said. "There's a national *dearth* of babies for adoption. People go to Romania and Russia and South America for babies. They'd line up for this baby. This baby could have a perfect home, lovely parents who'd been yearning for it."

At which point she remembered suddenly that this baby would be her grandchild, and fell silent.

And there they sat. Sophie poured herself a glass of orange juice. She said that her diet sheet recommended plenty of vitamin C. She told her parents that they mustn't worry, everything would work out okay. Of course she'd been pretty shattered when she realized, but she'd come to terms with it now, she felt quite positive about it. People had been just *so* supportive. She looked rather hard at her mother, at this point. She thought it would probably be best if she and the baby moved out, eventually, but there was no need to start making plans yet — after all, there were months and months to go, plenty of time.

Chloe eyed her daughter and saw someone she did not entirely know —

whom she hardly knew at all, perhaps. She saw that she herself had been knocked aside by the onward rush of things, this unstoppable process whereby your careful construction of order and progress is swept away by the malign hand of contingency. The too-careless conjunction of two adolescents, to be precise.

"Music college . . . ," she whispered.

Sophie said that she hadn't been absolutely fixed on music college, anyway. Perhaps. Perhaps not. We'll see. She finished her orange juice and said she had to go and wash her hair now — she was meeting people later and she needed to do some revising first. She avoided the eyes of her stricken parents. Upstairs the boys had their sound system on too loud, with the door open, and Chloe knew that she lacked the fiber to do a thing about it.

Over the next few weeks Chloe assembled herself again — gradually, painfully. This had come about, and must now be confronted. She told her friends, in a matter-of-fact, take-it-or-leave-it sort of way. The friends said that well, there you go, that's life, and exclaimed to one another — with perhaps a touch of satisfaction — that you wouldn't expect this in *that* family, *Chloe* of all people.

She found that she tiptoed around Sophie. At night, she lay awake rehearsing a scene in which she sat Sophie down and they had a good talk. Let's just look at the . . . the other option, she said to Sophie. Let's weigh up the pros and cons . . . awfully young still . . . your whole future . . . best for both you and — and it — in the long run. To which Sophie would say, these are just pros, Mum, where are the cons? And Chloe would contemplate the cons and fall silent. A silence that obtained in the clear light of day, as she tiptoed, asking Sophie if she had any washing that needed to be done, or if she would fancy risotto for supper.

There were other adults in Sophie's life now — benign, concerned people in pseudoparental roles, or so it seemed to Chloe. She had been elbowed aside. There were the counselor and the lady at the clinic and the Head, who was being so really nice and helpful about everything. Chloe saw that, in fact, society had taken over. Sophie was a child of her time, and society was ready and waiting for her, equipped with professional advisers and advocates and benefit provisions. Sophie was a social statistic; she was expected, the arrangements were already in place. She had made her choice of the alternatives that were on offer for one in her circumstances, and that was fine with everyone; there they all were, standing by to hold out the safety net.

Miranda turned up unexpectedly, as ever. She called from the local bus station to say that she was on her way home from a trip to see friends and had suddenly realized where she was: All right if she came to stay for a day or two?

When told about Sophie she was surprised. "Ooo . . . I say! I thought they were all so clued-up nowadays."

Chloe replied tightly that they were, apparently. Everyone was. Sophie was getting a lot of support. She found that she did not wish to look Miranda in the eye.

Miranda lit a cigarette, unchastised. "Well, I hope she's being allowed to have her say. No doubt they've been going on at her about adoption."

Chloe became busy pouring coffee. She fetched Miranda a saucer for her ash.

"They always do," said Miranda. "First thing that springs to mind."

Chloe gazed out of the window. She sounded very casual, when at last she spoke, except that she couldn't seem to find an ending for her question. "Did anyone . . . I mean, back then . . . Did people back then . . ."

"Oh, of course," said Miranda. "It was all arranged. And then I couldn't go through with it. I looked at you and thought: no. But it was all fixed up — they were coming for you the next day. So there was nothing for it but to be up and off. Find someone to stay with until I could work out what to do. I thought of cousin Sylvia."

Chloe remembered cousin Sylvia. Many families have a cousin Sylvia. She was someone's sister, or aunt, who had somehow fallen foul of the accepted procedures of a conventional middle-class family of the mid-twentieth century and lived a raffish and ramshackle life on the other side of the tracks. Almost literally — Chloe remembered a dilapidated cottage beside a railway level crossing on a branch line in the west country. Cousin Sylvia had once been married, but no longer was, kept chickens and was indiscriminately hospitable and welcoming. There was often a burly farmer around who seemed to have his knees well under the table. In Chloe's childhood, she and Miranda would stay with cousin Sylvia for days and weeks when Miranda was at a loose end or undecided about where exactly she wanted to go next.

"Yes," said Chloe. "Cousin Sylvia. I see."

She did see. She saw just how cousin Sylvia would have been a catalyst, would have served as the prompt for Miranda's reinvention of herself, for her crossing over from one way of life into another.

She saw also that this conversation — if such it was — should have taken place long ago. She did not know if she wanted to hear more, or not. Miranda had in any case gone off at a tangent.

"Sylvia's still going strong. I went to see her. Over eighty now, though you wouldn't think it. Still keeping open house. If Sophie wants anywhere to hang out at any point . . ."

"No!"

Miranda shrugged. "Come to that, she's welcome *chez moi,* if she feels like it. It would be odd to have a baby around again, but quite fun really. Oh God — I suppose it'll be my great-grandchild. Help!" She reached for another cigarette, temporarily fazed.

Chloe's voice was rather faint. "Sophie is fine here." After a moment she added, "Thank you all the same."

She felt indistinct. She was not herself at all. It was as though her vision of the world had been given a violent shake, so that now all was differently assembled. For a moment, as Miranda spoke, Chloe had seen her life reel away on some unimaginable course — her childhood passed amid faceless strangers, John unknown to her, the children consigned to oblivion. She looked now at Miranda and saw a person who was indefinably changed. But everything had been subtly skewed over the last few weeks; Miranda was just an extra twist. You think your grip is firm, and find that nothing is reliable. Above all, she saw procreation as some sort of malign joke, this random throw of the dice that determines who gets born and who does not. Words floated into her head: "There, but for the grace of God, go I. . . ." But Chloe knew full well that God has nothing to do with it; she was a rational woman, she was an atheist. All the same, she glimpsed the awful, pervading irrationality that sends people running for cover into the churches.

Sophie's baby would be a girl — somehow Chloe was sure of that. There were these lines of women that extended back and forth through time, mothers and daughters and grandmothers, an inexorable progression. But every birth was a fortuitous event; the child born was a chance in a million. It was the uneasy alliance of this haphazard arrangement with the orderly descent of generations that had Chloe in a kind of despair. It was as though nature were jeering — confronting you with a diabolical marriage of order and disarray. You are programmed to go forth and multiply, but your children confound you. She saw with awful clarity that nature and nurture are not in apposition but have made some kind of provocative deal.

She offered her mother another cup of coffee. She emptied the cigarette stubs out of the saucer and replaced it at Miranda's side. It was Saturday. The boys were off at a sporting fixture, or so they said. John was beside some reservoir, with a fishing rod, a packet of sandwiches, and a book of crossword puzzles. Sophie was upstairs, doing the exercises recommended by the lady at the clinic. Everyone was in place, except that there was no guarantee whatsoever that they would stay that way.

Chloe never was, and I did not become Miranda. If a place is haunted, it is perhaps with the ghosts of ourselves, both past and future. Not long ago, I sat in the Albert Hall, watching a production of Aida. *My daughter was playing in the orchestra; her own two girls sat at my side. There was spectacle on the grand scale — an immense supine sarcophagus figure that rose up on pulleys, great sphinxes, a cavalcade of priests and soldiers carrying lit braziers, priests bearing poles with the heads of Anubis, Horus, Isis, Osiris. Watching, it seemed to me that I saw with double vision. The cast of the opera — the bronzed spear-bearers, the slaves, the white-robed attendants, the priestess with great wings — all of these seemed to drift through the revelers of New Year's Eve 1951, through the Pierrots and the masked ladies and the 1920s flappers and the girl in jeans and a green-and-white-checked shirt who should have been able to look up and see an elderly woman gazing down at her. I felt as though I were suspended in time, existing both then and now. I knew what I know, about the years that lay between, but I was also that girl who knew nothing of all that, and for whom things might have spun off elsewhere, who might have become someone else.*

The Temple of Mithras

Dear Professor Grimes,

I have read the article in *The Times* about your excavation of the Temple of Mithras in the City of London. I am a second-year History student at St. Anne's College, Oxford, and I am very interested in archaeology. The article mentions that you have student volunteers at your dig. Please may I come and help with the dig during the long vacation?

Yours sincerely,
Penelope Low

Dear Miss Low,

Thank you for your letter. I am pleased to hear of your interest in archaeology and would have liked to be able to invite you to join us in Queen Victoria Street, but I am afraid that we already have a full complement of student volunteers. I am so sorry.

I do hope that you will keep up your archaeological interest. You might wish to consider doing a Diploma or an

M.A. in archaeology after your degree. If you should, I would be happy to give advice about the various universities at which you could do this.

Yours sincerely,
W. F. Grimes

Fictitious letters. I do not have access to Professor Grimes's archive, and in any case letters from importunate students are unlikely to have survived, or his replies to them. But Professor Grimes is real enough, and he did indeed excavate the Temple of Mithras in 1954. And the student was real enough also. I do have vestigial access to the person who wrote a letter that ran something like that. And there is a clear-cut impression of a considerate and diplomatic reply from the professor — disappointing in that it put paid to those daydreams of a summer spent importantly scraping away in the Roman remains, but flattering in its concern for my future. His suggestion was never followed up. I did not go to Durham or to Cambridge to confirm that archaeological bent, in which case the forking path could have led to many places. Instead, I got myself a rather dead-end job after I took my degree, married young, and, eventually, became a novelist, which had never been on the cards, or so it seemed. But archaeology has played a theme song all my life.

The Temple of Mithras is real enough also. Or rather, was real. I paid it a visit the other day. But it is not there. On a terrace north of Temple Court, off Queen Victoria Street, there is a reconstruction of the ground plan of the building; the actual site lies beneath the foundations of the neighboring fourteen-story office block. Buildings rear up all around, traffic flows; the Walbrook, beside which the Mithraeum stood, is gone. The Museum of London has a display of objects found on the temple site: marvelous marble heads — bearded Serapis, fine-featured Minerva, the torso of a river god. They seem more actual and permanent, there in their glass case, than that 1950s excavation, my twenty-one-year-old self, and the kindly Professor Grimes.

The distorting feature of anyone's perception of their own life is that you are the central figure. Me; my life. But nobody else sees it thus. For others, you are peripheral. You may indeed be of significance to them — of great significance, perhaps — but equally you may make barely an impression; either way, you are *not the seeing eye. You are an adjunct, a bit player.*

So in the interests of truth and reality, most of these alternative lives of mine abandon the solipsistic vision. I am around, but shunted to one side. Stepping in as the novelist, I have woven myself into the general cast — an aspect of a narrative, which is all that any of us can be.

It is 1973. We are on a hilltop somewhere in southern England. Or rather, they are: this group of people apparently engaged in some random earth-moving operation. The hilltop is a mess, pockmarked with holes, scarred by long gashes in the turf, littered with buckets and wheelbarrows and a couple of tents and a smaller structure and a canary yellow JCB. And people: a group, of varying ages — one gray-headed man, three in their thirties or forties (one man, two women), a handful of young figures of both sexes. An anthropologist would be puzzled about the composition of this gathering, the kinship implications. What do they have to do with one another? And what are they up to, anyway?

There is a fine view from the hilltop — green distances all around, ridged with the dark lines of hedges, the whole complex, eloquent mosaic of English rural landscape. The hill itself has a curious tendency to undulate, up here at its crest; the turf rolls up into ridges, the ground does not seem to be behaving quite as it should, there is a sense of irregularity, of interference.

And that is of course the whole point. This is August 1973, but it is also the first century AD, and very many other points in time as well.

Never take anything at face value, thinks Alice. Nothing is ever quite what it seems. She thinks this as she emerges from the Elsan, which commands a particularly fine view, of the dig itself against the backdrop of landscape melting away toward a hazy horizon. There is a stiff breeze, as so often up here. She stands for a moment, looking at the chaos of the site, which makes a sort of sense to her by now; she stands there in the summer wind, with a kestrel floating at eye level and great luminous cathedrals of cumulus cloud passing overhead, and she thinks about violence. Just here, where they are digging, the ground whispers of violence. Blows and blood and screams and pain are hidden a few feet below the turf, in which pretty blue harebells grow, and cowslips and eyebright. This violence is silenced. The whispered testimony is all that is left of it — the sword hilt that was found in the main trench yesterday and that prompted several celebratory rounds in the White Hart that evening, the bones that are being exposed every day, many of them bearing significant grooves and fractures, the purposeful barbs of arrowheads, the sling balls. Something went on here. Something grim and final.

Other things are going on now. From where she stands, she can see that Luke and Laura are working side by side over by the rampart. Mike Chambers and Professor Sampson are conferring outside the big tent. Professor Sampson turns suddenly and goes inside. Mike Chambers walks off, fast.

Alice registers these conjunctions, but she is thinking about this deceptive place, this tranquil vista. You are looking at mayhem, all over Wiltshire and Dorset and Somerset, those calm green counties with their sleepy villages and the cricket pitches and the primary school playgrounds and the pubs with the hanging baskets that drip petunias and lobelia. Surface veneer, all of it. Dig a few feet and you are into bloodshed. The arrowheads and the axes and the swords and the daggers. The Stonehenge skeleton with the flint barb in its ribs and the bones at Maiden Castle, chopped about by sword blows, and the split skulls here at Cornbury Hill. This landscape is howling, if you listen.

But all that is academic now, in every sense. It is fodder for books and articles and conference papers; it will bolster CVs and job applications. The disheveled topography of the dig, with its pits and trenches, has reduced the evidence of what happened here to an assemblage of plans and labeled objects. Alice is no longer shocked or stirred when she sees another of those battered bones; she achieves the proper level of professional excitement when the word goes out that they have another sword blade, or a spearhead. It is only at night that violence simmers in her dreams.

Mike Chambers is beside Luke and Laura now, saying something. He points to the main trench. Luke gets up, rather slowly, and walks away. Professor Sampson comes out of the tent and looks at the horizon, where dark clouds are massing.

Alice is twenty years old and does not expect to live for very long. She does not believe that the world will go on for much longer. She is waiting for the bomb to drop. Each time she sees the word "nuclear" in the newspaper she feels that lead sinker in the pit of her stomach. She has marched for CND, of course, she has done her bit, but deep down she knows that it can do no good. The world is hurtling to its fate, and she with it; everything is in the lap of the gods — or, rather, it is in the hands of frenzied generals and mad statesmen.

Doing archaeology should concentrate the mind. You should be able to take the long view. *Sub specie aeternitatis.* All these extinguished cultures, all these vanished people, leaving nothing behind except various muddles of stone and a great many broken pots and hunks of metal and a scatter of bones, which gives employment to the likes of Professor Sampson and Penny Sampson and Mike Chambers and June Hammond. But somehow it doesn't work like that; the long view is neither bracing nor consolatory — it simply makes Alice think that it is pretty thick to have been born into the generation that will see the end of the world. "We who live at the end of time." Where did she read this? Who said it? One of the monks at Lindisfarne, is it, waiting for the next Viking raid? Or someone expecting the millennium, in AD 999? Whatever, she knows how they felt.

Penny Sampson walks toward the tent, carrying a bucket. She passes her husband; they do not speak to each other.

Alice heads back to the small tent. She is working here today with Eva, sifting material from postholes. Eva has her period, which means that she is getting stomach cramps, and wears a pained, stoical expression. You become very intimate with other people's physical condition under these circumstances, striving away alongside all day and then sleeping together at night. Alice sleeps with Eva and Laura in the infants' classroom of the village primary school that has been turned into a hostel and the dig's command center. Luke, Peter, and Brian have another classroom, while Guy Lambert is on his own in a third, June Hammond has the sick bay, and Mike Chambers gets the teachers' room to himself, with its attendant cloakroom. The rest of them use the children's cloakroom, with much jollity about the pint-sized toilets intended for the infants. One of the school dinner ladies is earning some holiday money by coming in to do breakfast, and they are each provided with a bag of sandwiches and fruit to take up to the dig.

The Sampsons are staying at the pub.

Professor and Mrs.; Paul and Penny. It is apparently all right to call them that, except that in his case you somehow don't. He is not exactly matey. Perfectly polite, but in that "us and them" kind of way. It is clear that he sees students as a separate breed. When he explains something, it is in a brisk, functional manner — enough information for people to be briefed and efficient, but that's all. Whereas Mike Chambers gets all expansive and enthusiastic; he's the other kind of archaeologist, all beard and bonhomie. He's a field man, it seems, whereas Professor Sampson is a theorist. Alice did get one of his books out of the library, but she found it hard going — all graphs and diagrams and tables.

Penny Sampson is a lot younger than he is. Around forty, whereas he must be going on for sixty. Apparently she is wife number three — she was a student on his M.A. course, way back. You wouldn't have thought he'd be a lady-killer — *three* wives — but there's no accounting for taste. She doesn't actually have a job, it seems — not as such. The others here have university posts, or they aspire to, like Guy, or they move from dig to dig, like June, but Penny Sampson's always been a sort of assistant to her husband, working with him on digs and then helping with the deskwork afterward, getting it all written up. She's pleasant enough, but seems a bit semidetached, as though her mind might be on something else a lot of the time.

Archaeologists always marry each other; they never meet anyone else. Mike Chambers said that in the pub one night, laughing. The Sampsons weren't around. "Speak for yourself," June Hammond had snapped. There's a lot of to-and-fro between those two. He winds her up, and then she gets stroppy. But he's like that with everyone. He isn't married himself, it turns out. Nor is she.

June has come on this dig because Iron Age hill forts are her special interest. She is small and stocky, like a pit pony, and as tough as anything. She can move stuff like nobody's business. Mike said, "We don't need the JCB when we've got June," which didn't go down all that well.

And then there is Guy Lambert, who is a Ph.D. student, which puts him in a sort of no-man's-land between the professionals and the students, though of course he intends to be an archaeologist. The students are the bottom of the hierarchy — the six of them who have signed on for the whole of the dig, and the handful of others who

121

drift in for a few days or so, a bunch of sixth-formers from the local comprehensive, a couple of French girls who are students of some colleague of Mike's, various others.

We're the labor force, thinks Alice. Cheap labor, at that, but we're all volunteers and there's something in it for us, too. It'll look good on our CVs, or we're doing it to please our parents, like Laura, or we're at a loose end, like Peter and Brian, or we've been told to, like the sixth-formers, or we're just interested, like me. Actually, everyone gets interested, to a greater or lesser degree. It would be hard not to — even Laura got quite excited when June uncovered the shield boss. And everyone reacts to the bones; Peter and Brian make macabre jokes, and Laura comes over squeamish, or she did at first, but now even she is pretty blasé. We're the old hands, the veterans; we even get asked to keep an eye on the newcomers, to see that they're doing things right.

They are here for six weeks, the duration of the dig. Two of those weeks have already passed, and now it feels as though they have always been here. Everything is entirely familiar: the camp beds in the primary school are no longer so hard, muscles have become used to kneeling or squatting all day, wind and rain are ignored. They know each other with an odd intensity; the outside world has come to seem irrelevant. And something strange has happened to time: it proceeds neither fast nor slow but seems to have become an entity, unrelated to normal days or weeks. They are in a time scale that is specific to the dig. Which is apt, thinks Alice, given the way history treats time, chopping it all up into sections.

Prehistory has to be neatly divided into segments, and laid out in order: Paleolithic, Mesolithic, Neolithic, Bronze Age, Iron Age. They had to do that before anyone could get a grip on it; they had to establish a chronology. And the system fosters an entire way of thinking; you even look at the present century in terms of decades — the twenties, the thirties, the forties . . . Each with a particular climate and some kind of logo — a flapper doing the Charleston for the twenties, Hitler's ranting face for the thirties, the blitzed facade of a building for the forties. And here they were now in the seventies, which are as yet too close up and intimate to have acquired a flavor. Alice supposes that she must be a child of the seventies — you are deemed to have sprung from the decade of your youth. Does she feel attuned to the times? Well, not particularly. She does not like pop music and she would hate to go to a music festival. She has never tried pot or anything else. She does not feel impelled to explore her sexuality. She is not a virgin, but she cannot chalk up a list of partners, nor would she wish to. She assumes that she has not yet come across the right bloke, but supposes that she will do so one day. Compared with many of her peers, she is in the slow lane, which does perhaps indicate a certain lack of accord with the spirit of the times. She thinks she might have slotted in rather better with the twenties; she has always rather liked the look of that period — the chunky little cars and the girls in frocks and the wind-up gramophones.

Alice finds that she does a lot of thinking, as she kneels and scrapes up there on the hill. She thinks about the bomb, as always, and about the people they are digging up, for whom the Romans were presumably their version of the bomb, because it is the Romans who stormed the hill fort, left arrowheads and spear shafts, provoked sling stones. Other people up here, back then, were also waiting for nemesis. But she thinks too about the others on the dig, because you cannot help but be involved when you are all flung together like this. She thinks how assorted they are, whereas the people up here waiting for the Romans would have been very assimilated, all living the same sort of life, with the same sort of experiences and expectations. Alice, who grew up in Enfield and went to the grammar school, can hardly imagine what it would have been like to be Laura, whose home is called the Old Rectory and who went to Cheltenham Ladies' College. Or Mike Chambers, who comes from County Durham and don't you forget it, and whose father was a miner.

Alice's father works in a bank. His world is all about money. When he picks up a newspaper he always turns first to those columns of small print at the back. When he is with his cronies, they talk about the market and the pound and the dollar and stuff that sends Alice out of the room. Money is boring. Money is *so* boring. And people should not be preoccupied with money.

Actually, she is coming to realize, everyone is preoccupied with money. Certainly, up here on the hill money is a frequent topic. Professor Sampson and Mike Chambers, who are joint directors of the dig, are concerned about the funding. Resources are stretched to the limit, which is why they have only six weeks. Professor Sampson and Mike can frequently be seen poring over a sheet of figures, in the White Hart of an evening.

Peter and Brian are skint. They are trying to save their subsistence pay — the beer money, as it is called — for a spree to Paris planned for the last week of the vacation. So they nurse a pint and a packet of crisps for the entire evening, having eaten as much breakfast as they can and made their sandwiches last all day. Luke is worse than skint, according to him; the bank is getting nasty about his overdraft and he owes his mother and his aunt and the college buttery and Heffers. Not that that stops him making a good evening of it in the pub, or running that beat-up old MG that sits outside the primary school attracting much interest from the village. Eva is worried about whether or not she is going to get a grant to do her M.A. Laura has well-upholstered parents and doesn't have to worry about grants, but she wants to go to Spain with her boyfriend and the parents are getting tight-lipped about providing the funds for this; she is on the dig to demonstrate to them how industrious and committed she can be. She phones the boyfriend from the pub each evening to complain.

Alice herself has no surplus funds, but neither is she in debt and she knows that she can get by on her allowance because she is careful and provident. But in this climate of financial crisis that is clearly a rather boring thing to do — more boring than to be obsessed about money. So she bows to the prevailing culture and trades horror stories of indigence.

Money is in the air, up here on the hill. Not as such — nobody needs ready cash and it is seldom seen; you would hardly know that this group was part of a cash economy. Indeed, exchange and barter seem more likely; there is a good deal of give-and-take, over the sandwiches and apples and soft drinks, during the midday break. But money strums away there in the background, lest anyone forget where and when they are. They may be up on a hillside with their hands in the detritus of the Iron Age, but it is still 1973, with all that that implies.

How did money rate up here on the hill two thousand years ago? Was their world all about money? It was certainly about survival — about enough to eat, about cattle and crops and power, and that's money in another form, thinks Alice.

Occasionally, they dig up money. There are two Celtic coins and several Roman ones in the trays back at the school, neatly packaged and labeled along with all the other finds — the shards, the bones (ox, pig, sheep, human), the spindle whorls, the needles, the inscrutable lumps of metal which are in fact belt buckles or harness fittings or hilt segments or cuirass hinges or awls or gouges or pins. Artifacts. The position of each artifact has been planned — the place where it lay until one of them loosened the dirt around it with a trowel. This is the static record, and it is not the past at all but the present, since these artifacts exist today. Alice managed enough of Professor Sampson's book, with its indigestible diagrams and graphs, to learn that the task of archaeology is to ask questions about the past of this material which is no longer in the past but very much present. The archaeologist is interested in the dynamics of past society; the challenge is to find links between statics and dynamics, to make assumptions about the middle range, which is the space between the two. These assumptions guide the archaeologist from observation of the static artifacts existing in the present to general theories about the dynamics of the past.

But actually, thinks Alice, it is the other way round. Sorry, Professor Sampson. The dynamic is what is going on now, here, today, during these weeks that we are fossicking away up here. It is whatever happened back then that is static, unchangeable, finished with — whereas we are in this interesting capricious dynamic in which the story has yet to unfold. Luke is trying to get off with Laura. Mike Chambers fancies Laura, too, but he thinks no one has noticed. There is definitely bad blood between Professor Sampson and Mike Chambers — words in the trench yesterday that stopped just short of a full-scale row. And what is it with the Sampsons? You never see them together — they hardly speak to each other. None of this will feature in the account of the dig that will eventually be published, but it is this brew of human relations that is the narrative, the dynamic.

Alice is back at the small tent. Eva is looking martyred. She says she thinks she may have to ask to go back to the school early. Professor Sampson is approaching, to check up on what they have achieved today.

Paul Sampson stares intently at an artifact. As a processual archaeologist — indeed, as one of the pioneers of processual archaeology — Paul knows full well that the interest of this object is its context in the past. The artifact itself is in a sense neither here nor there — or, rather, it is very much here but no longer there, which is why it is an enigma. He must decode this object — wring from the uncommunicating contemporary static in front of him the teasing dynamic of the past.

In fact, the artifact does not require very much by way of decoding, since it is all too recognizably his wife's spectacle case. The green plastic thing in which she keeps her dark glasses. But why is it open, and lying half under the bed? And why is there a further challenging artifact — her blue T-shirt — on the floor by the dressing table? And why is the wardrobe door open? And why, above all, are these objects here, while his wife is not? The last time he saw the blue T-shirt it was on Penny's back, an hour or so ago, up on the hill. And the glasses were in their case, which was on the dashboard of the car, and the car is no longer outside the White Hart, but entirely absent.

Even the most primitive exercise in

middle-range assumption suggests that Penny has gone off somewhere in the car, having changed out of the T-shirt that she had worn all day — hurriedly dropping it on the floor and snatching up her dark glasses, allowing the case to fall under the bed.

Why? Where?

The principal guest bedroom of the White Hart has a double bed that sags disconcertingly in the middle, a walnut veneer wardrobe, a scratched deal dressing table, a violently patterned carpet and pink floral curtains. It is suffused with stale cooking smells, as is the rest of the pub. In fact, not much cooking goes on at the White Hart, since the food — on which members of the dig depend in the evenings — consists mainly of Scotch eggs, ploughman's, quiche with coleslaw and a tomato, chicken in the basket, or baked potato with cheese and chutney. The smell seems intrinsic, and indeed is vaguely reassuring. Mike Chambers calls it a cultural indicator: "You know you're in England by that smell."

Neither Paul nor Penny Sampson is dismayed by the facilities of the White Hart. They have known worse — much worse. They have experienced remote Turkish inns, they have camped in Libya and Greece and Scotland. Penny has not bolted from the White Hart as soon as she could after the end of the day's dig in order to sample the fleshpots of Shaftesbury or Blandford Forum. Nor has she gone shopping, because her purse is lying on the dressing table.

So where has she gone?

Paul looks around the room. Penny's anorak hangs on the back of the door, but in any case those black clouds he watched earlier have dispersed — the threat of rain has passed. Her brush and comb are on the dressing table. Her nightdress protrudes from under the pillow. There is a pile of books on her bedside table — paperback novels for the most part. Paul does not read novels himself, of course, and finds her addiction vaguely irritating. Surely there are better ways of spending her time? She has been reading other things lately, too. He can see authorial names in the pile that give him a tingle of annoyance: Germaine Greer, Kate Millett. He has found an attitude of amused skepticism to be the best thing where this sort of stuff is concerned.

Paul has a wash and goes down to the bar. He will have to do some hard talking to Chambers this evening, who is becoming rather too independent and high-handed. This dig is under joint direction. Chambers had no business sinking that trench without consultation. He does not appreciate the importance of more work in the flotation tank on material from the best stratified layers. It was a mistake to team up with him. He has a considerable reputation but no sense of procedure. And an exasperating personality.

Sampson is getting up his nose. Tight-arsed bugger. Okay, so he's considered the bee's knees these days where theory's concerned, but his fieldwork is nothing to write home about. And he's a menace on site — always on about how we need to have a meeting about this, and we haven't yet agreed the agenda for that. We'd grind to a halt if things were done his way.

Mike is enjoying the dig. He always enjoys digs. Digs are what he is for. And this is an absolutely prime site, one that he's been dying to tackle. Plus it's not a bad group, Sampson aside. Old June is all right, even if she can't always take a joke. Guy Lambert seems a decent sort, and prepared to work his socks off. Mrs. S — Penny — is a bit subdued but who wouldn't be, married to that bloke? The students are the usual mixed bunch. Reasonable lineup of girls, couple of nice enough lads. That Cambridge twerp Luke is a bit of a pain in the neck, with his public school drawl and his old banger of an MG. Daddy's a high court judge — that was made much of on his CV, and Mummy's some sort of second cousin twice removed of Paul Sampson, which is why young Luke is getting his hands dirty on Cornbury Hill. Something to keep the boy occupied and out of trouble for a few weeks of the vacation. Luke knows sod-all about prehistory and cares less, but that expensive education has taught him how to lay on the charm. June has fallen for it hook, line, and sinker, the silly girl — doesn't seem to notice that it's never Luke heaving the big barrow, and that when it's raining Luke's got himself the cushy job pot-washing in the tent. Well, I've got news for young Luke. Guess who's on Elsan duty tomorrow.

Alice does not want to be an archaeologist. She is interested all right, but some basic instinct for self-preservation tells her that this is not for her. She has no idea what she does want to do — if indeed the bomb spares her for long enough to do anything

— but she knows that she lacks a certain fervor that is required, and that she senses in all the professionals on the dig, however variously manifested. Admittedly, you can apparently be an archaeologist and seldom dig at all, if ever. You can spend your time in a lab, assessing bones or snails or pollen, or scrutinizing bits of pottery. You can behave more like an anthropologist and batten onto such hunter-gatherers as still exist around the globe, and note the physical effects on the environment of butchering or cooking, with a view to applying these insights to interpretation of the archaeological record. Actually, Alice doesn't think she would much fancy that — hunter-gatherers tend to live in the most disagreeable circumstances, by all accounts; Cornbury Hill on a wet day is bad enough. She tries to envisage the Sampsons in the Kalahari or Alaska, or indeed Mike; no such experience has been claimed.

Professor Sampson had a face like thunder in the pub this evening. First he and Mike were cloistered together in a corner of the saloon bar for an hour or so, not looking as though they were enjoying each other's company, and then Penny Sampson suddenly appeared and her husband got up and kind of herded her upstairs. Later, she came down by herself and ate a Scotch egg with June.

June wonders if something is up with Penny Sampson. She seems on edge this evening, and earlier June saw her getting into the car, having rushed off from the dig as soon as they'd finished for the day. Said she was meeting a friend. "Did you find your friend all right?" June asked kindly, but Penny didn't seem to want to go into that, so they had something to eat and talked shop. Paul was nowhere to be seen, though Mike Chambers was much in evidence, as usual, chatting up anyone who came into the bar and showing off like crazy if they displayed any interest in the dig.

From time to time June would like to clobber Mike. That stream of not-so-funny jokes. The professional northerner stance that assumes the moral high ground because he's more working-class more right-on more rooted more plainspoken than anyone else. Which means he's entitled to make fun of anyone with a posh accent, such as Luke. It's okay for him to tease Luke by imitating the way he talks — that officer-class voice, Mike calls it, with a grin and the twinkly look that's meant to say — just having a laugh, nothing personal, okay? But there'd be all hell to pay if anyone started taking the mickey where *he's* concerned.

Plus, she can't stand all that macho stuff. Strutting about the place in too-tight jeans, the testosterone radiating off him. His favorite word is "wimp" — anyone's a wimp when he wants to have a go at them. Always with the grin and the twinkle, of course. And he's an out-and-out male chauvinist pig, no question. He likes women all right, but for one thing only. He fancies Laura, as does Luke, which is another reason Mike has got it in for Luke.

In June's opinion, Luke is a really nice boy. Okay — he's public school and his dad's a judge, but that's hardly his fault. He's got manners, which is more than you can say for many students, and he's helpful and friendly.

June has never had an academic post, but she has dug alongside so many students that she considers herself an expert on the species. This lot are a pretty reasonable bunch, in fact — Luke especially, and Alice, who is a bright, serious girl and genuinely interested in the work. Peter and Brian are your typical twenty-year-old lads, all chat and cheek. Laura is a bit of a home-counties princess, but she is pulling her weight. Eva is rather a whiner, always fussing about her grant application. She wants to do an M.A. in archaeology and anthropology, which makes her the only one of them for whom this dig is a really significant CV item, and that is very much how she sees it. June has already been lined up as a referee. Eva really wants Paul Sampson, of course, but doesn't quite like to ask.

Paul took her upstairs as soon as she came back, and required an explanation. He needed her to help him with sorting the seeds and snails sieved in the flotation tanks, and she was nowhere to be found. The bedroom in chaos; the car gone. Why? Where? The day's work is not at an end when we come down from the hill; she should know that.

One of those women, apparently. This so-called group. Happened to be down this way and wanted to meet up. He had made it clear that there was no time for this kind of thing in the middle of a dig. And then she had declined to help with the sorting, said she had a headache, and went down to the bar.

From time to time Paul remarks that his wife has apparently joined the sisterhood.

He says this with a grin, which can be interpreted as benignly tolerant or sardonic, according to inclination. If the other person appears baffled, he spells it out: Penny is displaying feminist tendencies. But he does not pursue the subject. He lets it fall aside — a matter for observation, merely. If someone seems keen to develop the point — women, for instance — he listens with a quizzical look on his face, a faint smile, one eyebrow lightly cocked. Those who know him well are familiar with that expression: students, colleagues, wives. When the other person is through with whatever point they had to make he comes back with some quick and dismissive rejoinder and takes the conversation elsewhere. So much for that.

Alice cannot imagine being thirty, like June, let alone forty or fifty or sixty, and really old is quite inconceivable. Since she is unlikely to get there this is irrelevant, but she does find herself thinking about age, as she scrabbles away up on the hill.

The bones that they find are those of people who died young; life was short back then. Someone as old as Paul Sampson would have stuck out a mile; a person in his forties like Mike would have been thought elderly. Alice has a great-aunt who is ninety-three and still expressing forceful opinions. If it were not for the bomb, Alice too could presumably expect that she might fetch up thus.

The bomb is special to us lot, thinks Alice, but of course there has always been something around to give people the chop. You got picked off by an arrow or a spear, or you starved or you died of disease. We've got antibiotics and immunization but we've got the bomb too, so they kind of cancel each other out in terms of progress.

It is a golden day, up here this morning. A blue sky with rippling veils of cirrus cloud, a soft stir in the wind, bees and butterflies at work on the grassy hillside. The fields round about are studded with sheep, black-and-white cows are spread out in drifts against the green. Hard to believe that anything nasty ever took place here. But it did, it did. Witness those gnarled fragments of weaponry lined up on the trestle tables down at the school, witness the bones.

But those people must also have looked up and thought: Oh, it's a nice day. Or something along those lines. They must have noticed the wildflowers and the butterflies, even if they didn't make lists and check up on the names, like Alice does, which is profoundly twentieth-century behavior. Cattle would have been of extreme interest to them, though not in any aesthetic sense. And they would above all have been intensely conscious of other people, of one another. The hill would have been a hotbed of interaction, of observation, just as it is now.

Alice reckons that Luke and Laura have done it. They've been to bed together. There's that look about both of them — a sort of heightened, satisfied look. And they've been rather pointedly not paying too much attention to each other this morning. How did they manage it? Where? Certainly not in the school — we'd all have known. They must have gone off somewhere in Luke's car. And, yes, come to think of it, one didn't notice either of them around yesterday evening. Peter and Brian were in the pub and I went for a walk with Eva, but where were Luke and Laura? In a field somewhere, presumably — bedded down in a hay meadow, all very Thomas Hardy. Well, at least Laura won't be a fallen woman, wandering along the hedgerows with a baby in her arms. Probably she won't get pregnant. She's on the pill anyway, in honor of the boyfriend — she told me that on the first night here. Her pills are stuck up on the shelf in our room, so that she won't forget. Will she be mentioning Luke to the boyfriend? Laura believes that other people should be absolutely open and candid with each other — she explained all that when we were working in Trench B the first week, apropos of the boyfriend and the fact that they've agreed not to get engaged at the moment, which doesn't mean that they may not do so in the future, simply that they both think it's too early for an absolute commitment. But of course they sleep together, that goes without saying; Laura thinks that sex should just be free and natural. I wonder if the boyfriend will agree.

They're fucking, those two. It's bloody obvious. The looks they give each other. You can practically smell the sex.

All right, all right — I'm an envious bugger of forty-five and I wouldn't mind getting into her pants myself. Not that she's ever going to realize that, and nor will anyone else — I've always known better than to make a fool of myself over students.

Pity June turns me right off. No joy there.

Apparently a very famous archaeologist

is going to pay a visit to the dig. A Grand Old Man. Alice has heard of Sir John Causley, and so has Eva, but none of the other students have. The prospect of this visitor has both Professor Sampson and Mike Chambers in quite a stew. There is much polishing up of the site; a new trench has been opened. Alice is given the task of redoing some of the more scruffy labels, because she has nice handwriting, which meant a peaceful day on her own down at the school. The material on the table is more orderly in consequence, and she has learned a lot in the process, such as how to distinguish a pin from an awl, or bronze from iron when both are lumps of corroded metal. She doubts if this knowledge is going to be of any use in later life, but since she fully accepts that knowledge is to be valued for its own sake, that is not an issue. She is not after all studying history at university as a vocational training.

The children at Little Cornbury primary school have also been studying history. This is evident from the artwork around the room. Greek vase figures have been most convincingly reproduced by Sharon Curtis, age ten, and various others; there is a plywood model of the Parthenon, mathematically exact, that must have required many painstaking hours; portrait drawings of the Greek gods flank an impressive clay head of Zeus, with beard and flowing locks. Clearly, history has been good fun. Which is fine, thinks Alice, arranging another arrowhead in its little plastic pouch: thus do you engage the interest of ten-year-olds. She wishes she had been at a school like this.

On the other side of the room is Professor Sampson's table with the material garnered from the flotation tanks. Alice is not fond of the flotation tanks, but has gamely done her stint when required. You empty bags of spoil into a sieve which is set over a forty-gallon oil drum, and you then run water through this from the hosepipe that has been set up. Despite wearing waders, you get extremely wet, and your hands freeze. The resulting detritus left in the sieve is then taken down to the school, where Professor Sampson will sort through it in search of the emmer wheat, snail shells, and other clues as to diet and environmental conditions in the area back in the first century AD. Snail shells are particularly eloquent, it seems. The whole process is time-consuming, and a source of dissension between Paul Sampson and Mike Chambers. Mike wants to concentrate on stripping as much of the site as possible in the little time that they have. Professor Sampson wants valuable evidence about climate and environment.

Paul would also like evidence that Chambers sees this dig as a joint venture. The man's attitude seems to be that he is entitled to proceed exactly as he pleases, regardless of Paul's views. He makes it manifestly clear that he has no interest in examination of the wider context of the site. Open trenches right, left, and center, grab as many finds as you possibly can in the time, and that's it, as far as Chambers is concerned. He is apparently impervious to reasoned argument. Sits there with that grin on his face and then says, "Okay, okay — let's just play it by ear, shall we?" And the next day you find he's putting another trench through the rampart, and taking students off the flotation tank.

They could do with a few more hands, the way things are going. Paul regards students as a necessary evil. They are an essential workforce, but they require supervision, take up time, and contribute an unwelcome element of levity and personal interaction. He is careful to keep himself expediently distanced from them, unlike

Chambers, who spends half the day back-slapping and then holds court in the pub every evening. Paul just about knows their names, after three weeks, and that is quite enough and all that is required.

Time was, Paul was not quite so indifferent to students. Penny was of course a student on his M.A. course when he first met her. But that was a long time ago and irrelevant and in any case he is annoyed with Penny at the moment.

Alice finds herself cast in the role of confidante. Laura thinks that she may be falling in love with Luke, which creates a problem: she might not after all want to go to Spain with the boyfriend, in which case she need never have come on this dig in order to impress her parents. Alice points out that if she had not come on the dig she would never have met Luke. This elegant complication silences Laura, but only briefly; she then has the idea that perhaps she could go to Spain with Luke. That would kind of straighten things out. What does Alice think?

Alice has no thoughts on the matter because at this moment her trowel reveals a curious-looking metal object. They are working in Trench B, which runs diagonally across part of the site and through the complex of hut circles marked out by postholes. Any out-of-the-ordinary find must be reported, so Alice goes off in search of Mike Chambers, who joins them in the trench and examines the object.

"Well, I know what that is," says Laura. "It's a nappy pin. You see them exactly the same in Boots."

"It's a pin all right," says Mike. "But forget nappies. They would have used this to fix a cloak or other garment. Well done, Alice — that's a nice find."

They all three contemplate the pin, and Alice notes that Mike is doing his best not to contemplate Laura, who is wearing a tight skimpy top that leaves her with bare shoulders and well-exposed cleavage.

"Okay, girls, carry on," says Mike, rather briskly. He leaves them, and presently they hear him joshing Luke, over in the other trench. He is calling Luke a wimp for using a kneeler. There is a tacit code of practice on the dig that while it is all right for girls to use kneelers, any male definitely loses face by so doing. Consequently, all the boys have sore knees, and Mike himself is no doubt heading for a major arthritis problem in the fullness of time. Never mind, honor is at stake.

147

Laura listens to Mike and rolls her eyes. She says, "Really, he is a bit much, isn't he? Luke calls him Asterix the Gaul." She yawns. "I couldn't sleep last night. That's a symptom, isn't it?"

Laura is not the only one to confide in Alice. Eva is not exercised about love or Spanish holidays, but she is getting these headaches, and also she is afraid that the hard bed in the school is affecting a problem she has with her back. Plus, she thinks that the principal of her college, on whom she depends for a good reference in support of her grant application, does not like her. It seems to Alice that possibly Eva is not cut out for a life in the front line of archaeology, but she refrains from saying so. People do what they are going to do.

Or do they? When Alice was ten she was going to be a vet. At sixteen it was social work, and at eighteen she fancied something in Africa with Oxfam, and now she hasn't got the faintest idea what she wants to do. The future — given that there is one — seems like some impenetrable fog into which you are required to plunge, blindly forging ahead in some direction that leads goodness knows where. Alice has always been a careful person, and the awful randomness of this arrangement offends her. She rather

envies those who are carelessly uncon-
cerned, like Laura, who might try to get
into the BBC, or publishing, and actually
would like to get married and have children but of course you can't go round
saying that in this day and age. Or June,
who started out teaching in a comprehensive
school and was seduced into archaeology
by a chance visit to a local dig, which
spurred her out of teaching and into a
different life. "Thank heaven," says June.
"If I hadn't happened to drop by that site
and got totally hooked I'd probably still be
battling with fourteen-year-olds. Pure luck."

June does believe in luck. Or rather, she
can't see that anything much else directs
what happens to you. Luck, and hard graft.
June is a worker, always has been. She
can't abide skivers and slackers, and you
get a few of those on most digs, though not
too much on this one. This is a funny sort
of dig. Each one has its individual climate,
and the weather on this is particularly
unpredictable, and that is not just the rain.
Mike and the Prof are at loggerheads more
often than not. The Prof and his wife don't
speak to each other. A couple of the kids
are very obviously having it off — not that
that's either here or there, but it does

rather thicken the atmosphere.

And Mike gets on her nerves, which is a distraction. June is here to work, not to be riled by some testosterone-driven director. Okay, he's a good archaeologist, and actually June prefers his methodology to that of the Prof, with his environmental obsessions, but when it comes to people management, Mike is abysmal.

June simply wants to dig. She loves it. She gets all her thrills from digging: the point when you can suddenly make sense of what you're looking at, the moment your trowel comes up against something intriguing. All she ever wants to do is to dig. She doesn't want a posh job, or any more money than just enough to live on. She just wants to go on as she is now, hiring herself out month by month, year by year, into a future which she never considers. What's the point? It will arrive anyway, bringing with it whatever the fates have laid up for you.

I'm going to make it rule number one on any bloody dig of mine in future that female personnel cover up. They can wear burkas. No tits on view, no bums, no flesh. And anyone suspected of copulation will be dealt with accordingly. Fuck the permissive society.

Mike means this, and would like to blaze away along these lines right out loud, though he has more sense of self-preservation than to do so. He has a strong streak of old-fashioned working-class Puritanism which is as offended by the spirit of the times as another part of him is gratified by the license that allows sexual indulgence on all fronts. This discord makes for some confused reactions from time to time.

There is an element of subversion about this dig, no question. Though Mike cannot quite nail what it is; just a feeling that things, or people, could go off the rails in some way. And it is only a couple of days till the grand panjandrum shows up for this state visit, which is seen as a high compliment and has Sampson running round like a scalded cat. Mike himself has been mildly cynical in public about Sir John Causley's impending arrival, pointing out that the old boy hasn't had a major excavation to his name for decades, much of his work is now quite outdated, and this is just a photo opportunity. There has been talk of the local newspaper covering the occasion. Privately, Mike is rather looking forward to making himself known to Causley, who remains an influential figure, and he knows that a good spread in the local rag, with some nice shots of the site, would be advantageous all round, even if it does bring a few gawpers in its wake.

Penny Sampson has gone. Just like that. Yesterday she was here, and today she isn't. Nobody seems to know if she's coming back or not. June has taken over her area.

Alice has already noticed the way in which, on the dig, news hops from person to person, changing shape in the process. In this instance, Penny Sampson has gone to visit a sick mother, it is said. No, she is ill herself — having a breakdown. She'll be back at the end of the week. No, she won't.

Paul puts the envelope from his wife under a pile of shirts in the top drawer of the chest. He would not wish anyone to see this, under any circumstances. For some reason, it is more insulting and exasperating to have your wife disappear to join up with a so-called women's group than if she had run off with a lover.

"Sick mother, my foot. She's walked out on him," Mike tells June, who shrugs, and refuses to comment. None of his business, nor hers.

The dig settles to Penny Sampson's absence. It has its own momentum, and soon it is as though she had never been. Part of an infant's cranium is found in one of the pits; Mike's new rampart trench is revealing evidence of a defensive structure; Luke and Laura are caught by Mike snogging behind the tents and there are words. Mike tells them to bloody well keep that sort of activity off the site; Luke laughs and says, "Will do, squire." Later, Laura tells Alice that it was *so* embarrassing, but actually quite funny too.

Alice is aware of a kind of latent anarchy in the air. People are edgy. Professor Sampson has been tight-lipped and acerbic since his wife's departure; he says little to anyone unless he must. Eva had a migraine and spent an entire day lying on her bed at the school. Two German students who were supposed to be joining them have sent a telegram to say that they cannot do so after all; Mike is saying that they are now seriously shorthanded and everyone is going to have to pull their finger out. And the weather is not helping. There have been twenty-four hours of continuous rain; the trenches are now quagmires and the entire site is sopping wet. The time when they were rained off was spent washing and sorting shards and doing other house-keeping chores, which meant that everyone was cheek by jowl in the tents. Mike made sure that Luke and Laura were kept as far apart as possible; in consequence they spent all day casting smoldering glances across the trestle tables. Professor Sampson stood staring morosely at the waterlogged site.

Alice cleans shards with a toothbrush. The impression given by the assembled harvest of the dig is that the ancient occupants of the hill were people who spent their time breaking crockery and losing small objects. This fits nicely with the theory of processual archaeology, she realizes, because of course this stuff has been shunted into the twentieth century and has lost all contact with its original existence. Those bits and pieces are now teasing references to their context back then. Alice marks a shard — CBH '73 — thus placing it even more firmly in this day and age, and listens to the rain hammering on the roof of the tent. Chucking down; raining stair-rods. Presumably the Celts had their own colloquialisms for bad weather. She thinks about the language that should hang in the air up here, centuries of it, the reverberations of a million exchanges about love and war, birth and death, and what to have for supper. Instead of which all that is left is this entirely tangible array of broken rubbish.

A wet day in the Iron Age would have had everyone cooped up, getting on each other's nerves, just like today. Alice is trying to avoid Guy Lambert, as politely as possible. It is not that she has anything against him; he is unassuming, rather reserved, a pale, weedy young man in glasses, with a slight stammer — but it is becoming apparent that he is taken with her. Alice is a bit flattered, but she really doesn't fancy him in the very least, and it would be unfair to pretend otherwise, so she has to be a little discouraging while not conspicuously unfriendly, which is quite difficult under today's cramped circumstances. He keeps coming over to her table, ostensibly to take a look at her trays.

That evening, Mike Chambers and Paul Sampson have another argument. The dispute begins as they are coming off the hill and escalates later in the school, where it is impossible to ignore what is going on, with the pair of them locked in not entirely sotto voce disagreement in a corner of the big classroom, surrounded by the spoils of the dig — the domestic bric-a-brac, the fragmented weaponry, the crucial snail shells and grains of emmer wheat. People tiptoe around them, pretending not to notice, and eventually retreat to the pub. There, Peter and Brian play darts with the local regulars, Laura and Luke hold hands in a corner of the saloon bar, Alice and Eva do *The Times* crossword. Later, Mike comes in, drinks malt whiskeys and engages in raucous repartee with the landlord. Paul Sampson is not seen.

Next day, the rain has ceased but the site is still awash, and it is clear that the directors are barely on speaking terms. The only matter on which they are united is the need to get things cleaned up for their eminent visitor. There is much bailing out of the trenches. Mike is in a thoroughly bad mood. He orders everyone about, slags Luke off for his desultory labors in a flooded pit, and snaps at Eva, who is picking her way around in the mud with a martyred expression. The others give him a wide berth. Laura and Alice work together at the drier end of a trench; Laura confides that she and Luke are planning a couple of days away next week: she is going to take him to see her family — she knows Mummy will really like him. Alice perceives that the boyfriend's days are numbered.

She points out that the dig is supposed to be a six-week full-time commitment; Laura laughs merrily.

In the middle of the day, Eva announces that she has another migraine, and returns to the school.

June says that frankly that girl needs to rethink her career plan.

Alice finds a pair of tweezers. They are embedded in the muddy wall of the trench, and are so entirely twentieth-century-looking in appearance that she takes them for just that — a piece of contemporary flotsam. She owns something very similar herself. But no, Mike says that this artifact is from the Iron Age. At the end of the day, it joins the other finds in the tent, where Paul Sampson gives it a cursory inspection — he would rather have an array of snail shells, probably — and Guy Lambert takes what Alice feels to be exaggerated interest. For her, this homely implement is rather touching; for what finicky operation was it intended? Was its owner male or female, old or young? Female seems somehow likely, and Alice has this picture of someone around her own age, which in the first century would be the prime of life.

She does not see herself as being in her prime. She can vote, or join the armed forces, but she is corralled in a category that denotes youth, and immaturity — she is a student. The best is yet to come, she assumes, the time when she will be a fully paid-up member of society, with all that that implies. Whereas back then, up on the hill, everyone was paid up and liable from the word go. Except that everyone is liable, always, when it comes to spears and arrows and the bomb.

Is she the only person here who thinks about this sort of thing? Possibly. None of the others have been on CND marches, and indeed their eyes glaze over if the subject comes up. Patently, they do not suffer from nuclear angst. Well, lucky them.

But Alice's angst comes in fits and starts, like some chronic disease that flares up at intervals. And right now she is more or less free of it, on this summer day when the world is fresh and clean after the rain and you cannot help feeling an uplift, a cheery disregard of local tensions and indeed of the horrors of the human condition. It is good to be up here on the hill, in the sun and the wind, with the bees and the flowers and a lark somewhere overhead. Though she cannot help noting what a mess the dig has made of the place; before the JCB moved in, and the spades and the picks, there was just springy green turf. Archaeology is also desecration.

Sodding weather.

Causley arriving tomorrow, and the site still as mucky as hell, despite everyone's efforts, if you can call them that, which in some cases you can't. Well, the old boy will have seen worse. The point is to demonstrate a well-planned dig, show off the most spectacular finds, turn on the charm, and let him go away impressed with a well-run show about which he'll chat to his chums in the Society of Antiquaries and maybe mention one's name in the process.

You're a bloody creep, Chambers.

One should have doubled the number of student volunteers and put a group full-time on environmental material. With wisdoms of hindsight. Had one realized what Chambers's performance was going to be like. Too late now.

Causley of course is not too sympathetic to today's approach — any more than Chambers himself, who appears to be stuck in some professional time warp. All the more reason to show what a properly focused contemporary excavation is trying to do. The man may be sidelined these days, but he has significant connections.

The Grand Old Man arrives half an hour late, by which time the reception committee of Paul Sampson, Mike Chambers, and a delegation from the *Wessex Gazette* has run out of any small talk that it could muster. They are standing in silence when the car draws up, driven by a young acolyte, who helps Sir John Causley out and hovers respectfully with stick and folding chair to hand. The party makes a slow and deliberate progress up the hill along the well-worn track, which is now extremely muddy. There has been an attempt to doctor the worst bits with straw begged from a local farmer, but even so it is heavy going. Eventually the group reaches the site, where people are pretending to be hard at work.

Contrasting sartorial style is conspicuous today. Paul Sampson has put on a tweed jacket and tie, with cord trousers. Mike wears jeans and a red-and-green checked shirt. The students are much as usual, with Laura in hot pants and a bra top.

Sir John Causley also wears a tweed jacket. He is stout, bald, a little lame and, yes, well into his eighties. Laura, Luke, Peter, and Brian see simply an old boy about whom a lot of fuss is being made. Alice sees a person she knows to be somewhat famous and is a little awed; she has not much come across famous people. June, Guy Lambert, and Eva see reams of text loaded with tables, diagrams and definitive data; it seems a little odd that all this has sprung from the bent figure now struggling over the last fifty yards to this site. Mike and Paul Sampson are acutely conscious of legendary distinction, though neither would for one instant admit this, even to themselves, and have been careful in their different ways to voice their independence of the dinosaurs of their trade. For the reporter and photographer from the *Wessex Gazette*, this is just another assignment, though rather damper and more strenuous than most.

Mike has given thought to the handling of this event. He has in mind a conducted tour, during which there will be several staged photo opportunities that will feature himself and the great man, and himself gazing speculatively into a trench. He has already briefed the photographer on the most strategic point for a general view of the site. But it is soon apparent that their visitor is averse to tight control. He keeps veering off the chosen course, or lingering over some feature that takes his fancy. He also talks volubly; it is quite difficult for either director to get a word in, let alone a sustained explanation.

Sir John arrives at Trench C, which is Mike's new excavation through the rampart. Laura and Alice are busily scraping, while keeping a wary eye on the approaching group. Mike launches into an account of the newly revealed section of wall, but Sir John's attention is elsewhere. He focuses on Laura: "Why doesn't this young lady tell me about what is going on in this trench?"

Laura smiles charmingly. She puts down her trowel and says that, well, they're sort of opening up this bit and they're looking out for, well, anything important, and in fact they've just found this — actually I didn't, Alice did — this, um . . .

"Hinge?" suggests Causley.

"Right," says Laura, beaming. "This hinge."

Causley sits down in his folding chair. "Now, this might interest you, my dear," he begins. "When we were digging in Mesopotamia in '36 . . ."

He continues thus, at length. Laura is apparently entranced. The rest drift over from the other trenches. "Gosh!" says Laura. "That is *so* interesting. . . ." The *Wessex Gazette* contingent close in, the photographer busy. Paul Sampson and Mike Chambers stand a little apart, superfluous.

After some while the acolyte clears his throat and murmurs something.

"Good heavens!" says Causley. "As late as that . . ." He heaves himself up.

Paul Sampson steps forward determinedly, talking about the exhibits down at the school: ". . . give you a good idea of the kind of material we're finding so crucial now to establish the wider picture . . ."

The acolyte murmurs again to Causley.

"Oh dear," says Causley. "We've got this lunch date, you see. Can't keep our friends waiting. Have to leave that for another time, I'm afraid. Too bad."

The acolyte attends to the chair, proffers the stick. Causley beams upon the students. Laura bats her eyelashes and says, it was *super* hearing all those fascinating stories. The photographer takes another shot.

There is a royal progress back down the hill. Mike Chambers positions himself at Causley's elbow, but is unable to insert more than a few words into the departing discourse. Causley is now recalling Syria in '34 and Orkney in '57 and Brittany in '51. Cornbury Hill is eclipsed by legendary endeavors, put in its place, relegated. Age has pulled rank; Mike and Paul share a certain dismissive feeling for their visitor, as one whose day is done, but it would be quite impossible for either of them to display anything other than deferential attention. And so Sir John talks himself into the car, waves a benevolent hand from the window, and is driven away, leaving the directors of Cornbury Hill '73 to climb back to the site, more or less in silence. The *Wessex Gazette* contingent has already made off, and up on the hill the others are sitting around drinking Tizer and munching apples. "What an old sweetie," says Laura.

People return to the trenches and the pits, to the tents, to the flotation tank. The dig judders into activity once again. It is the middle of August, the middle of the time during which they will be here. Presently the place will be abandoned; in due course all evidence of their labors will be hard to identify. Their occupancy of the hill is but a passing moment. Nothing has happened, in terms of the hill's experience.

Except that it has, thinks Alice, as she kneels and scrapes. People have rubbed up against other people; they have squabbled, like Mike Chambers and Professor Sampson, or they have started a love affair, like Luke and Laura, or they have made some decision and disappeared, like Penny

Sampson, who apparently is not coming back and must be somewhere quite else now, getting on with things that we know nothing about. The thing that has happened, really, is that a whole lot of lives have briefly touched and will then spin off in different directions. Probably I'll never set eyes on any of these people again, but they'll always be in my head.

A few days later, the dig features in the *Wessex Gazette.* There is a photograph, but it is one that pleases neither director. It does not display the site to advantage, nor does it feature either of them demonstrating some point of interest to Sir John Causley. The photograph has Laura smiling up from an unidentifiable patch of disheveled earth, trowel in hand, a vision in a little halter-neck top and matching hot pants.

The *Wessex Gazette* has also a center spread which discusses the potential effects of a nuclear blast on the region. It shows a map of southern England over which are superimposed concentric rings indicating areas of total devastation, lesser devastation, radioactive fallout, and so forth. Alice studies this, though she would prefer not to do so. And, next day, she seems to see those concentric rings hovering about the landscape — the fields, the drifts of cows, the die-straight line of the road first laid out by the Romans, the melting green-blue distances. It's not fair, she thinks, it really is not fair to be living now, of all times.

I have taken considerable liberties, in these fictional projections of an alter ego. The disaffected Penny Sampson seems distinctly possible. I did indeed marry an academic, in real life; he was about as different from the misanthropic professor of this episode as is possible. But we are all conditioned in a sense by those to whom we are bound; my real-life husband affected the person that I have become. Without him, with someone else, who knows what twists of personality might not have come about. Miranda of the feckless lifestyle seems a wilder supposition altogether. I am a rather pragmatic and organized person. I was about to write "naturally pragmatic and organized" — but is that the case? Are such tendencies innate, or honed by circumstance? All I can say is that when I was young I much admired those who displayed artistic leanings, the more defiantly flamboyant the better, and when I was about nine I asked to be rechristened as Miranda, instead of my own plodding name. My parents declined.

The Battle of the Imjin River

Personal life is set against the background noise of public events. When I consider my own, each period is flavored with the times. In the sixties and seventies, I endured nuclear angst, like Alice; as a young mother, I looked at my small children during the nine days of the Cuban missile crisis and thought that they might never grow up. My next-door neighbor and I had a strategy worked out, should the four-minute warning go: I would mind our small children, she would dash to the primary school to fetch the older ones. In four minutes?

Before that, there were other points when private life was suddenly skewed by what was going on in the world. At the time of the Suez crisis, I was in Oxford, with that rather dead-end job, but also just getting to know Jack Lively, whom I would marry before too long. He was then a junior research fellow at St. Antony's College, and was at once in the forefront of those trying to coordinate the university's protest against the policy of Sir Anthony

Eden, the Prime Minister, in colluding with the French and the Israelis to invade the Suez Canal zone. I was right behind him, and remember those days as my first experience of indignation at an external event, and of political commitment.

Earlier still, there had been a more cataclysmic disturbance yet. I don't recall being much aware of the Korean War. I was in the hinterland between school and university when it broke out, being "crammed" for Oxbridge entrance at a boarding establishment in Surrey. The only American girl there was summoned home by her father, who considered that the Third World War was imminent. The rest of us went on mugging up the Industrial Revolution and the Tudors and Stuarts.

Jack was in the last months of his national service. He was twenty-one years old; it would be five years before we met.

His regiment was the Royal Northumberland Fusiliers, one of those detailed for service in Korea, along with the Gloucesters, the Royal Ulster Rifles, and the Middlesex. National service had been extended after the outbreak of the war in 1950, and Jack was devastated to realize that he would now be sailing for Korea along with the regular soldiers and reservists serving with the regiment. He had applied for a place at a Cambridge college. Three weeks before the regiment was due to embark, he heard that he had been accepted by St. John's, and was thus reprieved. Some national servicemen with university places were granted early release. But not all. The army seems to have exercised some form of capricious choice as to whom they let go. Jack was lucky.

And so, by a whisker, he missed the battle of the Imjin River, into which other national servicemen with the Northumberland Fusiliers were flung, some of them within days of their arrival in Japan for forward posting to Korea.

A thousand British soldiers were killed, wounded, or went missing at the Imjin River, one of the earliest and bloodiest battles of the war. The Gloucesters suffered the worst, and also gained great glory for their stand at "Gloucester Hill," when entirely surrounded by the Chinese advance.

I might never have known him. We might never have met. There might never have been our children, and theirs, and the forty-one years of love and life and shared experiences, and those long hard months at the end.

What follows supposes what so nearly happened: the fate of a young man who is a shadow Jack for whom events ran differently.

He stared out over the edge of the trench into the darkness. It was three o'clock in the morning. Oh, he had done this kind of thing before — maneuvers on Salisbury Plain. But that was then and this was now — an insane, incredible now that should not be. And the darkness of Salisbury Plain was an amiable, homely darkness, whereas this darkness was malign; at any moment it might hurl machine-gun bullets or a grenade at you. The darkness of Salisbury Plain was a great calm circle, but this darkness was broken by the jagged shapes of hills, it was lit every now and then with flares or a shower of green or red tracer, it emptied into the whine of shells.

He thought: This is not happening. This could not be for real — this place on the other side of the world to which he had been shipped and flown, a piece of human freight. He was not here. Really, he was in his room in a small house on a council estate in Newcastle-upon-Tyne; he was back in the time of reason, two years ago, his books spread out on the table — R. H.

Tawney and G. D. H. Cole and the Hammonds. There was a cup of Nescafé with wrinkled skin on it at his elbow, the lino was chilly under his feet, downstairs his mother had *Housewives' Choice* on the wireless. That was where he was really, not here.

They were on stand-to. Somewhere out there in the darkness, on the other side of the river, the Chinese were moving. Many Chinese. The enemy. The map that they had been shown had this looping river, the Imjin; north of it lay the menacing territory out of which would come the enemy attack, to the south were their positions, Twenty-ninth Brigade — the Gloucesters to the left, the Belgian battalion to the right, themselves in the center, the Ulsters behind, in reserve. He had craned to see this map, spread out in front of them by an impatient officer who had more pressing things to do than brief a bunch of newly arrived national servicemen. He was struck by the bleak number references accorded to the hills — the height in meters, 257 and 194 and 398 and so on — and it occurred to him, even in the trauma of his hideous arrival, that they must have names. The people here would call them something. He had remembered the Lake District, where he had walked —

171

Cat Bells and Langdale Pike, Skiddaw and Saddleback.

He thought he saw the darkness move. His stomach churned; his fingers tightened on his pistol. And then the movement defined itself: the shifting branch of a bush. A little gust of wind.

In his kit bag there was the War Office pamphlet: "Notes on Korea, August 1950." He had read this several times on the voyage out, sitting on deck amid the wastes of the Indian Ocean, or lying in his bunk in the cramped cabin shared with three others. Officers' quarters, relative comfort; elsewhere were the teeming fetid tiers below decks.

ON SUNDAY 25 JUNE 1950, SOUTH KOREA WAS INVADED BY THE NORTH KOREAN COMMUNIST ARMY; NOW YOU YOURSELVES ARE GOING TO FIGHT THESE NORTH KOREANS. WHAT IS OUR QUARREL WITH THEM? HOW DOES THIS AFFECT YOU? WHY, IN FACT, ARE YOU GOING TO KOREA?

Why indeed? But he knew why. It was because that is what history does to people. It picks them up by the scruff of the neck and puts them where they do not

172

want to be. It scuppers them; it condemns them to national service and then throws them this, as an extra treat. He was interested in history; at school, he had sat at the feet of a charismatic history master; he had won the sixth-form history prize. At this moment, he would prefer to stand aside from history.

A sound. Scurrying. Someone coming. He tensed again. Then the reassurance of a hoarse whisper — a Geordie whisper, a Fusilier whisper, one of them, an NCO going from trench to trench: they could stand down for an hour, brew up. The men alongside him shuffled with relief, slumped in the trench, lit cigarettes.

YOU ARE GOING TO KOREA TO HELP THE SOUTH KOREANS TO REPEL AGGRESSION; AND, MORE IMPORTANTLY STILL, TO UPHOLD THE CHARTER OF THE UNITED NATIONS AND TO FIGHT FOR THE PRINCIPLE THAT THE WORLD MUST BE GOVERNED BY THE RULE OF LAW AND NOT BY FORCE.

Ah. So that was what they were there for. For noble, enlightened reasons. Never mind that the goalposts had now been subtly shifted and it was the Chinese that

173

they must fight, and what had *they* been told, one asked? And a fat lot of consolation was all this high-mindedness out in the middle of the Indian Ocean, or in a transit camp in Japan, and least of all here, now, in a trench on a freezing hillside with people who intended to kill you somewhere out there in the darkness.

He was twenty-one. He was interested in social justice, the music of Mahler, Newcastle United, girls, books, and argument. He had been reading his way through Newcastle Central Library since he was fourteen. He played rugby, cricket, and the violin. He was a member of the Labour Party, the Youth Hostel Association, and the Newcastle Literary and Philosophical Society.

He owned a bicycle, a violin, a gramophone, three Beethoven symphonies and two of Mahler's, the Concise Oxford Dictionary, the complete works of Evelyn Waugh and eighty-nine other books, a compass, a map of the Lake District, and not much else.

Someone handed him a mug of tea. He must have dozed off for an instant, leaning up against the wall of the trench, and was jolted back to consciousness by a thud and then an explosion that he recognized as mortar, quite near. Gunfire too, closer than before. The platoon commander was telling them to get back on watch. He stared out into the darkness, which was leeched with light, a proposal of dawn, and was hectic now with flashes, flares, tracer, the sound of firing, of explosions. Intensified, continuous rather than spasmodic — something going on out there, down there, over toward the other company positions, three miles away, nearer to the river.

"That's Z Company getting it. And the Gloucesters." His own former platoon sergeant was next to him in the trench, the familiar voice somehow reassuring, known from Catterick, from Salisbury Plain, from that other life a world away. Most of the men around him here were strangers, regulars and reservists, their Northumbrian accents the only unity. The officer commanding this platoon to which he had been attached as observer and second in command was a regular soldier, the men a mix of veterans and the raw, newly arrived national servicemen.

Daylight came. Now you could see the lumpy green hills again, this queer artificial terrain that had seemed alien as soon as he set eyes on it — no landscape he had ever seen was like this, with the row upon row of jagged peaks, seemingly endless, receding into the distance. W Company was stuck up on the side of one of these, looking down on the road that ran to the river, which was shallow and easily forded, no obstacle to the enemy — the briefing officer had told them that. They could see a bend of the road, with armored cars and lorries and sometimes one of the Eighth Hussars' Centurion tanks, and a stream of the carts on which Korean porters brought up supplies. The river was invisible, beyond the next peaks, on one of which Z Company was dug in. And that was ablaze, it seemed — smoke, flying tracer, a barrage of noise.

The sergeant was looking at him: "You've lost your rose, sir." It seemed like a reproach.

They had been issued yesterday with red and white roses for St. George's Day, flown in specially from Japan, and many men still wore them, tucked into their battledress or their beret — limp, incongruous tokens.

Sir. The sergeant was older than he was. That "sir" always gave him a twinge of embarrassment. Army hierarchy offended his deepest instincts. The army trawled its catch and selected those who had higher educational qualifications or were apparently more intelligent — categories not always mutually compatible — and set them in authority. He was an officer because he was a grammar school boy and, yes, he was clever. And, yes, an army has to have a command structure. None of this made him feel easy with the sergeant's "sir." He and the sergeant shared a background — they spoke the same language, recognized the same codes; the crude dictation of the army had thrust him with public school boys whose attitudes and assumptions he despised, and who in their turn patronized grammar school types.

He knew that if the officer in command were killed or wounded he would have to lead this platoon, and a role that he had found possible at the barracks or on Salisbury Plain, if unnatural and occasionally alarming, became out here a nightmare. He thought of the time he had got lost on an exercise, with thirty men, and brought them back to base ten hours late. Here, a mistake could cost men's lives. His training had all been in anticipation of this moment; a hypothetical event, back then, but now an incredible reality amid these foreign hills. Others depended on him; somehow, the sobriety of this knowledge helped to steady him.

The sun came up; a bright, clear, spring day. There were new green leaves on the stunted, windswept trees, and shrubs that had purple flowers. And every now and then the ground shook, the hills were exploding, sending up bushes of white smoke, and the whole place was frenzied, manic, treacherous. He found that he was superficially calm, could do what he had to do, function correctly. But there was cold fear within. The thing was to keep it there — tamped down, in check. The routines of trench existence were a kind of solace; he was constantly busy — supervising the rotation of guards, checking signals procedures, overseeing the storage of greatcoats and surplus kit now that night was gone.

They had another brew up; they ate. He was surprised that he was able to do so, was even hungry. The ration packs were American and their contents seemed exotic — pork, beans, and pineapple slices, which were a luxury at home, a tin of them opened up for Christmas, or for Sunday supper. He sat eating, and the taste brought back his home, and the time before the army staked its claim.

He hated national service. In the initial weeks he had bitterly resented the way in which every minute of his time was allocated. He hated the bull, he hated having to change his clothes several times a day, he hated uniforms and weapons and sleeping every night on a thin hard bed, the blankets of which had to be folded in precise alignment every single morning. He hated the hours spent blacking boots and cleaning equipment. As an officer, he was spared the daily grind of basic chores, but his life was still commandeered. He had survived by counting the months, the weeks, the days. He was a rational being; he knew that this experience was finite. And then it had landed him with this.

The day inched on. There was intense activity down on the road, and several times mortar bombs fell close by. The action was still at some distance, and another sound was to be heard now. Bugles. A haunting sound that rose and fell, insistent against the crackle of rifle fire, the rattle of machine guns, the explosions. Chinese bugles — their system of command and communication.

He was straining his ears to evaluate this eerie, uncomfortable music when the officer came running from trench to trench: they were to prepare to advance. Z Company had been forced to retreat from the key hill position beyond them, which commanded the road junction. Both Z and Y Companies had withdrawn and were regrouping farther south. Their own company was to attempt an assault on the Chinese positions on the crucial hill: "Get cracking. We move in fifteen minutes."

It was then that time went haywire. Before, he had been aware of the passage of hours and minutes, of the turning of the world. Now, all was one continuous moment, a helter-skelter process of kitting up, scrambling through undergrowth, sliding on slopes covered with loose shale, following the man ahead, listening for orders, plunging this way and that through the trackless landscape. And all the while the gunfire getting nearer, a whole tree flying apart once, hit by a mortar bomb, an aircraft roaring overhead, an American fighter, spawning silver sticks that fell and whined.

Afterward, he had no idea what had sustained him through the attack, how he had been able to go on, to stumble up that hill, to fire a rifle, and fire again, swept up it seemed in some unstoppable, unquestionable progress. Once, he had fallen, hitting his knee against a rock, and the pain had kept him momentarily slumped there, his heart banging, a brief instant that raised the possibility of simply staying like that, of not getting up, not going on. And that instant had fused at once with the next; he was on his feet again, forging ahead, going on up that hillside, from foothold to foothold, rock to rock, toward the flashing summit from which came bullets and grenades.

The assault line ahead of him was within range of the enemy positions now: the men were firing continuously. And the Chinese were screaming, up there invisible beyond the thick curtain of scrub below the brow of the hill — a thin, chilling noise that was presumably intended to do just that — curdle the blood. It was at this point that everything seemed to compact, so that later he could remember only that at one moment they were going on and up, and then suddenly men were running back toward them, shouting at them to pull back. He remembered an intensified barrage of fire from the summit, he saw other leaping figures beyond their own men, mustard-colored uniforms snaking through the bushes, waves of them, it seemed. A mortar bomb fell so near that the blast made him stagger. An officer was coming down the slope above, waving and shouting. He realized that the assault had failed, and then he was sliding and stumbling his way back down the hillside they had just climbed, and there were bullets whistling past.

They regrouped half a mile or so farther back, on high ground, near to the positions taken up by X and Y Companies. The rest of the day was spent digging in, a relentless task battering at the hard stony soil with picks and shovels. His direction of a group of men was interrupted by the platoon commander: "We'll have to do without you for a bit. Pick a carrying party and get going — there's a mortar and ammunition to be brought up from HQ."

He was shown the map, given further instructions. Brigade HQ lay a few miles back. He should lead his group off the hill and join up with the road: "Report to Major Harrison. Watch it, though — you could run into an enemy assault party."

They made their way down the hillside, the men relieved to be released from digging in, but jumpy as they wove their way through trees and scrub. One of them grabbed his arm as they approached an outcrop of rock: "Sir! Something moved behind there . . ." It was a man from his own platoon back home, a stunted, anxious lad from Ashington, as ill at ease in the army as he was himself. He told the men to get down, and left them lying there as he crept round through bushes until he could see beyond the outcrop, his heart racing. He found nothing, and turned to wave the men on. The road was now clearly visible, with its confusion of activity. They would be safe down there.

There were jeeps, armored cars, carts, lorries, the occasional tank. A lorryload of wounded passed them, ashen-faced men clinging grimly to the sides, shaken and jolted as the vehicle navigated the ruts and potholes. At one point he halted his men to check with a sergeant who was bent over a stalled motorbike as to how far there was still to go. As they spoke, the sky was ripped by two U.S. fighters; they circled and then came hurtling down toward the rise beyond the road. The sergeant stared up at them: "The enemy's got a mortar position some-where in there — that's what those boys are after." White smoke plumed up from the hillside; the fighters disappeared.

Once on the road, they could make quicker progress, and he was relieved to see the tents, vehicles and bustle that iden-tified HQ, through which he had passed only a few days ago, on his way to the line. A time of innocence, that now seemed.

Major Harrison was a small, gingery man, preoccupied and brisk. "You're who?

Okay — I know, we're expecting you, there was a signal. I've got another job for you. There's some replacements for your company coming through at any moment, and you can take them up to the line. Send your men on ahead with the mortar. What's wrong?"

His expression must have betrayed him. He found himself dismayed at the idea of leaving the men on their own. "The lance corporal can take over," said the major impatiently — that clipped Sandhurst diction that he now knew so well but that still seemed to come from another planet. "Collect the equipment and get them going. You'd better go to the mess tent and hang on there till these chaps turn up."

He was given tea and a meal. He sat about, feeling displaced, uncomfortable, surprised by some unsuspected need that made him want to be not here but with his men, with the unit. An hour passed, and another. After a further thirty minutes he sought out the major, who was conferring with another officer and looked up impatiently. "What's the problem? Oh, didn't they tell you? There's been a transport hitch — those men won't show up till later. You'd better get back to the line on your own, pronto."

It was now late afternoon. There should be no difficulty about reaching the unit before darkness fell, but he resolved to try to get a lift if at all possible. In the event, every jeep or truck that passed him on the road was crammed; he resigned himself to the walk, suddenly grateful for this spell of solitude, the release from the monotonous swearing and repartee of the men, the sense of a fragile independence. Ahead, he could see the smoke of explosions, he could hear bursts of gunfire, fighters swept across the sky; he was going back into all that, and there was no alternative, but he was able to savor this brief respite. He felt concerned about his carrying party. Would they have made it back all right? Would they have identified the right hillside, and the route up to the company position? He felt guilt at having had to abandon them — pointlessly as it turned out.

These fears were compounded as he reached the line of hills and himself had some difficulty in identifying the right crest. He left the road and set off up the hillside, panicking at points when he thought he might be losing his way. This landscape was confusingly repetitive: it rose and fell, and each incline offered you a false crest, beyond which was a dip and then a farther slope. He had tried to fix his direction on the way down by noting features like a prominent rock or tree (again, walking in the Lake District came achingly to mind), and it was when he paused to consider a particular rock that a Chinese soldier stepped out from behind it, looking directly at him.

He reached for his pistol at the same moment as the Chinese drew back his arm, flung a grenade, and then vanished.

The grenade fell short, into a clump of bushes, and he was on the ground before it exploded, his face buried in the grass. Dirt and twigs and stones spattered down onto him. There was a belt of small trees to his left, and he began to edge toward the cover of these, watching the rock, expecting another grenade, another of those sudden figures, so instantly perceived as hostile, alien.

But nothing happened. This slice of hillside was apparently empty again. Presumably he had been judged not worth further investigation. Or did they think him the forerunner of an attack and were biding their time? He waited for a while, then moved forward cautiously under cover of the trees. The rock terrified him, and he swung round to keep it parallel, but when he could see behind it there was nothing there, and beyond he recognized with relief a gully that lay immediately below their own position.

He reported the encounter when at last he got back. The officer said laconically that he had been a bit lucky: "The chap was out having a look-see, probably. Thought there might be more of you. Anyway, you shooed him off. The new mortar's in position. I gather they roped you in for another job."

All day, they watched and waited. From time to time, news and information flew through the lines, arriving on the field telephones, passed from trench to trench: the Gloucesters were getting it badly, the enemy had bypassed the road, were moving behind their own positions. The word came more than once: "There are bloody thousands of them."

Night came. Another stretch of that treacherous darkness. They had gone twenty-four hours already without sleep, and those who were not on watch lay in the bottom of the trenches, clobbered with exhaustion. He did so himself, when his turn came, and fell at once into some pit of semiconsciousness that was laced with gunfire, bugles, and screams. He surfaced to find the sergeant shaking him, and shot up wildly, reaching for his pistol. But the sergeant was only telling him that he was due on watch again. The nightmare of his brief sleep gave way to the awful truth of that night: the noisy flashing darkness, the grim uncertainty. Nobody seemed to know what was going on, where the enemy were, how they were moving, whether their own positions were holding on.

All around him, there were Tyneside voices. They brought an incongruous homeliness to this benighted place. They evoked his city, and the Tyne Valley, and Morpeth and Accrington and all the places that he knew. He could tell where a man came from by subtle inflections, by the way he used a word, by the words that he used. He could place others, too: the officers' voices with their identifying vowel sounds, their overtones of the BBC, of masters at school, of his family doctor — the tones of authority. It seemed extraordinary that this entire elaborate social system could have crossed the world intact and asserted itself here among these Korean hills, amid this mayhem.

At daylight, orders came. They were to withdraw once more to a position half a mile farther back from the river, joining up with X and Y Companies. It was likely that the enemy would harass the withdrawal.

He anticipated attack at every step. Each line of rocks was a threat, each stand of trees. He was jolted out of his weariness by tension, waiting for the screams, the bugles, the grenades, as the company moved slowly across the hillsides. They were all on edge; he saw the sergeant scanning each rise ahead, silent and intent. He saw officers stop and turn their binoculars on the skyline, on the next ridge; he did the same himself. The place seemed to team with men, conspicuous and vulnerable — brown-clad figures moving through the scrub. His platoon was toward the front of the withdrawal; at one point they were within sight of the road, and saw trucks and lorries, a couple of tanks. From the hill beyond, there came mortar fire. And then, once more, U.S. planes came hurtling in, sweeping across that distant hill and the mortar flashes. In their wake there arose a line of dark red flame, a fiery snake against the green, and then great plumes of black smoke.

"That's napalm," said the sergeant. "Filthy stuff. Fries them, poor buggers."

Somehow, they arrived at the new position without attention from the enemy. All the noise was coming now from the range of hills beyond the road and nearer to the river, where the Gloucesters' positions were, and as the day went on, this intensified. They dug in, and lay there listening and watching. In their vicinity, there was little going on, just the occasional burst of fire from one of their own trenches as someone spotted movement. There was the sense that the enemy could be all around, waiting their moment.

Weary men brewed endless tea. Every hour or so, it seemed, he was handed a steaming mug, and drank automatically, grateful for a momentary alleviation of that nervous vigil. There were rumors now — word-of-mouth reports that hopped from trench to trench: the Gloucesters were surrounded, the entire brigade was going to pull out. He was so tired that he seemed to be beyond sensation, numbed into apathy, but with the talk of withdrawal he felt a rush of optimism. Never mind that after this there was heaven knew what else to come. Just to get away from these infested hills.

As darkness fell, the rumors were confirmed. There was to be a general withdrawal, by way of the road, the next day.

That night was quieter. They lay waiting — waiting for attack, waiting for dawn, for the prospect of getting out of this. There was speculation about their chances. He listened to the sergeant, who was acid about the order to use the road — "Bloody crazy. We'll be sitting ducks. We should keep to the high ground." — and thought that he was probably right. But most of the men were apathetic, worn out, and demoralized by their situation. News was filtering through now about the level of their own casualties in the counterattack on the hill — as high as 50 percent it was said. Several of his own men had been killed, his companions on the voyage out from England, including a man who lived round the corner from his home, with whom he had played street games when they were children. He thought of the mother, who would not yet know what had happened, going innocently about her business, perhaps chatting to his own mother at the butcher's or the greengrocer, in a world of routine and normality.

When dawn came, there was a thick mist. They were all anxious to move, and the mist seemed like useful cover, but the order to get going did not come until mid-morning, by which time the sun had broken through. There were U.S. planes swooping down frequently now, gunning for the Chinese mortar positions that threatened the road, and their own artillery trying to pick off machine-gun posts on the enemy-held hillsides.

They began to make their way down toward the road, following orders to report at designated checkpoints. He was surprised and impressed by the calculation of it all, the careful counting through of men, the determined imposition of some kind of order upon this anarchy. They wound their way over this now-familiar terrain — the grassy ridges, the stands of stumpy trees, the scrub and the sudden slopes covered with slippery shale — and he became aware of his blistered feet. He had taken his boots off at some point during the night, and had been startled to find his feet raw and bleeding. On the scale of things, this seemed a triviality; from the next trench he could hear the moans of a man who had taken a bullet through his thigh. He had put his socks and boots back on again, feeling vaguely ashamed. But now his feet felt as though he were walking on fireballs.

He was at the rear of the patrol, urging on stragglers. When a grenade exploded only yards away, they flung themselves down while the sergeant fired a few bursts with the bren gun at their invisible pursuers. Then they got up and plunged with new commitment over the last hundred yards toward the road — a chaos of vehicles and men. The gunfire was intensifying; it was clear that they were under attack from the hillsides both behind and beyond.

The road was a wide, rough track, busy with jeeps, trucks, and Centurion tanks. An officer was directing the men pouring down from the higher ground. They were to head south by any means available: "Hitch a ride if you can; otherwise, just keep moving." The pass ahead was held by the Ulsters, and the tanks were returning fire from the road, but the enemy was attacking the withdrawal: "Keep your eyes open, and take cover if you need to."

He heard the officer, looked at the cluttered road, the hostile hills, and thought: Where? He saw wounded men sitting and lying by the roadside, bloody field dressings on heads or limbs. He saw dead men. He saw tracer from an enemy machine-gun position on the opposite hillside. And then willy-nilly he became a part of this disheveled rout, men straggling ahead in groups, some of them helping out a wounded companion, vehicles crashing along the rutted dusty road, tanks with guns blazing.

He kept stumbling, made unsteady by exhaustion. The roadside was littered with debris — equipment that had been jettisoned, the occasional burnt-out vehicle. And when he looked back he realized with an icy twinge of fear that the enemy were clearly visible — the whole place crawling with figures, running along the ridges, leaping down the slopes.

Any truck that passed him was already filled with men, and equally the tanks that were also operating as evacuation vehicles, with men clinging to the hulls as they lurched over the uneven ground. The sergeant, walking beside him, said caustically, "Like Newcastle in the fucking rush hour. And we've missed the bloody bus. Have a smoke, sir." They paused to light cigarettes, and as they did so both heard the whine of a shell and flung themselves into the ditch that ran parallel to the road.

He lay facedown in damp reeds as the explosion rocked the ground. At the same instant, something hit his leg, slamming into it like a kick in the calf on a football pitch. When he sat up, gingerly, he saw smoke billowing from an upturned jeep, and a body on the road. He looked down; blood was seeping through his trousers. His leg felt entirely numb — not painful, just an absolute numbness, and he could only move it with difficulty, as though he were trying to haul someone else's limb.

He looked for the sergeant; he was still

lying facedown in the ditch. He crawled over to him, and then he saw that the back of the man's head was one sickening mess of blood and bone.

He tried to stand up, and could not. He was weak and dizzy. He knew that he should do something about the wound, and started to fumble for a field dressing. A truck loaded with men hurtled past, and another tank. A mortar exploded farther back along the road; the whole place was a cacophony of noise. He found the dressing and pulled his trouser leg up. And then someone was squatting down beside him: "Can you walk?"

He shook his head.

"Here, let's have a look." An Irish voice; a lieutenant from the Ulsters. The lieutenant bound up the wound, which was hurting now, a deep throbbing pain. "It's not too bad, but it's enough to get you out of this. You'll be going home, my friend. Just hang on — there's a carrier coming through behind with other wounded. They'll pick you up. Good luck."

He saw the man go, running to join other hurrying figures. He sat in the ditch, and became aware of more scurrying men, coming down from the hillsides, descending upon the road, dozens of them, scores, and he realized that these were not their own men; this was the enemy, these were Chinese infantry.

Two Chinese leaped across the ditch, only yards away, glanced at him, and ran past. He groped for his pistol, and realized that he no longer had it; he must have lost it when he and the sergeant flung themselves into the ditch. A tank came roaring up and he saw to his astonishment that Chinese soldiers were swarming onto the hull. Others were pouring after it up the road. The tank fired, two of the Chinese fell, the rest ducked down beside the road.

He tried again to stand, and found that he could, though pain shot through his leg. He began to walk, uncertainly: ". . . just keep moving." An Ulsterman with his arm in a sling caught up with him and they moved along side by side. Chinese soldiers ran past. He heard another tank approaching, and the burst of fire coming from it. The Ulsterman said, "Christ, better get down," and they dived for the ditch. There was searing pain from his leg, and he must have blacked out. When he surfaced, there were two Chinese standing over him, one of them holding a pistol.

He saw the Chinese gesture that they should get up, and knew that he would not be going home, not now, perhaps not at all.

Transatlantic

A few years ago, I met up with a woman I had known when we were both young. She had gone to work in the United States when she was twenty, had married there, and never came back. Now, she was a California matron, with children and grand-children, her voice and mannerisms entirely American except that here and there was just a hint, a flavor, of the English girl that she had been — like those elderly GI brides one sometimes sees on television programs, reminiscing against a backdrop of their former selves lined up on the quayside over half a century ago. Looking at her, listening to her, it was as though she had undergone some metamorphosis. She had not just grown older; she had shed one skin and assumed another.

After I left university, I worked for a couple of years as research assistant to the then professor of race relations at Oxford. One day, he was visited by an American academic colleague. Maybe they ran out of professional small talk, or maybe my employer had other commitments — anyway, he brought this man into my office after a while with the suggestion that I take him for a conducted tour of Oxford. Fine by me; it was one of those golden October days — far preferable to be out and about rather than moldering at a desk. I did the visitor proud: a choice selection of colleges, the Bodleian, the Ashmolean, Christ Church meadow, the river. He was entranced. We got on famously. I was twenty-two; he was — oh, old, forty at least, an avuncular figure. Let's be clear, this is not a tale of lost romance. Over a farewell drink in the Mitre he asked what I had in mind for the future — noting, presumably, that my present job was a pretty dead-end affair. I think I said something about wanting to travel at some point. He gave me his card: "My university has postgraduate programs that might appeal to you. Let me know if you're interested."

I didn't. That road not taken vanishes into mist. Not long after, I met the man I would marry.

In America, I have frequently experienced a sea change. Suddenly — on a plane, in a city, talking to a stranger — I have felt as though I brushed shoulders with some *other self, a person that I am not but easily could have been. It is to do with a transatlantic sense of expansion, of license, of possibility, the way in which people seem more relaxed, freed up, at one with the world. They talk to anyone; they talk to me. I have felt, sometimes, a sense of energy, of empathy. I have taken a sidestep and found myself acting differently, becoming a person who is still entirely me but also some extra self that I don't quite recognize. Is this a hint of an alternative destiny, an alternative persona responding to the requirements of another environment?*

Equally, once in a while, hearing an American voice, I know a peculiar nostalgia, as though I am listening to some echo, as though I am glimpsing an intimacy that I have missed, some other existence.

The first time I crossed the Atlantic, and woke to birdsong that was wonderfully wrong, I knew that evolution is true. I lay listening to the dawn sounds of a New England morning — blue jays, mourning doves, chickadees — and these were like some significant refraction of my Oxfordshire mornings with their wood pigeons, blackbirds, and robins — like, and yet quite unlike. I knew then that first hint of this alluring alternative universe. I have known the same sensation in Australia, once again, waking into the Wonderland of alien bird calls and being filled with wild exhilaration, a euphoric response to this diverse world.

To write fiction is to make a succession of choices, to send the narrative and the characters in one direction rather than another. Story is navigation; successful story is the triumphant progress down exactly the right paths, avoiding the dead ends, the unsatisfactory turns. Life, of course, is not at all like that. There is no shrewd navigator, just a person's own haphazard lurching from one decision to another. Which is why life so often seems to lack the authenticity of fiction. And when a writer contemplates her own life, there is an irresistible compulsion to tinker with it, to try out a crucial adjustment here or there. What follows is one such tinkering. The protagonist is not myself, her experience and her associates are invented, but she is perhaps a suggestion of another outcome.

She said, "We're almost there. Another mile or two, I guess."

Ben was driving. Carol had the map

spread out on her lap. They had progressed from motorways to major roads into this thicket of lanes, the car now squeezed by greenery as though they wound into the land itself. It was the first trip to England in eighteen months, the first since her mother had died, the first in which she had no parent to visit, no anchor. She was forty-nine, and she thought that this parentlessness felt as though you had gone to sea in a small boat and found yourself out of sight of any shore. There was no longer that distant, reassuring shape. Nothing now between you and the horizon.

Ben switched off the radio; he kept putting it on for the news. "Do you think Mrs. Thatcher is mad? I mean that. Clinically unhinged?"

The backdrop to this trip was the Falklands War. In hotel rooms, in the hired car, the disembodied babble of politicians, of government spokesmen, of Parliament, traveled with them daily. They knew by heart the names of ships in the British task force; they sounded like the language of hymns — *Endeavour, Invincible, Fearless*. The Argentine aircraft carrier was called *The Twenty-fifth of May*.

"If she is, then the rest of the Cabinet are too."

He patted her knee. "I don't hold you responsible for your compatriots."

She said, "You better not. Anyway, I'm not sure that they are, anymore."

He was her second husband, an economist at Harvard. They had been together for five years. Her first marriage, from which the children came, had melted away, diminishing from initial happiness long ago when he and she were young, through discontent to an ultimate indifference; both had been glad to step aside, without much rancor. The children were now in their early twenties and busy with their own lives. She had met Ben a year after the divorce, and knew a contentment with him that sometimes made them both incredulous. He too was on a second shift.

She did not know what to expect, at the end of these twisting lanes, when eventually they reached the house. She had not seen Aunt Margaret for years, except briefly at her mother's funeral. Let alone Uncle Clive. Colonel Clive Baseley. She stared out of the car window into the intimacy of hedgebanks and trees whose branches sometimes whipped the glass.

Each time she saw this country again it seemed so small. So neat, so dapper, so miniature. The little hedged fields, the dinky villages. It had surely shrunk? She had never seen it thus when she was young; it had been quite normal then, ordinary, expected. Now, it was a constant surprise. She found herself gazing in mild astonishment at landscapes that were eerily familiar, but also quite alien — those church towers, the flowery facades of pubs, terraces of tiny houses.

Ben had been amused, on their first visit together, penetrating parts that he had never seen on his previous brief scholarly visits, attending some conference or plunging into libraries. He had remembered that Mark Twain comment on the English countryside: "Too pretty to be left out in the rain." Suburban landscape made him laugh: "Why does everyone fence themselves off from everyone else?" — staring at the ranks of firmly segmented front gardens. They thought of the communal greensward of their own prosperous neighborhood back home.

"But look at all the roses," she said. And yes, the whole place was rampant, explosive with silken blooms.

In earlier years, when she had come back with her young first husband, then with babies, then with growing children, it felt each time as though she visited her own past. This place was not now, but then — the then of her childhood and adolescence, of her early youth. There it still was, a landscape that seemed to be less and less connected with her. She had left it behind, but it continued, impervious to her defection. It carried on, with its red London buses and its familiar accents and its Sunday roasts and its cups of tea; it did not seem to realize that it was somehow stuck, that it existed in some other time frame. At first, this had been endearing; she drank it all in, eagerly identifying sights and practices that she had half forgotten. They were comforting; they seemed to put her in touch with a lost version of herself.

And then, over time, something happened. What had been engaging and reassuring became vaguely threatening, even hostile. It was she who was out of step, who could not cope with changed circumstances. At some point there had been a subtle shift in the relationship; where once she had been the benign nostalgic visitor, the lamb back in the fold, now she was the outsider, someone who received the polite treatment meted out to any transient. An invisible door had closed, and she did not know if it was she who had conjured it up or those others in that now-distanced place through which she moved, a world in which things were done differently.

With both relatives and old friends, she often felt herself wrong-footed. People's expressions were opaque, but told her that something was amiss. She labored to speak as they spoke, to say "pavement" and "tap" and "flat." Yet this was a culture that had embraced McDonald's and Kentucky Fried Chicken and Levi's and Coke, whose television screens were filled with Hollywood movies, in which people said "Hi!" as often as they said "Hello." It was as though some double standard were in operation, one so elusive that she was incapable of identifying it. And, in a further twist, it seemed applicable less to either of her husbands than to herself. She did not see these shuttered looks in response to something that Ben said or did. She found herself always a little on edge, with those she had known since childhood, with those she had been at college with, as though she might be measured and found wanting. It made her behave expansively, urgently, like some propitiating puppy. She jumped up at people, she rolled on her back with all four paws in the air.

Equally, she felt constricted. It was as though she wore some restraining garment, as though she squeezed into a wet bathing suit each time she touched down at Heathrow. When she caught herself reaching out to put a hand on someone's arm, she held back. She would fall suddenly silent, conscious of having talked too much. She could not be herself, because of this disconcerting sense that her real self was likely to step out of line, to be incorrect in some way that was both unpredictable and uncontrollable.

She said to Ben, "What is it that I do? Did you see how they looked at me?"

He had considered this. He was a man who gave careful thought to other people's difficulties, and she loved him for it.

"Maybe they're not sure now who you are."

In her early days on the other side of the Atlantic, she had been fascinated by those visible physical mutations, by the way in which those graceful, brilliantly white New England churches echoed the spires at home — as she still thought of it — but were also newly minted, entirely indigenous. Wandering through gleaming displays of colonial interiors in museums, she saw that same delicate sea change in chairs, tables, mirrors, chests of drawers. They waved a hand at English antique furniture but had gone their own way — lighter, brighter, independent.

She had become an avid reader of accounts of early settlement. In imagination, she made that stupefying crossing of the ocean, battened down in some tiny, tossing ship. She endured those first winters at Plymouth Plantation, she cleared the land and grew crops and made a home in the wilderness. Again and again, she had arrived, she had established a new way of life, she had stepped westward, she had turned her back on the Old World. She thought that she had some appreciation of how those people must have understood the implications of that great divide, the thousands of miles that stood between one way of life and another.

But now she herself had crossed and recrossed the ocean, time and time again, and saw that today we abuse distance. Those few hours in an overcrowded metal cylinder made a mockery of space, they kicked aside the great sobriety of the Atlantic and pitched people without consideration from one set of circumstances to another, complaining about the food and the choice of movie. For her too, arrival was associated with the dishevelment of an aircraft cabin at the end of a flight, awash with blankets and discarded headphones, dawn staining the sky, lines of yawning people waiting for the toilets. She had lost any sense of awe, of wonder. Instead, the realization that there is still a crossing to be made came with something invisible and insidious, that unease that she now felt with people whom she thought she knew.

And now they would shortly be with Aunt Margaret and Uncle Clive, both of them unknown quantities. Her mother's younger sister, and her husband. She had written to Aunt Margaret proposing a visit several weeks before she and Ben were due to leave for this trip, which was centered around some work he needed to do with a colleague in Oxford. The card received in response to her letter had given pause for thought: "Dear Carol," Aunt Margaret had begun, following up with some anodyne comments on her own roundup of family news, and then ". . . Do by all means call in if you are going to be in our part of the world."

Ben read this. " 'Our part of the world' . . . I never heard that expression before."

She realized that she had not heard it for a long while. It had a musty whiff to it; at the same time, there was a familiar chime — yes, people had talked like that.

Ben was still examining the card. There was a neat strip of letterhead across the top: Colonel and Mrs. Clive Baseley, followed by the address. Ben was chuckling: " 'Our part of the world' . . . I love it. The sense of ownership. Military guy, is he, your uncle?"

"Well . . . ," she said. "Was. During the war, not since. I think he was something called a land agent. Retired now, of course."

"Once a colonel, always a colonel," said Ben. "Just as well to make your position clear." He studied the card again. "We are not being offered a bed for the night. Possibly not even a meal. Never mind, we are nothing if not resourceful."

Indeed, yes. They had a shelf of guides to farmhouse holidays and good bed-and-breakfasts and were now booked at a pub a few miles from the address on the postcard. At the last town through which they passed, Ben had said, "You know, I think maybe we need to ingratiate ourselves a little with your relatives. Show we're nice folk."

Carol had been initially dampened by the card, had felt somehow mortified. Now, she found herself sharing his amusement. They had taken to referring to

Uncle Clive as the Colonel.

"How?"

"I dunno. We'll go shopping and come up with something."

In the event, he came up with a bottle of whiskey from a supermarket. "All colonels drink whiskey."

She hovered over the cosmetics. Some perfume for Aunt Margaret? But perhaps she was not a perfume kind of person. In the end she bought a lavish bunch of lilies.

Back in the car, Ben looked at her. "I have to tell you that you've got an orange nose. Those things are evidently meant for looking at, not for smelling. Better warn your aunt."

She said, "I'm beginning to wonder what I have gotten us into."

Her father had died, and then, within a year, her mother. It was because of that that they were here. Indirectly, obscurely because of that. After her mother's death, something had happened to her perception of the past. Or rather, some latent need had been aroused.

She had said to Ben, "I don't know anything about my great-grandparents. I don't even know their names." She was thinking of her mother's parents.

Ben knew a good deal about his own

great-grandparents. He was of Scandinavian descent. His grandfather had emigrated to the Midwest from Norway in 1909 with a young wife and Ben's two-year-old father. Ben had visited the small ancestral agricultural community, had identified the graves of his forebears, had sought out relatives and checked family trees. He knew from whence he came.

"And this matters?" said Ben.

"Yes. For some reason. I've never thought about it before. It's to do with my mother. Her dying."

He nodded. "Then we better find out."

Most Americans know who they are, to a greater or lesser degree. Moreover, they signal myriad identities; they define the nation. They are Greek-American or Italian-American or Latino or black, they propose China, Japan, the Philippines — they echo the globe. They are a walking, talking mnemonic system, remembering arrivals and survivals, the Atlantic passage, the trek west, settlement and dispersal, calamity and prosperity, whispering still of the other place that is hidden in each person — the shtetls of Russia, Poland, Lithuania, the fishing villages and the farms, the fetid slums of cities, the plantations and the slave quarters. She and Ben had a friend called Mary Dixon, as Anglo-Saxon a name as you could find, but Mary herself was a figure from Greek tragedy, she was Electra, she was Clytemnestra, she was dark, dark, with great Byzantine eyes and rich black hair. And yes, indeed, Mary's great-grandfather arrived at Staten Island from Piraeus, with extended family and not a word of English, so that the recording clerk, defeated by the accent and the names, put down Mary's father simply as Dick's son, to have done with it. And Dixon the family became and remained, but Mary's face said otherwise.

"I must be American now," said Carol. "I need to know these things. When I was British, I wasn't particularly interested. The British know where they come from. They've been there all along."

She did know, up to a point. She had an image of the grandparental home in Henley, the large complacent house with the generous garden, from which her grandfather traveled daily half a mile to his solicitor's practice, five days a week for half a century, unimpeded even by two world wars, being rendered unfit for military service by extreme myopia. She remembered him, vaguely. She remembered also her grandmother, a person drowned in domesticity, her horizons restricted to family and neighborhood. Carol saw her yet, in a series of freeze-frames, static, unemphatic, attending to some task, in comfortable accord with her circumstances.

Carol had access also to her other grandparents, minimal data establishing only a seafront apartment in Hove, where her other grandmother first ministered to a husband sidelined by some unidentified disability and then lived out a long widowhood, walking a pair of Scottish terriers on the promenade and playing bridge with cronies.

Further back, there is nothing. No names, no faces. The family tree is leafless, its branches without labels. And now her mother was dead, one of her uncles too was gone, while the other brother was spending a sunny old age in the Algarve. There was no one available to question. Except for Aunt Margaret.

She said to Ben, "It's odd, but I hardly know this aunt. She and my mother never really got on. They saw less and less of each other. Of course, Aunt Margaret always lived in the country, and my parents were Londoners."

"That signifies?"

"Oh yes," she said. "You'll see."

And now they were about to do so. "Stop!" she cried. "We're there! The Old Rectory . . ."

They turned into an entrance between high hedges. There was a sweep of gravel in front of the house, bordered by copiously flowering shrubs. A lawn to one side, leading away to more glimpsed garden — paths, pergolas, beds brimming with flowers. The supermarket lilies on the backseat suddenly seemed tawdry.

The house was extravagant with period interest: mullioned windows, portico, weathered honey-colored stone. "Definitely too pretty to leave out . . . ," said Ben. "I hope they put a tarpaulin over it at night."

They parked the car. She tidied her hair, reached over the seat for the lilies, doubtfully.

"Here we go, then," said Ben.

The room reminded Carol of expensive inns in Vermont or New Hampshire: plump chintz-covered sofas and armchairs, ruched and pleated lampshades, piles of shiny magazines on low tables, sporting prints on the walls. Of course, this kind of place is the ancestry of such outfits. A flattering portrait of Aunt Margaret when younger over the mantelpiece; sparsely filled bookshelves. A large dog lumbered occasionally from one resting place to another.

They sat facing each other on two of the deep sofas, Carol and Ben side by side, as though lined up for consideration. Aunt Margaret dispensed tea from a little trolley. The timing proposed for the visit would seem to have allowed for this: hospitality, but not on a significant scale.

"Things seem to be going well down in the South Atlantic," said Uncle Clive.

Two days before, British missiles had sunk the *Belgrano*. Lives had been lost; there was controversy about the action. The Argentine fleet appeared to be in retreat.

"We've taken to watching the news," said Aunt Margaret, with a laugh, as though this were some kind of weakness. "Every *day*." She somehow matched her furnishings: floral, feminine, resolutely decorative. She would have been a pretty girl, time was. Carol could find no echo whatsoever of her mother. Uncle Clive was large, weatherbeaten, tweed-jacketed. The reception accorded to Carol and Ben had been politely adequate, without being effusive; there was something automatic about it.

The peck on each cheek from Aunt Margaret; Uncle Clive's firm handshake. They knew what should be done, and were doing it, you felt. They didn't particularly want to see us, thought Carol, but since they're stuck with it they'll go through the motions. She was intensely grateful for Ben's presence, for his reassuring lanky form alongside her, the glimpses of his profile, with that keen, half-amused look. He was not saying much; the occasional courteous comment.

"Mrs. Thatcher is a remarkable woman, in my view," continued Uncle Clive. He had his eye on Ben.

"Indeed yes," said Ben. "That I would not dispute."

The Baseleys evidently took this as a statement of approval, and looked complacent, as though she were their personal responsibility.

"I understand that she gets on well with your president," said Uncle Clive.

"I'm afraid so."

The Baseleys stared at Ben, baffled, it would seem, rather than alerted to any views that he might have. Uncle Clive cleared his throat. He seemed to decide that perhaps Ben was not following his line of thought, in which case it was not worth pursuing the matter. "Yes, well . . . Anyway, it's good to be showing a bit of muscle over this nonsense. Get the Argies out in a matter of weeks, you'll see."

Ever since she had stepped into this house Carol had been thinking of her parents and of their untidy, book-filled north London home, a world away from this. It still seemed incredible that they were gone. As others had become less reachable, they had remained constant. They did not change, except to grow older; unlike the landscape, they had not become smaller, or unexpected. And she did not catch from them that opaque glance, or feel that she had committed some solecism. Occasionally, her mother would say, "Goodness, you sound so *American* . . . ," or would laugh about some different way of doing things. When they crossed the Atlantic on visits, they were briskly adaptable. Her father approved of the more sedate freeway speed limits; her mother relished summer spells on Cape Cod as the children grew up. Over the years of such visits, each developed a transatlantic persona, without losing any of their essential cultural integrity. Carol was impressed by this; the rigidities that she found elsewhere were made the more apparent. She asked herself how they had been able to be thus, when clearly she had been unable to do so herself, but somehow she never asked them, or even thought to, until they died within a year of each other, and then it was too late.

They were metropolitan people, dug decades deep into the capital. Her father was a museum administrator, her mother engaged herself in a slew of voluntary activities. In Aunt Margaret's house, sunk amid fields and deep lanes, Carol felt as though she had crossed over into some other state, where the government was of a different complexion and the laws were otherwise. The divide between these sisters seemed now one sanctioned also by systems. But which had come first — inclination, or a way of living? Had this apposition been latent since their infancies, these lurking directives that would eventually propel one to college, political commitments, and an urban life, the other to a tranquil half century of gardening?

When the sisters were younger, there had been sporadic meetings; a statutory exchange of visits every year or so, Aunt Margaret making a disdainful trip to London, Carol's mother loading up the family for a determined foray west. As the cultural divide widened, these efforts became more and more sporadic until they petered out altogether. Christmas cards became the only solder to the relationship. Occasionally Carol's mother would say, "I really should try to see more of Margaret" — pause — "but we have less and less to say to each other" — sigh.

Carol's relationship with her own brother was more robust, and had successfully weathered the Atlantic crossing — indeed, had perhaps prospered from it. She sensed that Robert had come to see her as someone vaguely esoteric, a familiar feature of his landscape but one that had assumed added significance. They were not exactly close, but welcomed each other's news and company. He was not among those with whom she felt she walked on eggshells. He would tease her about some Americanism, refer to her as "my Yankee sister," but without that sense of distance, of alienation.

So how is this? she thought. He and I somehow rode out this mutation of mine — if that is what it is — but Mum and Aunt Margaret could not cope with a couple of hundred miles and their varied lifestyles.

She thought of the dimly remembered Henley villa, and pictured that shared childhood. The four siblings: Edgar, Lionel, Virginia, and Margaret. The upbringing that was rigidly conformist to an age and to a class. Nobody did anything unanticipated. The boys went to public school and university and then into the professions: law, medicine. The girls went to local academies and then got married. Only Virginia, Carol's mother, managed a sideswipe at this dictation by enrolling in evening classes at a London college, when in full bloom as a wife and mother, and taking a diploma in politics and economics. This propelled her into voluntary work for local charities, and a lifelong association with the Labour Party, the highspot of which was her service as a teller at the polling station on election days. She would sit in triumph outside the local primary school, politely accosting voters and startling neighbors from their leafy and expensive road who had not realized her political affiliations. Carol could picture her still — in her element, joking with colleagues, her hair untidy, wearing a T-shirt and grubby trousers.

Aunt Margaret has never worn trousers, she thought. Always a pleated skirt like today, and a blouse with a brooch. I'm glad we came, because I am seeing things more clearly. But I am not sure that I ever knew why I needed to come. Not just to find out what my great-grandparents were called, that's for sure.

She jumped into a conversational pause. "I've been remembering the house in Henley, Aunt Margaret. That garden — all those trees to climb. You must have had a wonderful time in it as children."

"Well, I was never a tree climber. The boys did, of course. And Virginia."

"She did boy sort of things?"

"Oh yes. Getting filthy, rushing about. Mother used to be driven distracted."

"And you weren't like that?"

"One was not," said Aunt Margaret. "Chalk and cheese, really, from the word go. Not that we weren't fond of each other, of course, but you know . . ."

Carol thought of Aunt Margaret at the funeral, somberly correct in a black suit, dispensing quick kisses. "Such a long time since I saw you, Carol. So sad . . ."

"And then of course later on we rather went our separate ways. A pity, but we're a long way from London and . . . both of us were tied up with our own lives. And so far as politics went, well, I had to beg to differ." Aunt Margaret turned to Ben. "My sister was a supporter of the Labour

Party." This was said quite flatly, but with regret, as though it were a reference to some physical disability.

"The left-wing party," the Colonel explained, also focusing on Ben. "Socialism, you understand."

Carol put down her cup with a crash; tea slopped into the saucer. She knew Ben to be almost saintly in his powers of tolerance, but every man has a breaking point.

She said, "Ben is an economist. He knows rather a lot about politics too."

Ben reached out and helped himself to a sandwich. "May I? Your uncle is concerned about terminology, I imagine. It's true that the word 'socialism' is less familiar on our side of the Atlantic. We have other epithets for the left." He gave the Colonel a sunny smile.

"Well it's all mumbo jumbo so far as I'm concerned," said Aunt Margaret briskly. "This -ism and that -ism. All I know is that Virginia did seem to me to have got in with the wrong crowd. Anyway . . . Where exactly is it that you are living now, Carol?" Political discussion had been put in its place.

Carol explained.

"That's a nice English-sounding name, Lexington. Is it in the country? A village?"

Defeated by the prospect of trying to re-define the Massachusetts landscape within these terms, Carol replied simply that they did not live in a city. Aunt Margaret nodded; it was clear that her interest in this theme was petering out in any case.

Uncle Clive was talking now about the house. "Basically seventeenth-century. In Pevsner, of course."

Ben said, "Is that so? I must check it out."

Bless you, Carol thought. For your good manners.

They had come here directly from Oxford. He had had a lecture to give, and a couple of seminars. They had been wined and dined; there were many people who wanted a piece of Ben — colleagues, students. It had been a busy, easy time for both of them. Ben was comfortable, stimulated, relaxed, enjoying the company and the exchange of ideas. Carol too had found these strangers congenial, on the whole. Occasionally, she had detected a whiff of parochialism, but no more, she told herself, than you find in any academic community. Ben found the collegiate formalities entertaining rather than oppressive: "On a permanent basis, no way. But it's a gas for a few days."

Carol had spent one lengthy High Table dinner in enjoyable conversation with a young historian. At the end of the evening he had come up to her: "I've just been talking to your husband, and I'm so embarrassed. I never realized you're *English*. I took you for U.S. born and bred."

She had laughed. "Why is that embarrassing?"

"I suppose because our conversation would have run differently."

"Then I'm glad you didn't . . . realize."

She had thought about this later; she had compared the ease she had felt on that occasion with the constraints on a visit to an old college friend the week before. Their exchanges had been prickly and awkward. The friend lived in a part of London Carol did not know. When she said as much, Linda was cool. "Well, you wouldn't, would you? This is the sort of place people like us have to settle for, given the housing market. I imagine you live in some colonial mansion." "No, no . . . ," Carol said. "House prices are high where we are too." Their shared youth seemed now quite eclipsed by achievements and possessions, or lack of these. When Linda talked of her children's progress, or her own concerns, she would break off suddenly: ". . . but you wouldn't know what I'm talking about, the system's different over there, I know." Carol thought that probably they would not meet again.

The Colonel had been giving an account of the house and its history. He had explained to Ben that in the seventeenth century there had been a civil war and that the then owners of the house had been Royalist supporters ("I'm glad to say") and, according to legend, had sheltered a Royalist officer in flight from the Parliamentarian forces. "The other side, you understand." The man had carved his initials on the wall of his hiding place, still to be seen.

"We use it as the larder," said Aunt Margaret. "Nice and cool. A bit parky for him, poor chap. Anyway, it makes a nice story." She smiled graciously at Ben. "I dare say you find this sort of thing rather fascinating. We have so much history in this country."

"Indeed," said Ben. "Though we do have the odd smattering of it ourselves. Have you ever visited the United States, Mrs. Baseley?"

Aunt Margaret looked surprised. "Oh no. We always used to go to France or Italy for holidays." She reached for the teapot, a continent eliminated. "Another cup, anyone?"

"There were American troops billeted near here during the war," said the Colonel. "Of course, I wasn't around myself, but my parents were living in the area and had a tale or two to tell. A lot of the men were black, apparently. Caused a stir with the local girls. Quite a few coffee-colored babies around later on." He chuckled.

"Really, Clive!"

"A further dimension to the special relationship," said Ben. "Quite timely, so long as no one was too inconvenienced."

Aunt Margaret gave him a look of perplexity. "Well, I shouldn't think the girls' mothers were best pleased." She began briskly to pile cups and plates on the trolley. "We really should show you the garden while the sun is out."

"One ran up against the Yanks quite a bit in the 1940s," said the Colonel. "Overpaid, oversexed, and over here — that's what we used to say. No offense meant, mind you. My own experience was mainly when I was in the army, which was a bit different. I knew some fellows from the American zone when I was in Berlin in '46. Very decent people, I have to say. One chap used to slip me stuff from their . . . what d'you call it? Like the NAAFI."

"The PX, I believe," said Ben.

"That's it. Camel cigarettes and bourbon — that sort of thing."

"Ah-ha!" said Ben. "Then I've been keeping up a tradition."

"What? Oh, yes, I see." The Colonel cleared his throat, looking momentarily embarrassed.

"Garden," said Aunt Margaret firmly, rising to her feet.

Ben, too, rose. "Carol, why don't you go with your aunt? Colonel, I'd really appreciate a look at that graffiti you mentioned — the Royalist officer. We can catch up with the ladies later."

This is so that I can have a heart-to-heart with Aunt Margaret about family matters, thought Carol. Bless him. Except that it is now clear that Aunt Margaret does not go in for that sort of thing and I am no longer at all sure what it is that I want to know, or why.

She followed her aunt. In the hall, the bottle of whiskey, still in its wrapping, stood beside the lilies, which were beginning to wilt. "How *lovely,*" Aunt Margaret had said, but evidently she had neglected or forgotten to put them into water.

They went out of the open front door and down the steps. "The hydrangeas are rather special," said Aunt Margaret. "Not at their best till later in the year, of course."

There was a wide lawn alongside the house, flanked by a pergola draped in roses and clematis. Beyond this could be seen a sunken area with complex plantings, and farther still more lawn reaching away to trees.

They walked slowly, Aunt Margaret providing a commentary. Quite a problem getting help these days, but luckily we have a good man at the moment. Of course, one still does a good deal oneself, but alas *anno domini* . . . Those old fuchsias should come out, but somehow I haven't the heart. You're lucky — you've come at just the right moment for the peonies. Look at the mildew on this tree lupin — we've tried everything, to no avail.

They reached the far end of the garden, where a woodland area gave way to open countryside. Cows — rich, red-brown cows — were grazing belly-deep in buttercups. Hills tipped this way and that, etched with dark hedgerows. A green sweep of hillside was dotted with the white hummocks of sheep.

"Of course we think nothing beats these parts," said Aunt Margaret. "Though I will admit that west Somerset is quite attractive."

Carol had once lived somewhere like this — briefly, long ago. She had this vague memory of walking with her mother and brother in a deep lane splodged with cowpats; the ripe organic smell came back to her now. It was in 1941. As the bombing of London intensified, her mother had at last given way to her father's insistence and agreed to evacuate herself and the children, with the utmost reluctance. She did not want to leave her husband, involved in a wartime job in Whitehall; she did not want to leave the city, her essential habitat. For many discontented months the three of them perched in a rented cottage. Carol no longer knew where this had been, but the landscape that she now saw evoked that time. She remembered the yellow sheen of buttercups, the slow chomp of cows grazing, the quicker snatch of sheep, ice on puddles, her mother struggling with a sulky stove, a dead mouse in the trap, owl cries, a fox that ran into a ditch.

When the raids on London abated, her father could no longer hold out against her mother's entreaties; they were allowed back to London, her mother jubilant with relief. Carol and her brother simply accepted circumstances, as children do, but Carol had been left with this vision of another world, where things were as qualitatively different as in some storybook. She had never been able to see the English countryside in the same way again, but recognized that childhood perception as having a special quality.

She said, "When we were evacuated, in the war, Mummy took us somewhere that felt rather like this."

"Well, lucky for you," said Aunt Margaret. "I never could understand Virginia's fixation on London."

There were bluebells here under the trees, and the smell of wild garlic — a place of contrived informality. The two of them stood at a fence that shielded it from the open fields and their occupants. Carol thought of woodland in Massachusetts, which goes on and on, deeper and deeper, secondary growth that has obliterated the patterns of earlier settlement. That would happen here also, she supposed, if by some quirk of history everyone moved away. She imagined oak, ash, and thorn surging across those manicured hillsides.

"Mummy was unusual. Most people have an atavistic feeling that the country is where they really belong. Which makes sense, in a way — most of us are descended from peasants."

Aunt Margaret gave a startled laugh. "What on earth makes you think so?"

"Well — eighteenth- and nineteenth-century migration to the cities. The Industrial Revolution."

"I wouldn't know about that. Our people came from the south coast, I believe."

"Your grandparents?"

"Mmm . . . ," said Aunt Margaret vaguely. "So one was told."

"What were they called?"

"Oh, heavens," said Aunt Margaret. "Carey — my mother's mother. Mildred. And she married Walter Notcutt. And the other side were Harpers, of course. My grandfather Lawrence and . . . I can't think . . . Oh, Edith. They've all been dead since goodness knows when. Why do you ask?"

"I just wondered." With relief, Carol heard voices behind them. "Here come Uncle Clive and Ben."

The Colonel was armed with a walking stick, which he used to slash at nettles. Ben had his arm round Carol: "Hi, there! Your uncle has been giving me a lesson in British politics. The Cavaliers and Roundheads become the Tories and the Whigs, in the fullness of time, it seems." He was wearing a beneficent grin — the one Carol recognized as concealing secret merriment.

"Exactly," said the Colonel, equally benign, as though approving an assiduous pupil. "Simple, once you get the hang of it. Not much different now, either, by and large."

"With a few minor adjustments, to take into consideration universal suffrage and social change, maybe?" suggested Ben.

"Eh? Well, we know where we are with Mrs. T, that's for sure."

Aunt Margaret was getting a trifle impatient. "I hope he's shown you the garden, as well as all this talk."

"He has indeed," said Ben. "Delightful."

"You don't see anything like this on your side of the Atlantic, I imagine. Gardening is definitely an English thing."

Ben nodded gravely. "Quite so. A national strength."

I can't take much more of this, thought Carol. They were standing in a group now, in this little belt of woodland, the Colonel occasionally reaching out to swipe at some unwelcome growth. Birds sang continuously, in turns, it seemed, as disciplined as the tidy fields and hedges and the elegant contours of the hills. That childhood experience of country resurfaced, and she knew now that in fact it bore no resemblance to this ordered place: back then, there had been some latent sense of threat, of menace. The mouse in the trap had been bloodstained; she had lain in bed wide-eyed, hearing the owls.

Aunt Margaret was talking about fertilizer. "We try to be entirely organic, but of course the farmers spray with anything and everything. Disastrous for the wildflowers. You see hardly any orchids these days."

The Colonel had wandered off, and was decapitating thistles.

Ben wore an expression of polite attention but was probably concerned with something entirely different. He would have slid off into a private train of thought; he would be doing some work, or contemplating current affairs, or wondering what breed of sheep those were. He was a man with an inordinate range of interest, and one who never wasted time.

He might, of course, be studying Aunt Margaret's diction. The variety of accents over here fascinated him, but also gave him trouble. He said, "Excuse me?" quite often. Asking directions, he was sometimes defeated by the reply, or he would stand at a shop counter with furrowed brow: "I'm sorry?" He found Cockney difficult, Cumbrian had been impenetrable; in these parts he sometimes had trouble with that soft, blurred west-country speech. Carol translated, and was surprised to find that her own ear could still make the adjustment without effort — she simply heard familiar words differently spoken. Indeed, the speech itself was familiar; it chimed in with the language. This was how people spoke English and ever had. She had said as much, earlier today, after Ben struggled over an exchange with an elderly man at a small petrol station.

"And what is it that I am speaking, then?" Ben said. They both laughed.

But now Carol was hearing Aunt Margaret's speech as strange, alien, even off-putting. Oh, she could understand well enough, but it all seemed to come from a long way away — that bell-like clarity, those pinched vowels. In that other life of hers, in her youth, at college, she had had a friend from the north, a blunt Yorkshire girl, who had a word for that kind of speech — pound-note voices, she called them. Back when a pound was something to be reckoned with. Lots of pounds in Aunt Margaret's voice — old pounds.

Perhaps this was what Ben was listening to, for he turned suddenly to Aunt Margaret with a smile. "Back home we have a yard — Carol does her best to achieve

British standards, but I have to admit that we fall short."

Aunt Margaret stared at him. "A yard? Oh . . ."

Carol knew what she was seeing: some fetid urban square of concrete. Probably Ben knew also; that particular smile was his tease smile, but Aunt Margaret was not to know that. She was seeing a washing line, dustbins.

Carol said, "It's mainly just lawn — the easy option." She squeezed Ben's arm. "You know, I really think we should be on our way. It's been so good to visit with you, Aunt Margaret."

Aunt Margaret inclined her head. "Lovely to see you again, and to meet" — she groped unsuccessfully for Ben's name — "your husband."

"My pleasure," said Ben. "A most enlightening afternoon."

Aunt Margaret appeared gratified by this comment. The four of them moved back to the house. Carol retrieved her purse. At the front door, they exchanged kisses and handshakes, their farewells erupting simultaneously so that nobody much heard what anyone else said. Later, only the Colonel's emphatic bass would lie around in Carol's head: "Tell your president to keep on backing up our Mrs. T."

In the car, heading for the pub in which they had booked a room for the night, Ben said, "So? Did your aunt fill you in on the family tree?"

"Up to a point. But I rather think I may have fallen off the family tree after today. Or jumped."

"Come now, they weren't so bad. A different climate of mind, put it that way."

"You can say that again!"

He laughed, and reached across to hold her knee. "Look at it as life experience. I don't often get to meet a guy like your uncle. It's an education. A man of firm views and a fine contempt for the evils of book learning. I was careful to play down my trade."

"He patronized you," said Carol.

"Of course, what else? A raw colonial."

"I was embarrassed."

"People are not responsible for their relatives. And in any case, you're making too much of it. Personally, I enjoyed myself."

"It's all very well for you," she said. "You're detached."

But that evening, in the pub, she felt an interesting surge of liberation. They drank a lot of wine over dinner; Ben came up with a rather crude imitation of the Colonel which had them both convulsed with laughter. She saw that her uncle would become an icon, one of those private jokes that are the bedrock of a marriage. She felt an absurd gratitude to him.

She said to Ben, "You know, this trip has had a peculiar effect. Maybe it was not just you who is detached." An image kept coming into her head — she kept seeing those geological maps in which land masses are shown in a state of fission, splitting apart into the familiar shapes of the modern globe: continental drift, America shaping up, floating free of its anchorage. Maybe people do that too, she thought, maybe it's what they have to do.

A few days later, they flew out of Heathrow. I am going home, Carol thought. On previous visits, over the years, she had always experienced at this point a faint sense of loss, as though in lifting off into the sky — taking out her book, glancing at the menu — she left a shadowy fragment of herself behind, down there among the boxy houses, the checkerboard fields. This time, she knew that she was whole. Whatever it had been, that shadow self, it was gone now — gone with her parents, perhaps. She was heading home.

I have lived in a century of mass migration, the time when millions slipped from one culture into another, were born with one identity and died as someone else. Such shape-shifting is a wonder — that people are so flexible, so permeable. Today, I am a Londoner. Cities absorb; new arrivals creep into cracks and crevices. They re-invent both themselves and the place. The minicab driver from Turkey, here just a month, but already able to navigate his way around — after a fashion; the Indian corner-shop proprietor who came from Uganda decades ago and whose children now have the speech of north London. I look at the faces of the city's migrants, which reflect other worlds, and wonder if I could have done that.

Comet

A faithful exercise in confabulation would proliferate like an evolutionary tree. I should write not one book but hundreds; I should pursue each idiosyncratic path. Not an option, clearly, and to follow a single outcome seemed like a constriction: more inviting to pounce on remembered climactic points and let speculation run free. And how they do cluster within a particular time frame, those portentous moments. When we were young. When we were least well equipped to make rational and expedient decisions, when we blew with the wind, when we lived for the day.

There was an explosion of choice, back then. The paths do not so much fork as flourish. Up here? Over there? This way? Or that? In the mind's eye, they mirror the evolutionary tree in which a brief central trunk throws out a series of branches, each of which divides yet again, and none of which is the inevitable course, arriving eventually at Homo sapiens. Contingency: the great manipulator. Under the laws of contingency, human evolution is an over-whelming improbability. In the Burgess Shale of British Colombia, there has been found a range of fossil animals about 570 million years old, most of which are unrelated to any existing fauna: dead ends, victims of evolutionary contingency. There is a creature with a nozzle like a vacuum cleaner, another that appears to be an animated bath mat, another like a lotus flower, another that resembles a feather duster. Bizarre elaborations; the routes that evolution might have taken, the alternative scenarios. I look at these and find myself thinking of the lives I have not had. Shall I be the lotus flower, the bath mat, the feather duster? What if I had followed the advice of the University Appointments Board and applied for a job with Shell? Or got serious and taken the civil service exam? Or gone abroad as a teacher of English?

I was young in the middle of the twentieth century. The year 1900 was history; the millennium was science fiction. We had wind-up gramophones and stockings with seams; we bought Chianti in straw-covered bottles, we smoked Gauloises and admired French films and American musicals. Sex was out in the open, but a *nice girl did not go into a pub on her own. We got married, on the whole, and some lived happily ever after, unaware of looming divorce statistics. Our babies wore real nappies and drank ersatz orange juice supplied by the government; our toddlers were guided by Dr. Spock. We bred early, usually on account of unreliable contraceptive methods. When we made choices, we did not look back; life seemed to have its own momentum.*

From time to time I stay in a hotel in Oxford that was undergraduate lodgings in the 1950s. I spent many hours there, back then; it harbored a group of my friends, young men who wore duffel coats and drank a lot of beer. The wind-up gramophones worked overtime in smoke-filled rooms. Today, the sixteenth-century stone building with mullioned windows has been reinvented as a classy establishment catering for the discriminating visitor. The warren of small personal dens is gone, replaced by tastefully comfortable rooms with all facilities. The pillows are fat and the water is hot; the barman prepares Irish coffee with elegant dexterity. But every now and then I seem to hear distant, scratchy melodies: "Begin the Beguine," "La Mer," "These Foolish Things."

What I feel is curiosity, not nostalgia. The girl in the bat-wing sweater who propped her bike against the wall is not so much an alter ego as another person. I am not she, because of all that has happened since; she is an ancestor, it seems, and I am just one of many possible descendants. I wonder what she would feel about me? Dismay, I imagine; when we are twenty, we are never going to get old.

Two boys are out shooting birds on an Italian hillside. Two boys, two guns, four dogs. They have strayed far from the village, up into the hills, farther than they have ever been before, high into the rocky, scrubby bird haunts of the high slopes, where they blast off happily at all and sundry. Few people come here; it is a barren place, and treacherous, with deep unexpected gullies and crevasses. And now, at the end of the day, one of the dogs has got itself into one of these clefts and cannot scramble out. They can hear it, whining and yelping, down there in a morass of twiggy, prickly growth, invisible and insistent.

What to do? They eye the gully without enthusiasm, but the dog is useful, they are fond of it, and neither is going to chicken out in front of the other. So there is nothing for it but to get in there and effect a rescue.

They slither down the rocks. They bash a path through the bushes, collar the frantic dog, and prepare to climb back out.

And then they see it. Some sort of seat, wedged between boulders, half-smothered in brambles; a rusted frame, amid which there are rags of material and a bundle of collapsed sticks or something. They peer closer; they understand. And they are out of there like a dose of salts, back up the rocks and away, bawling at the dogs. They are not going to hang around here; this is not one for them — this is for the *carabinieri*.

Sarah Low said to her friend and colleague Clare, "I have had a very odd letter. An official letter from an official person at a very official address — the Foreign Office, no less — asking if I am my father's daughter. If I am, they will be in touch again with some information."

"Dear me," said Clare. "And are you? There's not some dark family secret?"

"None that I know of."

"Money? An unexpected inheritance?"

"I think not," said Sarah. "I think," she went on after a moment, "that it is going to be something about my half sister. Penelope."

Sarah has received, wrapped in polythene, a rectangle of water-stained, sunbleached, insect-chewed leather, attached to a long strap, equally degraded. This was once a handbag. You can open it, still. It has a flap, like an envelope, and on the front of the flap there are three rusted metal initials: PML. These initials made identification possible. They set in train the process of consulting files and lists, collating, eliminating, searching, enlisting the help of Somerset House — the process that led to the arrival of that letter. The initials, the bag, its contents, the strap by which it hung across its owner, have lain on an Italian hillside for nearly fifty years, waiting to give testimony. They have lain there since before Sarah was born.

The bag had contents, which are also neatly wrapped. A pair of sunglasses, quite well-preserved. Some Egyptian coins. A corroded circular metal object and an equally corroded metal tube. These last, she realizes, are a powder compact and a lipstick. She finds them peculiarly disturbing. They are mundane, and intimate. She imagines them back in pristine condition: the shiny compact, with some pretty design on the front, and the mirror within (there are shards of glass); the lipstick selected for shade and brand. Elizabeth Arden? Max Factor?

There is also a wodge of fibrous brown matter. It is possible to see that this is many-leafed, like a mille-feuille. Even so, she would not have realized what it was were it not for the inventory that accompanied the package. This is the remains of a British passport. How are the mighty fallen.

It would have been one of those old blue ones, she thinks. The real McCoy — the dark blue gold-embossed stiff-covered booklet from the days when a British passport was just that, and no qualifying coda about European Community. It would have had a photograph in it; somewhere in this wodge of matter there is the ghost of a face, a face that would be eerily familiar.

She has seen photographs of her half sister. She has seen in them her own myopic look — the thick-lensed glasses, the look that is a legacy from their father. And his nose, she has seen — his slightly beaky nose on that face, echoing her own.

In the family albums, photographs of Penelope cease. She is there, and then she is not. Everyone else gets older; babies and children appear. She is simply an absence. There is one further item in the package, separately wrapped. This is clearly recognizable as a locket, still attached to the chain on which it hung around a neck. The locket is heart-shaped; it is blackened and battered — there is a dent at the back, the hinge is broken. It is just possible to make out intricate patterning on the front, and there are inlaid chips of some other material. She rubs at one with her finger and sees that it is blue. Some of the chips are missing; there are tiny empty sockets.

"A Comet," Sarah tells Clare. "Apparently they were rather given to dropping out of the sky. It was 1956. In the run-up to the Suez crisis. She'd gone out to Egypt to teach in a language school, and then Brits were advised to get out. She was twenty-three."

"After all this time . . ."

"Quite. And now there's only me. Closest surviving relative."

"And you never even knew her?"

"Of course not. I was the second family, by the second marriage. She was just a legend. A sad legend, mentioned less and less."

"Oh my goodness," says Clare. "And now I suppose you'll have to do something about . . . well, arrangements."

In the chapel of the crematorium, there is a miasma of embarrassment. Hardly anyone here actually knew her; they are attending the funeral of a stranger. Most of them are unknown to each other; various people are unknown to Sarah. The mourners do not fill the room — far from it. They are scattered about, glancing furtively at one another. A couple of cousins remember Penelope, vaguely ("But we never saw her that much, you know. All the same, we felt we must be here"). A very old man has gamely struggled up from Bournemouth, leaning on a stick; he knew her father well ("Nice girl — such a shame"). The cousins' husbands are dutiful but a touch restive, wondering about traffic conditions and the route home. Clare has come, and a few more of Sarah's friends. There is an elderly woman who was at college with Penelope ("Thank goodness I happened to spot your notice in the paper"), attended by a patient daughter. And there are others, as yet unidentified.

They wait in silence, staring at the coffin, on which there is laid a sheaf of white lilies. And then the priest arrives, the mourners rise to their feet, and the process of dispatch begins.

Sarah tours the room. There is finger food, soft drinks, a glass of wine for those who would prefer. She has done her duty by the cousins; Clare is looking after the old chap from Bournemouth. And now this man is bearing down on her, one of the strange faces noted earlier. He carries a plateful of food and has preferred red wine.

"Tom Sayers. I was in Cairo."

In fact, it emerges, he ran the language school at which Penelope taught, for that brief time she was there. "We old Egypt hands tend to keep in touch, and someone told me about this, so I thought I'd come along."

"That was good of you."

He inclines his head, graciously. He must be eighty, at least. "I thought there might be some people I knew here. And one's not that busy these days. An outing's quite welcome."

"I take it you do remember my sister," says Sarah. Cool, now.

"Oh, indeed I do. Mind, there were quite a few expat girls around. My staff came and went like anything. Here today, gone tomorrow. Some of them left more of an impression than others. The bombshells, you know — and she wasn't that. Nice girl, though. Tall, wore glasses." His glance strayed over Sarah's shoulder. "Truth to tell, I don't see anyone here I recognize from Cairo days. Pity."

"I'm sorry you've wasted your time."

He waved his glass at a passing waiter. "Red for me. Not at all, not at all. I wanted to pay my respects anyway. Nice girl, as I say. Of course, one heard all about the crash at the time. Terrible thing. And we all took those flights home. There but for the grace of God, one thought."

Sarah eyed him. This old horror had lived to be eighty, shoving his way through life. There is no selective system, none at all. Let's not talk about God.

"Please excuse me," she said. "There are people I haven't yet spoken to."

She had written to the aunts and the uncles and the cousins. You will remember my half sister, Penelope, she wrote. Well, there is this news . . . I feel we should commemorate her, she wrote. A small event for family and friends. I very much hope that you will be able to come. It occurred to her that these were quite the oddest letters that she had ever had to write. And, no doubt, for others to receive. Puzzled spouses and partners would say: Who? Elderly aunts would be anxious about travel arrangements and frame guilty excuses.

She had put a notice in selected newspapers: discreet, succinct. There might be others interested.

And there were. For now there is this second stranger standing before her, explaining himself, but hesitantly, with diffidence. He, too, had been in Cairo. John Lambert. He had known her sister. He had known her very well. At first, his diffidence makes it hard for him to get to the point. He, too, had been teaching in Cairo, at the university. He had met Penelope soon after they both arrived. And . . . well, they had become quite close. Very close. In fact, he says, eventually, the idea was that we were going to get married, in due course.

"Oh . . . ," says Sarah. "Oh, good heavens. I don't think my father ever said . . ."

He tells her that nothing was exactly formalized. She hadn't told her parents or anyone. "People got engaged in those days," he says. "The ring and so forth. We hadn't got around to that, but it would have come." He smiles, embarrassed. "I hope you don't mind hearing this, but I felt I'd like to tell you."

Sarah said, "I'm so very glad you're here. And of course I don't mind."

"It was a shock, coming across your notice. It's something you do at my time of life" — a wry grin — "You tend to trawl through that page to see who's popped their clogs. And so I saw it. It made me feel very odd, I can tell you. It's not that I don't think of her — I often do. But it made the whole thing seem new again. Hearing about the crash, back then. What one felt. And I sat there looking at your notice and thinking that if that hadn't happened, my life would presumably have been very different. My wife was pouring me a cup of coffee and I thought: I'd never have known you. You'd be somebody I never met."

Sarah nodded. There seemed no appropriate comment.

"Mind, I'm devoted to my wife."

She gazed at this man: lean, slightly stooped, long thin jowly face, old enough to be her father. Somewhere behind and beyond all this there lurked another person entirely — a man who had been young with her sister. Penelope had stopped; he had continued. But he carried her still in his head; she survived in his mind, an

251

untransmittable image.

Fazed by this thought, Sarah hardly heard what he was saying. She saw her father's old black-and-white photos: that face with resonances of her own, the height and build that reflected hers. But this man would see her in color.

He was talking about Egypt, back then.

"Terrific place to be if you were young and up for anything. And then of course it fell apart. The Suez crisis. We Brits were persona non grata. Best to get out, if you were in a position to do so. Most of us were on short-term contracts anyway. She left a month before I did. We were all set to get together back home." He pulled a face, shook his head.

Sarah said, "I'd like to hear more about that time. I wonder if we could meet again?"

He looked alarmed. "We live up north, you know. I don't really come to these parts. I don't think my wife . . ." He paused. "You look like Penelope. It's eerie, seeing what she might have been like when she was older. I suppose . . . I suppose I could write to you. Actually, I'd find it quite helpful to put a few things down."

"Please," said Sarah. "I'd be so glad if you would."

★ ★ ★

At forty-seven, Sarah occasionally felt that life had her by the scruff of the neck. Mostly, you could ignore the passage of time; that is to say, you tamed it, you reduced it to diary pages, to dates and days of the week, to the setting on the alarm clock or the start of a television program. You ignored the darker implications, the stalking footsteps. And then, once in a while, she would wake in the night, often after some dream in which she had been a child again, or some younger self, and would lie there thinking: I am forty-seven, for heaven's sake, and I don't know how this has come about. It was as though there were some baleful presence alongside, forcing her to stare at this unrelenting fact: look, look hard, and don't you forget it.

She was alone, but not lonely. Once, she had lived with a man. She knew all about being half of a couple — about living with someone else's views, foibles, habits, their way of folding a newspaper, washing a plate. She knew that curious fusion of companionship and private distance; she knew about good sex and bad sex and sudden quarrels and the warm glow of reconciliation. She had wondered about having a child, and believed that he did the same, though nothing was said. And then something happened: feeling had withered, she no longer smiled at the sound of his key in the lock, she found herself treasuring time to herself. And she saw that this was so for him too. They became like courteous strangers, skirting any serious engagement. And, eventually, fell apart.

Sometimes, nowadays, she missed all that. At others, she relished her independence and self-sufficiency: the freedom to do what you wished without consulting anyone else, the small comfortable indulgences of solitude. She had friends, she had her work, she spent much of her time with other people; she felt herself largely fortunate.

That said, she knew that there were gaps. There was the significant gap of childlessness. There was her solitary status, which, while now statistically respectable, one understood, still offended against expectations. The man with whom she had once lived was married, with offspring; so were many of her friends and colleagues. She would not, now, have children, and accepted that; she balanced the regrets that sometimes surfaced against the satisfactions of an unfettered life. So far as companionship was concerned — love, even, if one were to be so specific —

she kept an open mind. Maybe, but quite possibly not; and if not, so be it.

After her parents died, Sarah had gone through a period when she felt untethered; those from whom she stemmed were no longer there, she had no child to carry forward aspects of herself. Genetically disadvantaged — this was the term that sprang to mind. Except that, no — that implied something rather different. She thought of the ways in which she resembled a parent — features, eyesight, asthma, skin that burned in the sun. Such were the discernible aspects; goodness knows what unquantifiable inclinations, capacities, and tendencies lurked there also. Advantages and disadvantages — the genes served up both, indiscriminately.

She had relatives, though none who were close to her; various aunts, uncles, cousins with whom she exchanged Christmas cards. But she had a friend who had no living relatives known to her whatsoever. When this was first mentioned, Sarah had been quite startled; her friend seemed grimly isolated, without that biological network into which most people are plugged. Christmas cards took on a new significance; Sarah tightened up the friendship.

When she was a child — an only child — she had invented brothers and sisters.

These were a versatile crew, constructed and reconstructed to suit the needs of the moment: a companionable, confiding sister, a tomboy sister with a taste for shared exploits, a masterful older brother. As she grew up, these useful shadows faded away: she rather missed them. She saw this lack of siblings as another gap, but perhaps not a seminal one. Plenty of people do not get on at all with their brothers and sisters; you can also get along without any.

Work had become central to her, all her life: far more than just the source of an income. She had been drawn to museums since she was a schoolgirl; her degree had led her to various jobs as a curatorial assistant, until a burgeoning fascination with conservation work sent her in pursuit of further qualifications. For ten years now she had been a conservator, responsible for that department in a leading museum of ethnology. Clare was her deputy. With the help of two or three interns, they labored to arrest the destructive effects of time and the malevolence of the environment. Ideally, the objects that passed through their hands should emerge not restored but preserved for eternity in their authentic condition.

Sarah's workroom sometimes looked like some outrageous car boot sale, or the attic harvest of a family with peculiarly bizarre tastes, she thought. Shrouded in polythene, there might be face masks, basketry, feather headdresses, moccasins, weapons, a paper kite, a skin-covered drum, strings of beads. An ethnological collection is eclectic in its tastes; a conservator requires wide-ranging skills. Sarah spent her days pondering decay: how to arrest insect damage and corrosion, how to bring a textile back to life, preserve degraded paper. The game was to step in and halt the natural progress whereby everything disintegrates. You interfered, tactfully and technically; you shone the bright light of science upon the object and froze it in the here and now. Literally, sometimes, as new acquisitions or those that had been on display were plunged into the freezer to eliminate insect larvae. The artifact in question would grow no older, age would not wither its stitches or its paint or its feathers; it would defy time, safely delivered into the care of the museum. It would no longer be used, or worn, or played; its function now would be to serve as evidence for the interesting vagaries of human behavior. People would look at it and be intrigued, or shocked, or impressed; they would wonder about the making of it, and about the lives of those for whom it had been significant — or they might simply drift past, looking around for their companions, thinking that it was time for lunch, locked into a mind-set of their own.

Ethnography takes the long view, when it comes to mind-sets: dispassionate, un-equivocal. Sarah was not an ethnographer, but as a conservator she found herself exposed to some pretty provocative stuff. The objects that she handled frequently suggested attitudes and assumptions that were a far cry from the lifestyle of a forty-seven-year-old western European woman; they spiced up her days, provoked fantasies and speculation. She spent her time with things that referred her to unknowable others, that conjured up practices and beliefs that she could barely envisage. She pored over the insect tracks in a feathered hat, or the indications on the sole of a moccasin that once someone wore this, and from somewhere far away and long ago there came an echo of voices that she could not understand; imagined sights and scenes drifted above the sheets of polythene on her table, the bottles and the brushes and the instruments.

"Look," said Sarah.

She unwrapped the locket and laid it in front of Clare.

"It was my sister's. I want to restore it, and wear it. What do you think?"

"Easy enough to clean it up. That dent would be quite tricky to do, though, and the hinge. The inlay is turquoise, I imagine."

The two women considered. They passed the locket from hand to hand, made suggestions.

"Tell you what," said Clare. "Why don't you show it to Barry Sanders when he comes next week. Isn't he supposed to be the last word where metal is concerned? He'd have ideas about how best to deal with the dent."

The museum made frequent use of free-lance specialists on short-term contracts, when there was an accumulation of work in some particular area.

"Good idea," said Sarah. "I'd forgotten he was due."

Somehow, the tarnished and broken locket had assumed a curious significance; it seemed necessary, for its original owner's sake, to revive it, and use it. Perhaps I have become obsessed with objects, Sarah thought: a hazard of this trade. She dealt daily with things whose makers and users were long since dead; the perverse survival of fur and skin and feathers, palm leaves and parchment, iron and ivory, jade and flint — these manifestations of the physical world stood in for a shadowy human populace. The artifacts suggested systems of belief, customs, methodologies — but in the last resort they were just things. If you could not set them within a context, they became meaningless. Like framed sepia photographs in a junk shop. The locket was poignant, because of its circumstances, but its impervious survival seemed also vaguely indecent. To wear it would be to tame it, to give it a context once more — the link between one woman and another. Some sort of catalyst.

"May I show you something?" she said.

She had known Barry Sanders only from correspondence, and by reputation. It was the end of the working day, the second of his stint in the museum; a cordial working relationship had been established — why not presume on him for a moment?

He held the locket in the palm of his hand. "Middle Eastern origin. Turkish, perhaps. There's a scrolly sort of pattern that you can't really make out at the moment. Turquoise insets. Easy enough to get it into apple-pie order again. You'd clean it up, sort out that dent. New hinge. You could make substitutes for the missing insets with Milliput. Why don't I do it for you?"

"Oh," she said, embarrassed. "That wasn't what I had in mind. Heavens! Don't think that. I just wanted an opinion."

"I'd enjoy it — I like to keep my hand in. I'll take it home. I'm always tinkering with something. Things that turn up. This was my line, once."

"Jewelry?"

"I fancied myself as a craftsman, after art school. I made jewelry, for a while, but found I wasn't much cop on the design side. So I moved over into restoration — became a silversmith. And thence, eventually, into this business. We all come from different directions, don't we?"

He was a dark, burly man — beard, bushy eyebrows. Fiftyish. At a glance, you would have placed him in some quite different sphere. He made Sarah think of accessory players in a Shakespeare play: the attendant lord or knight, the spearholder. You could imagine him in armor or archaic costumes, not shirtsleeves and rather grubby trousers, sitting at a worktable contemplating a piece of battered jewelry. He looked like someone who should be engaged in strenuous physical activity, but there was also something calm and concentrated about him.

People identify themselves, in some subliminal way. You know very soon into which category they fall. You know that you would like to see them again; or you definitely would not, or you don't much care either way. Sexual attraction doesn't much come into it; that's another matter with its own agenda. The basic thing is simply this question of empathy, as though the other person wore some coded emblem that you recognize. It can happen with someone who serves you in a shop, or a person you talk to at a party, or a neighbor or a colleague or the man who comes to read the meter.

He was still examining the locket. "How did it get in such a state?"

And so she told him. All of it. The crash. The Italian hillside. This long-ago girl whom she never knew.

"And I just thought I'd like to bring it back to life, and wear it."

"Of course. That's exactly what you

should do. Leave it to me. I'll enjoy it."

"Well, thank you," she said. "That's extremely kind."

The letter from John Lambert took her by surprise. She had not forgotten his suggestion, but had thought it more than likely that he would not follow it up.

"Dear Sarah (if I may)," he began. "Well, here goes. I said I'd try to get down something about that time — about her and me.

"I should explain myself briefly, to kick off. I'm a schoolmaster — was, rather. Forty years in a north-country boys' school. Egypt pointed me in that direction — it was there that I found out I rather liked teaching. I suppose Egyptian students were good induction material — bolshy and feckless and provocative and sometimes delightful. Much like the British male adolescent. Except that these were somewhat older — university students. They used to go on strike at the drop of a hat. They'd sidle up to you with sob stories at exam time. They were cheeky one moment, subservient the next. I taught them Shakespeare and the Victorian novel and the Romantic poets and so forth — wonderfully irrelevant, you might think. They needed English for career purposes, but Egypt didn't need the British any longer and that was becoming more and more apparent.

"I thought it was an amazing place. I'd hardly traveled at all — camping holidays in France were my idea of abroad. And now here one was in another world — one that was hot and brilliant and ancient and spoke half a dozen languages. I can still smell Cairo. And hear it — that endless jostle of traffic, everything from trams and beat-up lorries to donkey carts piled high, strings of camels. I've been back once, ten years ago, and by then they'd smashed flyovers through the place and lined the Nile with Hiltons, but back in the fifties much of it was still the real thing. I loved it. I was in a state of happy culture shock from day one.

"But it's her you want to know about. She'd been born there, of course. She was twelve when they left, just before the end of the war. She told me she'd always felt homesick, all through her school years in England. I'm not sure what going back was supposed to do. And the truth was that she'd gone back to a place that now seemed as alien to her as it did to the rest of us expats. She used to say that she felt like two people — there was part of her for whom the place was familiar and homely, and another for whom it was a foreign country, baffling and intriguing and deceptive.

"Maybe what she'd really gone back for was childhood, and that's not on offer. I think she was quite confused, that whole year. She'd thought it would be a sort of homecoming, and it wasn't. She had a smattering of Arabic and she knew her way around a bit, but she was really as bemused as any other new Cairo hand — as any of us who used to meet up at Groppi's or the Gezira Club, all the flotsam out there teaching or peddling culture for the British Council. We were all young, with nice new degrees, cavalier about our futures, wanting a bit of experience. There were a few old-timers around, long-term residents — engineers, and cotton people and oil people and so forth — but we didn't have anything much to do with them, except for anyone you were actually working with. I had my professor, who had been there since before the war, and all through it — one of those professional orientalists, nothing he didn't know about the Middle East, and most of it he told you. And she had the bloke who ran the language school, an awful hack. Actually, he was at the service. He didn't recognize me, and I steered clear. I suppose he must have introduced himself to you. She couldn't abide him.

"She shared a flat in Zamalek with another girl. That's how we met. The other girl worked at the university, so I knew her, and there was some gathering on the terrace at the club one evening, which included Penelope and . . . it just built up from there.

"We all pair up at around that time in life, don't we? Most of us, anyway. Maybe more so then than now. You expected to get married, probably sooner rather than later. She was twenty-two; I was twenty-five.

"We went for a picnic up in the Moquattam hills, one of the first times together. I'd borrowed a car from someone I knew, and we drove out of Cairo, up into those hills that are a wonderful sort of mauve color, and we found a nice rock with a view and ate our sandwiches and our bananas and drank iced lemonade from a thermos. She remembered coming there when she was a child and being disappointed because the sand was just ordinary buff, not mauve. And I remember that afternoon so well. Most of all I remember how I felt — happy and excited, as though the world had some huge potential I'd only just discovered.

"This probably sounds foolish. I'll sign off — for now."

"The locket is coming along nicely," he said. "I only get home at weekends, so it's a spasmodic process. Another week or two. Coffee?"

Space had been found for Barry Sanders in an annex adjoining the main conservation workrooms. Periodically he would emerge and head for the museum's cafeteria, sometimes pausing to seek company. The interns. Or Clare.

Or Sarah.

"There's no hurry at all," she said. "Please . . ."

They had talked shop on the first occasions: the tasks in hand, museum gossip. Then their conversations tipped into personal life. She learned something of him. He lived by himself in a village outside York; he had adult children; he enjoyed hill-walking. In his company, she felt an uprush of well-being. Which meant nothing, of course — nothing.

"My first repair job got me a good

bollocking," said Barry Sanders. "It was my grandad's fob watch. Hadn't worked in years. I thought: I can fix that. I was always making stuff — meccano, those balsawood airplanes, you name it. Apple of the woodwork teacher's eye. Cocky twelve-year-old. So I took the back off, and there's all these cogs and wheels, and I poke around with a nail file and a pair of tweezers, and presently I've got it pretty well dismantled — very interesting, very satisfying. But then there's the question of how to put it back together again. You can guess the rest. Don't worry, I've made progress since then."

"Junk shops," said Sarah. "A flea market was my idea of heaven. Normal adolescents like to cruise round Woolworth's. I was in perpetual search of a promising junk shop. Things. The more inscrutable the better. I spent birthday money on candle snuffers and paper knives and pincushions. My bedroom was a latter-day cabinet of curiosities. I seem to have been programmed, from an early age."

"I don't mind middle age," he said. "I mind it less than I expected. I run out of steam on a steep fell rather sooner than I care for, but that's about the size of it. The senses stay in good nick, it seems to me. Was youth such a big deal? One was always skint or in a tizz about some girl or wondering what the hell to do next. And I was a northern boy who wasn't interested in football, which didn't help."

"Being young in the seventies was a status, wasn't it? We girls drifted around in cheesecloth and strings of beads and flared jeans that trailed in the dirt, and you were supposed to smoke pot except that I tried it once and freaked out, so that was that. I was never fully-paid-up young, and I didn't know the tunes. When they run those TV programs re-creating a decade, I seem to be watching other people's lives — it wasn't much like that for me. Or do we all feel that about past contexts?"

"What do you think about when you're working?" asked Barry. "It's not always the matter in hand, is it? Or rather, half of the mind attends to that and the other half is adrift. I was drifting in the Bronze Age this morning, working on those spearheads. Don't know much about the period, but you start imagining a way of life. I suppose the likes of me might have done reasonably well back then — skills to offer that would have come in handy. I might have been a central figure in society, instead of on the eccentric fringe."

"Vulcan. You could have been a god. Bashing out armory in a cave. Can you forge? Well, you would have done back then. You'd have inspired awe and reverence. They weren't the prosaic lot that we are. Sometimes I think it odd, given the stuff we handle. I don't believe in sympathetic magic. Magic of any kind, indeed. Mysterious forces. Ley lines and all that send me up the wall. But most of the material here has magical connotations. We treat it with the utmost respect, but we have no truck with what it represents."

"Those blue stones in her locket — your locket — were to ward off the evil eye, of course. They don't seem to have done the trick. I remember once seeing a newspaper photo of the Pope kneeling to kiss the ground after descending from an aircraft. The comment, of course, was — well, wouldn't you if you'd just flown Alitalia? Sorry, that's a bit off-color, given the circumstances. Hope you aren't annoyed."

"I'm not annoyed," she said.

"Next installment," wrote John Lambert. "You apparently felt that my last letter was of interest, and I find I'm a bit obsessed with that time. There's no one I can talk to — my wife wouldn't relish it — and there's something therapeutic about getting things down.

"The thing is that she is disappearing. Penelope. I have to struggle to remember her. I can see her face, hold it for a moment, and then it dissolves. Other times, I can't see her at all. But I have all these snatched scenes in which she features. I am there, she is there, Egypt is there loud and clear. And occasionally, I hear something else she said. The way words can hang in the head for ever.

"She's talking about when she was a child, during the war. We're beside the pool at the Gezira Club and she's wearing a green swimming costume and she turns to me and she's telling me about the soldiers that used to stay at their house, on leave from the desert. She says, 'They were the same age that I am now.' And I can still hear the surprised note in her voice, as though something had fallen into place for her. And I hear that and I see the green swimming costume and the high diving

271

board above the pool. I used to dive off that; so did she.

"But the other thing is — what I remember best is how it felt, back then. How I felt. Those moments of euphoria. They don't come so thick and fast, fifty years on. But they leave an aftertaste, believe me. You sail into the horizon, when you're young — you're unstoppable, and it's always going to be that way.

"And I was in love. Well, we've all been there — most of us, anyway. Well-trodden ground. But that doesn't make it any less — unique. Does it?"

Sarah pauses to consider. She looks up from the letter and stares at the packet of cereal on her kitchen table, the mug of coffee, the fruit bowl. Love? But I've almost forgotten, she thinks. How was it, exactly?

We went to the Cairo Zoo. That was another time-travel trip, for her. Apparently she went there pretty well every week, when she was a child. She said, "It's so much smaller than I thought. And scruffier." We stood looking at a pathetic mangy polar bear in a pool of murky water, and she said that. I think she meant the whole place, not the bear in particular. We ate pistachio nuts from paper cones and fed the monkeys. The keeper was shoving green clover at the hippos with a pitchfork — *berseem,* that ubiquitous Egyptian animal food — and we sat and watched. Holding hands. One of the euphoria moments. Hippos, and happiness. She felt sure they were the same hippos as when she was a child. What is the life expectancy of a hippo?

I consider myself a rational man. I've spent my life teaching children to use their powers of reason. I've tried to apply the same rules to my own behavior: act sensibly, and expediently. Which works, by and large, over most things: career choices, financial decisions, relations with others. But where the system collapses entirely is over love.

Actually, the first time I met her wasn't like that. On the terrace at Gezira, with a bunch of other people. I noticed her, yes, and we talked a bit. It was in Alexandria that I knew, a couple of weeks later. The same bunch of us had arranged to go up there for a long weekend, staying at a pension on the Corniche. Beach parties; exploring the old city. Later, back in England, when *The Alexandria Quartet* started to come out, I pounced on those books and I have to say I was mystified. Durrell must have been moving around on some other plane entirely. But none of us had ever heard of Lawrence Durrell, that weekend, and we didn't know that this was a city of dark secrets and outrageous characters. Exotic, yes, and quite different from Cairo — Mediterranean, rather than Islamic. Speaking with tongues — Greek, Arabic, Yiddish, you name it. And the sea, those beaches, the cafés, the trams, the villas with gardens that overflowed with poinsettias and bougainvillea and morning glory.

We went to the catacombs, the whole gang of us. Roman? Greek? I forget. But I remember the place all right — I'll never forget that. Deep and dark and cool after the blistering heat outside. Long narrow passages with tier upon tier of shelves carved out of the rock, where they laid the dead. That was when I knew, down there in the gloom. It was difficult to see where you were going, and she tripped on the uneven floor and almost fell. I caught hold of her elbow, and she turned and said thanks or something, and I knew. Oh my God, I thought.

Why? Why her? There were lots of girls around. She was quite nice-looking but not one of the femmes fatales. Quiet and serious some of the time. Read a lot — we courted with books, like you do. Gave each other Penguins. Working our way through Graham Greene and Evelyn Waugh and Faulkner and so forth.

So there it was — the bolt from the blue down in the catacombs. And after that I spent the rest of the weekend trying to engineer that I got her to myself. Slipping into the seat next to her in the tram or the café, spreading my towel out beside her on the beach. And one evening we all went to a nightclub place where there was dancing, and by then she'd got the message. The rest of the crowd we were with might as well not have been there.

Why does love provoke love? Why do people fall in love right back? Well, they don't always, of course. But it happens, doesn't it?

When we were in Cairo we went to the Mouski one day and I bought her a silver locket with blue stones. A statement of intent, I think.

Barry Sanders had said, "I'm not going home this weekend. The drive's getting me down a bit. Thought I'd hang out here, and look around. If you're free, I wondered if you'd care for a walk and a pub lunch?"

"I was married for fifteen years," he said. "Then it went wrong. It was hard on the kids, but we muddled through. They're fine now — turn up and chivvy me around every few weeks. Girls. They think I can't boil an egg. Actually, I do a mean Sunday roast."

"I've never been married," said Sarah. "Attached, yes. Quite firmly attached, indeed. But then detachment came. I was young at the point when marriage was beginning to go out of favor. We were the lot who felt that that compulsory search for an official partner before you hit thirty seemed rather old hat. We thought we could take it or leave it, on the whole, and we lived with others, and if it led to marriage, well and good, and if it didn't, there was always another day."

They were in a Red Lion or a White Horse somewhere, which seemed as good a place as any in which to talk about such things.

"I make it sound very heartless," she went on. "It wasn't, of course. The standard amount of emotion all round."

"I grew up in Leeds," said Barry. "In the working-class north people didn't consort out of wedlock, even then. I dare say it's caught on now, but not in 1975, when I got married. At least, there was plenty of consorting, but if it was at all serious, you had it properly certified. There was an older generation breathing heavily in the background who had standards."

Around them, there were couples — young couples and old couples and in-between couples with children — and a gaggle of men at the bar and an old chap on his own with the newspaper in the corner by the window.

"I suppose we were the degenerate south," she said. "And of course the word 'liberated' was knocking around in quite a big way. We made much of our liberations."

"That never reached me. I don't remember having that line to hand when I was arguing my dad into letting me go to art school. And my mum. They've just about come round to it now, but you tend to give up the fight a bit when you're pushing eighty."

They walked across fields, down through woodland, heading for the river. Pausing at a gate, they spread out the map and sought the footpath, head to head. He rested his hand on her shoulder, and the world seemed to tilt a little. What's this?

she thought. What's this?

Dear Sarah: — I am relieved that you were not put off by my maunderings about the operation of love. I thought afterward — for heaven's sake, she doesn't need this kind of stuff, all she wanted was to know a bit more about her sister, and that year in Egypt. But you even seemed rather interested. I like your theory about an immune system — weak in youth and increasingly robust as life goes on, but always susceptible to failure. If this is the case, mine has been impermeable for many a year. Just as well.

The locket. How extraordinary. That gave me quite a shock. All this time, and it survives. No, please keep it. I like the idea that you will wear it. I like the thought of it being restored. A kind of regeneration.

I certainly do not feel that your interest in that time is intrusive — rather the opposite. I am glad to take it out and look at it while I still can. I am one of the few people who remembers her. I am seventy-four. When I go . . .

When we came back from that weekend in Alex, it began in earnest. We were both working pretty hard so we could only see each other at weekends and the occasional evening. She was finding teaching quite hard — not cut out for it. I guess. Her language school catered for the well-heeled Cairene young who wanted to spruce up their English — spoiled girls and boys who were more interested in each other than in paying attention to her efforts. My lot at the university were more satisfying, probably — at least acquisition of a degree was of some importance to them. Anyway, she rather endured the school, though she was fascinated by the students, and always had choice anecdotes about their goings-on. She said: never again, teaching — at least I know now what I *can't* do. She liked the idea of journalism, but didn't know how you got started. She tried sending articles to the *Egyptian Gazette*, and one got taken, I remember. But the point was simply to be in Egypt for a while, for both of us, and after a bit the point was to be together as much as possible.

Every love affair has its own trajectory, I suppose. The first kiss, the first time you say it, the first time you make love. Don't worry, I'm not going into all that. And then the calming down, the settling into the longer term. Marriage, if it is going to be that. But of course we never got beyond the heights, because of what happened.

We went out to Mena, in those early days. Camel ride round the pyramids, tea at Mena House Hotel — the classic program. They served English tea, at the hotel — Earl Grey with a slice of lemon, cucumber sandwiches, little iced cakes — sitting in the gardens with gravel paths and palm trees and rose-covered pergolas, and hoopoes strutting around on shaven grass. I told her I'd been doing the Romantic poets with some of my students and I'd had them do some learning by heart — that was still educationally respectable back then. Which set us off on a sort of mad career through all the stuff we had in our own heads, seeing how long we could keep going, trading line for line: "The splendour falls on castle walls / And snowy summits old in story . . . A Book of Verses underneath the Bough . . . In Xanadu did Kubla Khan . . . The boy stood on the burning deck / When all around . . ." The game was to keep going for as long as we could, without touching down, as it were: "O Wild West Wind, thou breath of Autumn's being . . . Earth has not anything to show more fair." We flung Shakespeare at each other: "Friends, Romans, countrymen, lend me your ears . . . To die, to sleep: To sleep: perchance to dream . . .

The quality of mercy is not strained . . ."
In a state of hilarity, we were — of exuberance. It was one of those defining moments — the beginning of that archive of shared experience that you need, the treasury of private jokes and references. And even now, those snatches send me back to that afternoon, and the *suffragis* in their white robes and red sashes, doling out silver trays, and we two twenty-somethings rapping out the canon — tea and laughter.

She was twenty-two, I was twenty-five. That seems younger now than it did then. Youth wasn't an official status, in the mid-fifties. You leapt from the quarantine pen of undergraduate life onto the level plain of adulthood. Nobody dressed young; girls looked like their mothers, we men wore gray flannels and tweed jackets, with the suit for interviews, weddings and funerals. And you expected to do the grown-up thing: get married.

My wife and I have been together for forty-five years. We met in 1958, two years after I left Egypt. I have never talked much to her of that time, or indeed to anyone. It seems now like some disturbing hiatus in my life, an unfinished story.

"It's the big day," said Barry. "The

locket is finished."

Sarah was examining some new acquisitions; she looked at him across a bag made recently in Tobago from old matchboxes, a nice example of recycling. "How exciting. Can I see?"

"No. I had in mind a ceremonial handover. Maybe I could call in at your flat this evening?"

She bought fillet steak, new potatoes, sugar snap peas. Stilton. Grapes. A Chilean Merlot. She knew his tastes by now — a meat-and-two-veg man. She knew his tastes and some of his views and the way he pursed his lips when he was considering something and the mole on the back of his hand and the sound of his laugh. She knew the blue shirt and the red one and the black sweater and the brown leather jacket with worn elbows. She knew that he liked to play grand opera full blast when driving, had a weakness for onion-flavored potato crisps and did the *Guardian* crossword over lunch. She found herself disproportionately interested in all of this, and was alarmed.

"So . . . ," he said. "Behold!"

It lay in his palm — a plump shiny disk, patterned with incised fronds and twirls, inset with sky blue stones.

"The chain is the original, that's come up nicely. And it opens well, with the new hinge. You'll have to decide what to put in it. A photo is traditional, is it not? Or a lock of hair."

She took it from him. "It's lovely. I don't know how to thank you." She put the chain round her neck, and began fumbling with the fastening.

"I'll think of some way, in due course. That steak will do fine, for now. Here — let me."

He came round behind her. She felt him push her hair aside, and then his fingers against her skin. Please do that again, she thought. Go on doing it.

"We went to Luxor," wrote John Lambert. "By train. Days, it seems to have taken, in recollection. Pottering along beside the Nile, stopping at stations where men sold oranges and soft drinks through the train window. We couldn't afford sleepers, so we sat up all night, and I remember the dawn sky over the river, reflected, molten copper; she was asleep against my shoulder and I woke her up to show her — you couldn't miss that. And at Luxor we stayed at a cheap pension run by a Greek lady who took us for man and wife. We didn't disillusion her — it made us feel adventurous and complacent, both at once. And anyway, I'd asked Penelope by then. I won't go into that — suffice it to say that we knew where we were heading, or so we thought. I had to get a proper job, once we were back in England, and then she'd have told her parents.

But the Suez crisis was starting to rumble. Eden sounding off; Nasser defiant. Demonstrations in Cairo; anti-British feeling on the up. My students would march around with banners denouncing Britain, and then rush into my office to assure me it was nothing personal: "Not your fault, sir." We all felt pretty fed up about it — we thought Nasser had a point, several points indeed, we thought the Israelis might start something, we mistrusted Eden. But it seemed like background noise — we were too busy with our own lives to pay much attention. Especially she and I.

So we just got on with things. Work — and as much play as we could get in. Once, we went to find her childhood home, the house where she'd grown up, outside the city. Cairo was creeping outward by then; the open country around was being slowly gobbled up by slum building. But the three big houses with their gardens were still

284

there. The driveway to hers had an avenue of eucalyptus trees, and I remember her being quite emotional at that point — she'd had a thing about those trees, when she was a child. We introduced ourselves to the Egyptian family living there, and they were very friendly, very welcoming. But I think that for her the whole occasion was rather disturbing.

We'd both been wartime children, though our experiences were very different. She'd been in Egypt throughout, with the Germans steaming across the desert toward them, in the early 1940s. She said she was never in the least bothered; war seemed the natural and normal thing — the way in which children just accept the circumstances they are landed with. I remember feeling very much the same, as a boy. I was in Suffolk, with my mother and brother; my father was called up, of course, and we used to trace where he was on the map, when we knew, sticking in red pins — training in Scotland, then India, and eventually Burma. It never crossed my mind that he might not come back, and he did, but I barely recognized him. Penelope's family made a dash for Palestine, when a German invasion of Egypt looked imminent; what she remembered best of that time was collecting cowrie shells on a Palestine beach, and seeing General de Gaulle once in his dressing gown, in the high commissioner's house in Jerusalem.

Looking back now, I'm startled to realize that there were only a dozen years or so between that wartime, and the peace, if that is what it was, in which she and I were stepping out in Cairo. No time at all. But to us, then, it was an age: we'd gone from child to adult, we were other people.

There's a house in Cairo called the Beit il Kritiliya, beside the mosque of Ibn Tulun. It's a building that survives from the Mameluke period — sixteenth or seventeenth century — all kitted out with the most amazing collection of oriental furnishings. Courtyards with fountains, and *mashrabiya* windows, and alcoves lined with Turkish rugs. She had loved going there when she was a child — it had seemed like the *Arabian Nights* brought to life. She fantasized about it, apparently — told herself stories in which she played as Scheherazade and everyone else.

We went there. One blazing-hot afternoon; inside it was cool, as though you'd gone into another world. And I think we each saw a quite different place. I thought it was wonderful — exotic, romantic, essence of the East. And she was rather quiet and glum. She tried to explain. It was that she couldn't any longer see it as she once had: now, it was interesting and strange, but it had lost its power. The magic had gone — whatever it was that turned it into something mythical. She said she realized that the change was in her, not the house; it was to do with having grown up. She talked about how she'd felt out of place, in England, all through her adolescence. Now, she knew she wasn't at home here anymore. "It's gone," she said. And we started to make plans about what we'd do when we got back to England.

Sarah found a note on her worktable: "I wondered if you might fancy spending this weekend up north. Think it over. I'll understand if you don't — at least, let's say I'll put a brave face on it."

She found that she did not need to think it over.

They drove north after work on Friday, up the motorway, Verdi on the car radio, loud; whatever comes of this, she thought, that music will be forever charged now. Loaded, for ever.

His house was one of a brick terrace in a

small village. Two up, two down, kitchen and bathroom; workroom extension occupying most of the garden.

"My bedroom," he said. "And the spare."

He put her case in the spare, and that first night she slept there, alone.

They walked. Sarah thought that she had never walked so far, and with such exuberance. She could have walked over the horizon, she felt.

"Tell me when you've had enough," he said. "This doesn't have to be an SAS training exercise."

They ate sandwiches in the lee of a stone wall. "All right?" he inquired.

"I can't remember when I was so all right," she said, and he put his arm round her. She knew then that she would not spend the coming night alone in the spare.

In the small hours of the morning he said, "When I suggested this weekend I had no idea if we'd end up like this or not. I won't say I didn't have ambitions, but I wasn't at all sure how you felt."

"And are you now?"

"I reckon so."

She sat in an old basket chair in his workroom, reading, while he dismantled a carriage clock he'd found at a car boot sale. "I'm not so hot at clocks," he said. "Some I can do. This one's a bugger. If I get it sorted, it's yours, as a memento of now." He looked across at her. "This is odd. I feel as though you've always been sitting there, reading your book while I potter about."

Later, in the car, he put his hand on her knee. "Tell me things," he said. "Anything. Just talk. Keep me awake."

So she did. Afterward, it seemed to her that she had gone into a kind of free flow. She had talked about last week, and about thirty years ago; she fished her life for stuff that might entertain or inform. The motorway roared by, a procession of light, and she cruised her past, trawled up incident and opinion, people and places. This is reckless self-exposure, she thought. "Have you had enough?" she said. "Aren't you tired of me?" And he touched her knee again: "I think it'll be quite a while before that happens."

"I'm getting toward the end," wrote John Lambert. "1956. You couldn't any longer ignore what was going on. Suez. Nasser and Eden. Most of the Brits were starting to pack, and we knew we'd have to go. Anti-British feeling was high, and if the balloon went up, it would be a sight worse. I gave in my notice at the university, and my students all trailed in to shake me by the hand and say: 'Not your fault, sir. Down with Anthony Eden!'

"We'd had a habit of walking beside the Nile, at sunset. Penelope and I. When she was a child there had been some great trees beside one of the bridges, and she remembered how the egrets used to come in from the cultivation outside Cairo in the evenings, to roost there. She described the trees studded all over with the white birds, and more floating in, the sky full of them, and the reek of guano on the pavement below. The trees were gone now, and the birds with them, and the bridge wasn't called the English Bridge anymore, it was El Tahrir Bridge, though the lion statues at each end were still there, making you think of the Trafalgar Square lions.

"We met by the lions, the last time we walked there. I watched her coming, picking her way through the crowds, wearing a blue cotton dress and a white floppy hat. When she got near I could see at once that something was wrong. She'd had a letter from her father, sending a check for a flight home, and this messed up all our arrangements. We had planned to go by boat to Marseilles and then up through France — explore a bit. But apparently there was some family event — a wedding — and her father thought she'd like to be there, and was standing her the flight, which was expensive back then.

"We leaned against the railings on the bridge, looking at the river. 'Damn!' she said. 'Oh, *dammit!*' She felt she couldn't send the money back, say no. Her family didn't know about us yet; I thought I should equip myself with a real job back home before we went public, as it were. We were disappointed, with the prospect of that leisurely wander back to England together evaporating. She started to dither, wondering if maybe she could tell them now, explain, send the check back. I said, no, she shouldn't, no point in starting off on the wrong foot. I'm a pragmatic sort of bloke, always was. There'll be plenty of other chances to explore France, I said — we've got all the time in the world.

"So we walked by the Nile. Another sunset — the last. She said she still missed the egrets: 'It seems all wrong without them.' There was construction work all over the place — tower blocks going up, the old buildings coming down. It was all change, in Cairo.

"We had dinner at our favorite café, and then we went back to her flat. A few days later, she got on that plane, and the rest you know.

"I'll finish now. There's no more to say, really."

"Do you ever take that locket off?" asked Clare.

"Occasionally. When I have a bath."

"Well, it suits you. Or something does, these days."

Sarah had told Clare about John Lambert's letters. "He's finished now. End of story."

"Sad."

Except that it seemed also to be a beginning. But she was not going to say that. She had reread all the letters, and thought — fifty years ago, nearly half a century. And something comes full cycle. Love, again.

She found that she had entered some other time sphere, one that she had visited before but had almost forgotten. Its climate was familiar, yet also subtly different. Happiness is never the same twice over.

The days were flavored now by phone calls, by the approach of the weekend. Barry had gone home again, his contract with the museum ended. Then he was off elsewhere, on another job. Each day, there lay ahead the solace of the evening, when they could talk; each week, the hours ticked by until the moment when she would drive up north, or he would come to her.

There was now, and there had been the time before, which seemed like a period of half-life, or unknowing. And yet, she thought, it was all right, or so it seemed; I was not unhappy, I was not discontented — just, I did not know about him, about this. She was losing the solipsism of life alone; she began to think in terms of "we" and "us." Sometimes, she was alarmed: Is this rash? Is this what he wants? Is this what I want? And then the evening would come, or the weekend, and she would know that in fact rationality did not enter into it — what was bound to happen, would happen.

And so it was that after a while — weeks? months? — he said to her, "This won't do, will it? All this to and fro. I can't be having it."

"No," she said. "Nor me."

"So there's only one thing for it, isn't there?"

Forgive this tardy acknowledgment of your last letter, wrote John Lambert. I've been unwell. They're not sure what it is, but discouraging noises are made by the men in white coats. All very tedious. I won't bore you with it.

I'm all the more glad that I sent you that stuff about Cairo. About her. At least now there's someone else who has an idea of how it was.

This time I really am signing off. But before I do so, may I offer all my congratulations and good wishes on your forthcoming marriage.

Yours,
John

Comets did fall out of the sky. I was never on one, but I remember reading in newspapers of those air disasters back in the 1950s; once, the plane was carrying passengers from Cairo, and there were names that I knew.

I never did go back to Egypt then, though I thought of doing so. I still felt the occasional gust of homesickness. A stint abroad after university was a favored option, cashing in on the one salable asset that we all had — the English language. I made a few inquiries about language schools in Cairo, and then the prospect of something else came up, my attention was diverted, and that was that.

I went to Oxford, rather more tamely, to the job as a research assistant, which offered no career prospects but brought me Jack, and, in due course, marriage and motherhood. I forgot about my brief flirtation with the idea of a job in Egypt until eventually I did go back, far into adult life, and experienced then that eerie sensation of being in a place that was both deeply familiar and entirely alien.

I have no half sister. My parents were divorced when I was twelve, and by a subsequent marriage my father had two sons, when I was in my twenties. As a solitary child, my fantasies featured a mythical sister, along with the cast of The Iliad *and* The Odyssey. *Maybe Sarah is the last gasp of this unfulfilled need, in which case it is only natural that I should wish to give her a happy ending.*

Number Twelve Sheep Street

I drifted into writing. Today, there is a career structure, it seems: master of arts degrees in creative writing are available up and down the land from prestigious universities. At a lower level, serious aspirants can cut their teeth in writing groups, or on writing courses. If there was anything like that around in the 1960s and 1970s, I did not know, and would have been alarmed at the idea, I suspect. I was entirely ignorant about publishers and had never heard of literary agents. Writing my first book, I could not imagine that it would arouse any interest, but why not have a go?

I was not particularly young. The whole process felt fortuitous, and only gradually did writing come to seem inevitable: what I did, and now would always do. At that early stage, some sharp discouragement would have deflected me easily enough, I now think. Or perhaps not; alongside that memory of being surprised, ambushed almost by what had happened, there is another one — of private absorption and

296

application. Where should I go next? Which new ideas should I seize? What I was now doing felt like a kind of neat reversal of what I had always done: reading had become writing.

I did not go to any school until I was twelve years old; until then, my home-based education centered entirely upon reading — pretty well anything that came to hand, prose, poetry, good, bad, indifferent, any page was better than no page. At a barbaric boarding school, where the authorities saw a taste for unfettered reading as a sign of latent perversion, I went underground and read furtively, hiding books like other girls hid Mars bars or toffees. At university, there was that great swath of required reading, which was fine, but I liked to read off-piste, shooting into English literature, which was not supposed to be my subject, and into areas of history ignored by the syllabus. There was never enough time. Grown-up life — syllabus-free, exam-free — came as a relief; now, there was the day job, but also the opportunity for unbridled reading. I became a public library addict, dropping in several times a week for my fix, and this continued into married life and motherhood, when I read my way through the small branch library of our Swansea suburb, pushing the pram there with the baby in one end and the books in the other.

You write out of experience, and a large part of that experience is the life of the spirit; reading is the liberation into the minds of others. When I was a child, reading released me from my own prosaic world into fabulous antiquity, by way of Andrew Lang's Tales of Troy and Greece; *when I was a housebound young mother, I began to read history all over again, but differently, freed from the constraints of a degree course, and I discovered also Henry James, and Ivy Compton-Burnett, and Evelyn Waugh, and Henry Green, and William Golding, and so many others — and became fascinated by the possibilities of fiction. It seems to me that writing is an extension of reading — a step that not every obsessive reader is impelled to take, but, for those who do so, one that springs from serendipitous reading. Books beget books.*

Would I have become a writer if I had been denied books? Plenty of people have done so. Would I have gone on writing in the face of a blizzard of rejection letters? Others have. Unanswerable ques-

tions, but they prompt speculation. Looking back at that diffident beginning, bashing out a story on a typewriter whose keys kept getting stuck together, the endeavor seems precarious indeed.

And if it had foundered, what then? Short of specific skills — derisory shorthand, inaccurate typing — I had nothing to offer but a degree in history and a brief experience as someone's research assistant. Oh, and a few years' intensive child-minding. At the time, I was rather taken with local history, with exploring the landscape. And, of course, I read. I read myself into one preoccupation after another.

A house that contains books has concealed power. Many homes are bookless, or virtually so, as any house hunter discovers. And then suddenly there is a place that is loaded — shelf upon shelf of the things — and the mysterious charge is felt. This house has ballast; never mind the content, it is the weight that counts — all that solid, silent reference to other matters, to wider concerns, to a world beyond these walls. There is a presence here — confident, impregnable.

Books invade; they arrive, and settle. They are a personal matter, as in book-affected homes, but they are also commercial, archival, official. A map displaying the distribution of books in Hawkford, a historic market town in midland England, would show serious infestation in the High Street (the sites of George Bain Books, the Country Bookshop, and the County Library), with light local occurrences elsewhere, and entire streets and housing estates virtually untouched. The County Library, at this point in the early 1970s, is still in a prelapsarian state. These are the good old days of card indexes, a table with newspapers, and books. No screens; the Internet and the online catalog are a mere gleam in someone's eye. There is a swath of fiction — straight, romance, crime, sci-fi — a respectable cross-section of history, a gesture toward psychology, philosophy, sociology; some photography, upholstery making, tie-dying and quilt making for the hobby-minded, plus all the usual suspects in travel and biography.

The Country Bookshop deals in cookery, gardening, nature, humor, children's picture books, popular fiction, and biographies of sportsmen and actors. This is where you find a Christmas present for an aunt or something for a godchild. The range reflects both local demand and the taste of the proprietor: nothing too taxing, nothing that will sit forever on the shelf, sex and violence in the strictest moderation.

George Bain Books, Antiquarian and Second-Hand, is on the other side of the street and very far away indeed in mood and method.

George Bain himself sits behind a stacked desk at the back of the shop, so screened by books and papers that he is virtually invisible to customers, which is the idea. It is not so much that he does not wish to inhibit browsers as that he is defending himself from importunate chat while still being able to keep an eye on what is going on. At any one time, he is well aware of exactly who is in the shop and what they are doing. Right now, he is inspecting a pile of sale catalogs, but his chameleon eyes keep covered the entire premises; he has noted the chap with the rucksack checking through old Everyman editions, the couple muttering together in Poetry, and the woman in the back room, intent upon the Local History section — a young woman in a long wrap-over cheesecloth skirt, brightly patterned in shades of yellow and orange, worn with a black T-shirt and a rope of brown beads. She has been in once or twice before. He watches her as she pulls books out. She has a way of

301

pushing her glasses up on her nose with one finger.

I know the type, thinks George. Bored, energies smoldering, kids at school, hubby bringing home the bacon. Latter-day blue-stocking, raring to get her teeth into some enterprise. Not canals and railways, dear, they've been done to death, and anyway that's a man thing. Ah, that's better — W. G. Hoskins: *Local History in England.* Torn jacket, scuffed. Thirty pence, if I remember rightly, but I'll probably let you have it for twenty-five. And now you've found Ekwall — *The Place-Names of Oxfordshire.* Quite hard to come by, that — you're in luck. And you know it. I can tell by the expression — quiet exultation. Mind, I see that look quite a lot in here. The smart cookies try to conceal it, thinking they've got a bargain. It's the innocent who come over to the cash register all gushing and chatty: I'm *so* pleased to have found this, been hunting for ages, completes my set, special passion of mine, blah-blah-blah.

People are a necessary evil of this business. George Bain is not mad about people. The occasional drink after a book auction with some chap he knows, Christmas with his sister, and that's about the size of it. The flat above the shop; the dog who spends the day snoozing in the office at the back, occasionally emerging to snarl at a customer. And books.

Books, books, books. George is not awed by books, but he is amazed by them. He does not read a great deal; he dips and samples and is thus intensely aware of this indestructible, apparently self-perpetuating commodity which provides him with a modest living, and which will flow on after he has gone, after his customers have gone, passed from hand to hand, an unstoppable progress through time, these small, eloquent, impervious blocks of matter. He has the measure of them, though. He knows a rarity when he sees it, he knows values, he can gut a sale list with half an eye. He can sieve through the stuff on the shelves of some deceased person and do the heirs a favor; once in a while you hit the jackpot, mostly you don't. The books win, always; they win by sheer numbers, by their dogged diversity. He sometimes sees them as a kind of chronic invasion — a culture that blooms where it can, and grimly proliferates when it gets a hold. The books always have the upper hand: silent, inert, ineradicable.

They also *are* the culture. George Bain

Books is a repository, pretty well, for the intellectual heritage of much of the Anglophone world, if you care to see its cluttered interior in those terms. For a fiver, you could pick up the entire canon of English poetry — a battered *Complete Works of Shakespeare* for thirty pence. Tennyson at twenty, Keats fifteen, Wordsworth ditto, *The Longer Poems of Robert Browning* a giveaway at a five pence on the odds and sods table. The culture may be tenacious, but it is also a snip; it would cost you a great deal more to equip your kitchen at Cotswold Homes and Interiors along the street.

The woman in the long cheesecloth skirt has completed her browse and is approaching the cash desk. George comes out from his lair to attend to her. She has collected five books. George tots up the total, knocks five pence off the Hoskins, pointing out the torn jacket (always impresses a customer, that gesture of superfluous honesty). She makes suitable acknowledgment, says that she was so glad to have found the Ekwall, and writes out the check. He notes that she is a Mrs. P. M. Lively, puts the check in the drawer, she leaves, and within the hour he has forgotten her, except that all customers are filed away in some recess of the mind, along with every book that has passed through his hands.

A market town has fluctuating populations: resident, intermittent, transitory. This one earned much of its keep then by way of tourism, with a celebrated church on offer, a museum, a fine array of oolitic limestone buildings dating from the sixteenth to the nineteenth century, and a substantial infrastructure of antique and gift shops. It was doing what a market town does — lure the punters. The number of occupants rose and fell, hour by hour, season by season — swarms of people on an August afternoon, just the inhabitants on a January night. The place could be gridlocked with traffic; drivers in search of a parking space circled like stacked planes.

Most of the day visitors tended to perambulate the High Street, check out the shops, and maybe dip into the church and the museum. The more adventurous would explore the side streets, with their substantial stone houses from the days of the town's commercial prosperity. This was once a center of the wool trade; number twelve Sheep Street, one of the more impressive survivors, is picked out by Pevsner: "C16 refronted 1730, five bay front, keystoned windows, doorway with pedimented hood on brackets approached by semicircular steps. Inside, stairway with fluted balusters and carved handrail. C16 stone fireplace with a molded lintel and quatrefoils in the spandrels." The discriminating tourist would have admired the exterior of the house, but also deplored its present condition, the stonework crumbling, the steps cracked and broken, the front door in dire need of a coat of paint. Nobody is putting on a show here, not anymore. Number twelve Sheep Street may be one of the most impressive houses in Hawkford, but it has lost its clout; wealth has moved elsewhere.

Hester Lampson, aged eighty, was born here and has found no reason to leave. Her parents bought the house in the 1890s. That speculative map of book distribution in the area would show a serious concentration at number twelve Sheep Street; here it was that Hester's father assembled his remarkable collection and lived as a man of leisure, cushioned by private means. These had diminished alarmingly by the time of his death, though he appeared not to have noticed. The house was full of good furniture and small valuables, acquired over the years by Hester's mother, while the books occupied every available space. There was not much rhyme or reason to the collection; Walter Lampson liked old books, attractively bound books, interestingly illustrated books, books on quirky themes. He read a great many of them. He was not a bibliophile but a man who found books irresistible. He saw; he bought; he read. Gradually, the house filled up; books covered the walls, overflowed onto landings, squeezed into cupboards and alcoves. Marian Lampson protested from time to time, but was herself entirely occupied with her garden, a fine walled space in the heart of the town which became her life's work, and which would in due course be taken over, with equal fervor, by her daughter Hester.

Thus, number twelve Sheep Street, on the doorstep of which there arrived one afternoon a young man called Max Binns. Shortly before, he had paused outside George Bain Books to ask a woman in a long orange-and-yellow skirt who had just come out of the shop if she could direct him to Sheep Street. As it happened, she could. Max thanked her nicely; he had been well brought up, though some might be surprised to hear this. His long, unwashed hair hung to his shoulders, his flared jeans were torn at the knees and brushed the pavement, his shirttails were knotted around his midriff. He carried a rucksack.

Hester Lampson opened the door, and contemplated her great-nephew without enthusiasm. She had last seen him as perky ten-year-old and would not have recognized him had he not been quick to explain himself. The explanation was somewhat confused, but the gist of it seemed to be that he had found himself in the area, had been seized with a desire to see his dear aunt again, and, not to put too fine a point upon it, was proposing himself as a houseguest. There he stood, wearing a beguiling smile.

Grudgingly, she let him in. She made it clear that this would have to be a brief visit. She indicated one of the several spare bedrooms, where Max dumped his rucksack on the bed and followed her downstairs again, talking effusively. Hester could hardly understand a word. His diction sounded most peculiar, and much of what he said did not seem to her to be English, or at least not English as she knew it. She suggested that he look round the house and the garden, to get rid of him for a while, but he then caught up with her in the kitchen, where — in some annoyance — she was putting together a meal of tinned spaghetti hoops in tomato sauce followed by Edam cheese and cream crackers.

Max noticed the books only as a pervasive form of furnishing. He did not read. He could count on the fingers of one hand the books that he had read from end to end. Books were a bore — who needed them? They reminded him of school, which he had considered the most appalling imposition on a free spirit. Having left at the earliest opportunity, without any discernible attainments, he was now free to realize his potential, and had been doing so for several years now, notching up a dozen brief spells of employment, rather longer on benefit, and a few run-ins with the police, who did not seem to understand his preferred lifestyle. He did not like to be tied down anywhere for too long, and had a taste for hanging out in unoccupied buildings with like-minded souls; he needed to smoke a joint most days, and if funds were short, well, you have to be resourceful, don't you? From time to time he went home, where his parents would receive him with resignation and routine strictures. After a period of rest and recuperation, and a clandestine handout from his mother, who was always susceptible to a bit of sweet talk, he would be off again to see what might come up.

It was his mother who had mentioned Aunt Hester, in conversation with his father over supper one night.

"The old girl must be worth a packet," his father had said. "That house . . . Crammed with valuable stuff."

"Who's Aunt Hester?" demanded Max.

"Oh, Max," scolded his mother. "You know perfectly well. We've been there several times. I've always tried to keep in touch. Goodness, I wonder who she'll leave it all to. . . ."

Max had pricked up his ears. Some thoughts were prompted, and thus in due course he knocked on Aunt Hester's door, wearing his most winsome smile.

Max's attention was not on the books, as he toured the house, thinking that it would be a great place for a squat. He had been more interested in various small ornaments and knickknacks that he spotted. It was Hester who alerted him, telling him crossly not to lean against the bookcase in the drawing room. He was giving her an extended account of a visit he had made recently to a rave in north Wales, hitch-hiking there in five hours flat, which he considered a feat. Carried away by his narrative, and made a touch unsteady by the half bottle of sherry he had found in the dining-room sideboard, he had rested against the nearest vertical surface. "Don't do that," said Hester. "Those books are valuable, or so I'm told."

And so it was that when Max left the next morning, Hester having made it clear that this was the limit of her hospitality, an ivory fan, a silver cigarette box and the Nonesuch Press edition of the poetical works of John Milton, with illustrations by William Blake, left with him.

Hester was not aware of this, though she had not been fooled by her great-nephew. There was only one reason why a young man should suddenly start to display concern and fondness for an elderly relative he scarcely knew. She had considered him, over the breakfast table, and had thought: I wasn't born yesterday, you know, my lad. She had long since made her arrangements, in any case: a clutch of legacies (from which he was excluded, along with his parents), the bulk of the estate to be divided between the Canine Defence League and the Gardeners' Benevolent Association.

George Bain knew when Max came into the shop that this was someone you kept tabs on. In the event Max merely cast a cursory eye around before approaching the desk. He had remembered this place from the evening before, and realized that it was probably just what he needed right now. He presented the Milton, with the explanation that he was disposing of it for a friend. Since this is the standard ruse under these circumstances, George Bain was not taken in for one moment. He examined the book briefly, and said that he would need to work out a price, if Max cared to return in an hour or so, this being a routine stalling procedure, where there seems to be doubt about the provenance of an item.

Max went off to check out the antique shops, in the interests of the fan and the cigarette box, while George set about a more leisurely inspection of the Milton.

The invoice from a London bookstore was folded between the pages, dated 1926, and with a price that George found to be highly gratifying, knowing as he did what Nonesuch Press editions fetched these days. There was also a name and an address: Mr. Walter Lampson, 12 Sheep Street, Hawkford. George stared hard at this, and reached for the local telephone directory.

Ten minutes later he was knocking on the door of number twelve. He did not know Hester, but recognized her when she opened the door as that large woman in brown clothes whom one saw pulling a shopping basket on wheels. Hester, needless to say, had never been into George Bain Books, but had seen George around and also reacted to a vaguely familiar face. She was marginally less frosty than she would otherwise have been, and allowed George into the house.

In the drawing room, they considered the Milton. Hester acknowledged her father's invoice. She said she didn't recognize that particular book, there were so many, after all, but she had a feeling there were some like that in the case over there. George crossed the room to have a look, found more Nonesuch editions, and a most suggestive gap. He returned to Hester, tutted, and asked if she knew the young man concerned. At this point he mentioned the going rate for an edition such as this.

Hester was astonished. She gave only a passing thought to Max — shifty little blighter — and focused entirely upon this matter of price. She knew little about money, having been brought up in the understanding that it is vulgar to display an interest in income, or the value of possessions. She had been aware that elements of her father's collection were "valuable"; the word knocked about the house during her youth, a familiar local sound that made little impression. Equally, some of her mother's ornaments and trinkets were "precious"; there was a fuss if something got broken. For most of her life, money had been something that the bank supplied according to need. However, over recent years this process had become less straightforward. The bank manager kept writing tiresome letters. He had drawn her attention to the dwindling balance in her account, and to the diminishing sums paid in each quarter from securities. For some while now she had been in the red, a condition mysterious to her until the bank manager had explained. He was becoming more and more pressing; it was all a confounded nuisance.

She eyed the Milton, and asked George Bain if he would care to buy it.

Now George was startled. Fortunately, he had somewhat understated the going rate, so there could still be a respectable profit. He said that he would be happy to oblige. He inquired what he should say to the young man, when he returned. Did

Miss Lampson want the police involved?

Hester had entirely lost interest in Max. She felt no great rancor; indeed, she realized that he could be seen to have done her a favor. She would not miss the fan and the cigarette box for several weeks, by which time they seemed like water under the bridge. She told George to get rid of Max in whatever way he saw fit, graciously accepted George's check, and parted with the Milton, which she had never been aware of in the first place.

When Max returned to the shop, George gave him a terse account of his visit to Hester Lampson. After a brief moment of dismay, Max smiled sweetly and remarked that he must have entirely misunderstood his aunt, he had been under the impression that she wanted the book valued, old people can be a bit confusing, can't they? He then left, rather hurriedly.

George had not had an opportunity to inspect the bookshelves at number twelve Sheep Street, but he had been intensely aware of them. They had glimmered at him from all sides; he had felt as though he had walked into an Aladdin's cave. And it was clear that the old girl hadn't got the foggiest interest in them. He pondered.

When her doorbell rang again two days

later, Hester felt as though she were under siege. This time there was a young woman on the step, wearing one of those ridiculous skirts down to her ankles that girls wore these days. Apparently she had written Hester a letter, some while back, asking if Hester was in possession of the deeds to the house, which would be valuable source material for a history of the town on which this woman was working. A search at the County Record Office had failed to locate them.

Hester's expression indicated that if people would insist on writing her letters, that was their problem. Her instinct was to close the door firmly in this person's face, but the woman was quite insistent, nattering on about the age and interest of the house. If Hester was not in possession of the deeds, never mind — but would it be at all possible to have a look round? That would be such a help to her project.

Unwillingly, Hester said that she supposed she could manage a few minutes. She stumped ahead; the woman followed, making noises of appreciation. She took an interest in the books, lingering in front of the cases, which irritated Hester, who wanted to get back to the long border. "They're good wall covering," she said.

"You don't need to repaint a room that's got plenty of books. Not that I go in for repainting."

At this point the front doorbell rang — a delivery of coke for the Raeburn, which required supervision by Hester. When she returned, the woman was still scrutinizing the books, moving from shelf to shelf. "I hope you don't mind," she said. "I took the Camden *Britannia* down for a moment, just to have a look. And the Leland. What an amazing collection . . ."

Hester asked her rather sharply if she wanted to see the rest of the house, and headed for the stairs.

The County Archivist, Charles Benson, was acquainted with Hester Lampson's keen young woman visitor. She was a frequent user of the archives at the County Record Office, with a favorite seat at the end of the long table in the public searchroom, where he would see her staring worriedly at some hearth tax assessments, adjusting her glasses with one finger. He knew that she had trouble deciphering early script, and had given her a hand from time to time. Charles Benson was a scholar; he was a highly competent paleographer, he had a good working knowledge of Anglo-Saxon, his Latin was excellent, and his dog Latin, his low Latin, and his medieval Latin were superb. He moved with ease amid Hundred Rolls and poll tax assessments, manorial surveys, enclosure awards, chantry certificates, and parish registers. This woman wanted to write a history of Hawkford, and good luck to her, but Charles Benson wondered if perhaps she had rather overstretched herself. However, it was not for him to comment; amateur she might be, but enthusiasm should always be encouraged. He had made various tactful suggestions. She was currently accumulating information on the town's earlier houses. He had helped her with a search for the deeds that he held, and understood that she was engaged on a house-by-house inventory.

And so it was that the books at number twelve Sheep Street reached out once more, signaled their presence, asserted their power, spoke out. Charles Benson found himself buttonholed one morning by this woman, who had an excited account of a house in which there was this amazing collection of books, among which were rare and important topographical works. He listened. He knew Hawkford well, of course — the County Record Office was situated elsewhere, in the county town —

and remembered Sheep Street as architecturally rather fine. This image of a somewhat curmudgeonly old lady holed up in a historic building ("marvelous staircase . . . this carved stone fireplace") that was apparently falling to pieces around her did not surprise him: small ancient English towns seem to breed such people. But this book collection was an unusual feature. Some of the titles mentioned were ones that would sit very nicely in the Record Office library, which was not that richly equipped. Still, he did not see any way in which he could come by them, short of theft, and there the matter might have rested, if the books had not signaled once more, exerted their curious power.

Hester was now intensely aware of them. She had never before thought of them as a commodity. They were part of the fabric of the house, so far as she was concerned, the backdrop to her life for as long as she could remember. They had never interested her, though she granted them a certain respect as the legacy of her father's passion. She was no reader. She could not be doing with fiction — all that made-up business, what was the point? The heavy stuff was not for her — history and biography. Poetry made her think of the posturings of the drama teacher during her schooldays. Her own library consisted solely of books on gardening; her regular reading matter was the *Journal of the Royal Horticultural Society*, alongside a quick daily skim of *The Times*.

And now the books had achieved this startling potency. She found herself staring at the familiar spines — tall, short, calf, cloth, gilt-lettered, insect-nibbled — and saw that she had underestimated them. She felt quite detached about this; evidently others found value and significance here, while she did not. That was their concern, not hers; she did not need to pursue the matter further. Nor did she propose to devote time and energy to learning just what it was about certain of the books that generated such attention. Apparently there were books, and there were rarities — a distinction that she could appreciate, as a plantswoman.

She stared at the books as she moved about the house, and saw money. At least, she saw not money so much as the solution to a problem. She could cock a snook at the bank manager; she did not need banks — she had her own. She had not the slightest interest in acquisition, unless it was the pursuit of some choice plant. She seldom bought clothes, and, if forced to do so, usually found that the local Oxfam shop could meet her needs. She had inherited a fully stocked house; all that was required was to keep it functioning. The house's own gradual disintegration she barely noticed. The roof leaks were a bother, but could be contained by strategically placed buckets. There had been cracks and flaking paint in her parents' day; if these were now rather more pronounced — well, time takes its toll, doesn't it?

After a few days of reflection, Hester paid a call on George Bain. George received her with an excitement that he was careful to keep tamped down. He had not been able to get those books out of his mind since that glimpse a few days before. He had felt their smoldering presence, just a few hundred yards away, and now, apparently, they were being offered up: ". . . might be prepared to part with a few more . . . don't mind if you come in and have a look." An arrangement was made.

When George set about his close inspection of the books, he realized that this lot was in a class of its own. He had met many book-stocked houses, but never anything like this. The collection was disheveled, to put it politely. If ever there had been any sort of order, any smack of firm librarianship, that had long been abandoned. Among the bound back numbers of *Punch* he found a fine copy of Plot's *Natural History of Oxfordshire*, and the 1720 edition of Ogilby's *Britannia Depicta*. The works of Mary Webb — that thirties edition with the speckled binding that had clogged his shelves for years — sheltered a couple of T. S. Eliot first editions. A second edition of John Locke's *Treatise of Civil Government* lurked in the midst of a nineteenth-century set of Dickens. It seemed that from time to time Hester had found books handy for various domestic contingencies — as props for unstable pieces of furniture, as doorstops. The two volumes of an early nineteenth-century edition of Johnson's dictionary had for a long while been doing duty as a flower press, in the service of Hester's collection of botanical specimens.

And the old girl hadn't a clue, that was clear enough. She didn't know her arse from her elbow, where books were concerned. This put George in a spot. He was not an innately dishonest man, but he was running a business, not a counseling service.

After making copious notes, he sought out Hester, and made a proposal, only to find that she had her own agenda. No immediate bulk selective purchase; individual sales, at regular intervals, according to her dictation. He saw exactly what she had in mind — a revenue stream; he tried to point out the advantages of a capital sum, but she was inflexible. And when he touched on the delicate issue of pricing, he found that here again she had done some thinking; she told him coolly that she would probably be taking a second opinion.

George left, purposeful, but with a feeling of having been to some degree outflanked. He had regular customers who would be interested in various items that he had listed, but he was disturbed at the thought of the involvement of any of his rivals, some of whom he knew to be distinctly unscrupulous. Apart from that, he felt a particular obligation, given the nature of one particular element of the collection.

The County Archivist and George Bain had a working relationship. Whenever George came across something that might interest Charles Benson, he would let him know. He would tell Charles what this item might be expected to fetch; Charles would consider his budget, and George would then undertake the negotiation on his behalf, or put in a bid at an auction, charging a small commission. This arrangement suited both parties, for various reasons; Charles Benson was made aware of things he might have missed; George saw it as a piece of diplomatic public relations. From time to time they would meet up for a drink, to keep the relationship oiled. George saw that it was the moment to suggest such a meeting.

It was one short step from the County Archivist to the Conservation Officer. Hester had been confused about Charles Benson and let him in because she was under the impression that he was an antiquarian bookseller whose name she had found in the yellow pages (her threat to George Bain was not an empty one). Charles Benson was as struck by the house as he had been by the books. The Camden was the abridged eighteenth-century edition, of course, not an original, and the Leland the 1906 publication, but both would still be handsome assets for the Record Office library. However, he was aware of what the market values were likely to be, and knew that they were well beyond his current means. There were other things that he would like to get, also — the Plot, several early travel books of local relevance. He decided that this was an occasion when the expedient move was to appeal to a person's conscience and sense of social obligation. He said to Hester that he understood that she was prepared to dispose of some elements of her collection. As a lifetime citizen of Hawkford and of the county, would she not like to make a generous gesture and donate some appropriate works — here he handed her a list that he had compiled — to the Record Office? Mistaking Hester's stare of incredulity for one of interest, he gave her his card and said that he would look forward to hearing from her.

After he had left, the County Archivist found that he was as much concerned about the house and its condition as he was about the books. He could not get it out of his head, and when, fortuitously, he ran into the county Conservation Officer in the Town Hall a few days later he began at once to talk about it: interesting building, in rather desperate need of attention, imagine you know it . . .

The Conservation Officer paid attention. As it so happened, he did not know the place, with any intimacy, and so was wrong-footed. He had walked past number twelve Sheep Street on various occasions, had noted its facade and that it was not in great shape. Now he realized with some guilt that here was a listed building which he had ignored. Time to put that right.

Hester stared mutinously at the figure on the doorstep. Another jack-in-office. Another of these men in suits who wrote intrusive letters and then turned up, carrying a briefcase. Well, go on then, she told him silently — come and pester me if you want to, but a fat lot of good will it do you.

The Conservation Officer toured the house. Hester followed him, breathing heavily. He noted the superb carved fireplace in the drawing room. He peered at the interesting little cupboard set into the paneling alongside, and asked if he might open it. Hester shrugged. He did so, and saw a pile of old magazines and a great many mouse droppings. The paneling itself was intrinsically very fine, but chewed up by woodworm, pockmarked by drawing-pin holes and currently serving as a pin-board for various bills. The floorboards creaked ominously, and there was a funny smell; the Conservation Officer became concerned about dry rot.

As they climbed to the first floor, he admired the staircase with fluted banisters and carved handrail. He ventured to suggest to Hester that this was probably eighteenth-century, inserted during the makeover of the building at that time. The earlier origins of the house were apparent in the mullioned windows that he had already spotted at the rear and the small lancet windows high up at one side. Warming to the theme, he pointed out that this was a process very typical of the period — a prosperous family using architectural display to demonstrate position and resources. This is an early eighteenth-century house, he said, within which lurks its ancestry of the sixteenth century and quite possibly earlier. That window. Those beams.

Hester observed that her father had always said it was quite an old place. They were standing at one of the rear windows (mullioned, with four lights) that over-looked the garden — which the Conservation Officer did not appear to notice, despite its midsummer glory. There was staking to be done in the big border — the delphiniums reeling — and Hester was itching to get out there. The Conservation Officer had just spotted a ceiling beam painted with ball-flower and crosses, and was getting excited about this. The attics, he was saying, may have some interesting clues.

It was clouding over. Hester could stand this no longer. She must get into the garden before the rain started. She decided to leave this fellow to his own devices — he didn't look the type to start nicking the silver.

Somewhat relieved, the Conservation Officer continued on his tour alone. Up in the back attic, he was thrilled to see fragments of what looked to him like late sixteenth-century wall paintings — a bit of scroll patterning, a medallion, and even the suggestion of an inscription. But he was appalled by the pervasive damp, and the buckets and basins whose purpose was only too apparent. The roof must be in an appalling condition. He came downstairs and inspected the kitchen area. He found a stone archway in the passage which looked to him fifteenth-century, but the rear elevation had him really worried. An alarming crack, and a bulge that suggested even more serious instability. He was busily making notes on his clipboard. This was a much more significant building than he had realized; he had checked out the entry in Pevsner, of course, but that now looked somewhat cursory. The place was in a very bad way; there should be extensive repairs and renovations forthwith. He was going to have to have a word with the old lady and remind her of her statutory requirements, as the owner of a Grade II listed building. You are obliged to keep the things standing up.

Hester received his comments with a basilisk stare. She was thinking about botrytis and black spot. She followed his pointing finger, as he indicated the crack running up the back of the house, and that bulge, and made a mental note to give the old climbing rose a really good pruning in the autumn. The Conservation Officer was talking about house repairs, which were none of his business, frankly. What a nerve. When he mentioned that he would be writing to her about this, just to clarify matters, she told him under her breath that he could do what he bally well liked, gave him a wintry smile, and began to herd him through the house to the front door, where they parted. Hester returned to the garden; a tussle with some bindweed soon put the tiresome fellow out of her mind. The Conservation Officer found that his car had collected a ticket, for being six inches over a yellow line; his notes about number twelve Sheep Street became a degree more excitable in consequence.

A few days later Hester glanced at the

Conservation Officer's letter with distaste, and dropped it into the wastepaper basket. The letter was three pages long and had numbered paragraphs, a style she found offensive. There was stuff about features of historical and architectural interest, and other stuff about essential restoration, which she did not wish to hear. She had the same sense of being got at by officious meddlers as when she received one of those missives from the bank manager. She was far too robust in character to feel persecuted; rather, she was put on her mettle. There were these importunate people closing in; it was up to her to fend them off, them and their blustering titles — Conservation Officer, County Archivist. Her father would have done the same. She had binned sackfuls of petulant documents after his death.

The Conservation Officer's fears about number twelve Sheep Street were entirely justified. Like the carcass of an animal, it was experiencing a process of corruption; it was being gnawed and bored, it was crumbling, it was festering. There were woodworm and death-watch beetle, damp rot, dry rot, fungal invasions, and the rear elevation was slowly falling apart. Left to itself, it would disintegrate, over time, with all that was therein — the books, the bric-a-brac, the furnishings. It was under attack; nature and the laws of nature were closing in, just as society was closing in on Hester Lampson.

She had kept society at arm's length, hitherto. She took no part in the town's activities. She had not seen the need for friends; she had dealings with only a handful of acquaintances. Relatives were tolerated but had to make all the running. As for the social operation itself, she had steered well clear; she ignored political discussion, she did not vote, she availed herself of the various freedoms and safeguards of democracy without any sense of obligation. She was lucky to live in the twentieth century; it would have been less easy to get away with this level of detachment at any other time.

But the world had caught up with her, in the form of the County Archivist, who was appealing to her conscience and her sense of responsibility, and the Conservation Officer, who became insistent, in further letters. He was courteous, if cool, and reminded her that he had certain powers, which he would be reluctant to enforce, but . . . And then there was George Bain, who spoke for the world of Mammon, with which she had never before been concerned.

Far away, Max Binns, who began it all, was most satisfactorily installed with a group of new friends in a decaying mansion in Hove, where indulgence of every kind was a condition of residence. Eventually, this exercise in freedom of choice and defiance of the law would be terminated by a very public police eviction of all concerned; Max's parents would find a photograph of their son, cheerily brandishing a banner of defiance from the windows of the invaded building, spread across their morning paper. As for the aspiring author of the history of Hawkford, who had also had a hand in the exposure of number twelve Sheep Street and its contents, she continued to beaver away, frowning over the indecipherable handwriting of the past, and occasionally wishing that you could make things up when the surviving evidence is either too thin or too dull. Number twelve Sheep Street would merit a passing mention in her book, which was published by a small press and was to enjoy a small but steady sale in the Museum and the Country Bookshop.

Thus are we all fingered by the actions of strangers. Hester Lampson, who had spent a lifetime trying to avoid involvement with other people, was now locked into a cycle of exchanges with the County Archivist, the conservation people, and George Bain, a process that she would succeed in prolonging without giving any satisfaction to either of the first two, until a fatal bout of pneumonia one winter put paid to any further negotiations.

The books rode it out, of course, having done what books do — changed people's lives. Though perhaps not in the more usual sense. Unread, they still managed to manipulate, to have an effect. And so it would go on; eventually they would be dispersed, would float free of their temporary mooring at number twelve Sheep Street, and continue upon their way, primed with their insidious power.

A History of Hawkford by Penelope Lively. Followed up perhaps with a few articles in not especially learned journals, and the occasional piece in Country Life. *Books could well have shunted me in that direction, and the great and good W. G. Hoskins was indeed a formative influence, though not in a scholarly way; rather, his interpretations of English landscape came to seem a metaphor for the interlacing of past and present.*

I would like to have been George Bain; a life in books seems an attractive proposition. And I would have liked to own number twelve Sheep Street; my real-life houses have all been elderly and in varying states of decay. I am a skeptical woman and have no truck with ghosts, but I do prefer a house of substance, a house that has experience.

As for Hester Lampson, I see her as a symbol of the universal plight: we can any of us be picked off by strangers — our lives derailed, our tranquillity disturbed. And such strangers continue on their way impervious; frequently they do not even know what they did.

Penelope

Is there some directing factor, from day one? Some cast of mind that will always prevail, that will insist that we go in one direction rather than another? Is the plump, curly-haired toddler riding on my father's back in Alexandria in the photograph of 1934 already programmed to become addicted to reading and writing, to prefer thoughtful, argumentative men, to want children, to need to live in one way rather than another?

I am still here because my mother took us to Palestine rather than to Cape Town in 1942, because I did not get onto a dodgy plane in the 1950s, because of myriad other evasions. Happenstance. But I am what I am, doing what I do, perhaps because of some mysterious innate steering system which twitches the wheel at crucial moments. No, not that way; keep clear of the reef, mind the sunken vessels. And listen to that persuasive inner voice that says: Try this.

When very young, I fed on fiction, and

*created private narratives. And today I
feel an eerie compatibility with that solitary
child with a handful of books and a taste
for invention. Was she pulling the strings,
even then?*

*My driving literary influence was Homer,
by way of Andrew Lang's* Tales of Troy
and Greece. *And here the most compelling
attraction was that I was right in there
anyway, with a leading role: Penelope. I
read and reread, steeped in that late-
Victorian interpretation of the ancient story.
The wine-dark sea, rocky Ithaca, battles,
warriors, and gods became as real and urgent as my own world of palm trees, the
Nile, the convoys of tanks and armored
cars on the road to Alamein, the roistering
officers on leave from the desert whom
my parents entertained. But the trouble
was that I was there with the wrong part,
and the story line was not entirely satisfactory. It is made clear that Penelope is
not nearly as beautiful as her cousin
Helen, who is the fairest woman that ever
lived in the world. Penelope is wise and
good, qualities that did not have much appeal. Moreover, Ulysses is short-legged
and has red hair; evidently not a patch on
Hector or Achilles. And that addiction to
weaving is tiresome, let alone the shilly-*

shallying over the suitors. Some reconstruction was in order, it seemed to me.

Andrew Lang trod carefully; he stuck to
The Odyssey for the story of Ulysses and
Penelope, and ignored other, off-stage
versions, thus excising the more unac-
ceptable elements of the story. He does
not mention the events said to have suc-
ceeded their reunion — the banishment of
Telemachus and the death of Ulysses at
the hands of his own son Telagonus, the
fruit of a dalliance with Circe. Above all,
he ignores the allegation that Penelope
subsequently married her dead husband's
bastard while, in a nice symmetry, her
own son Telemachus set up with his father's ex-mistress. He leaves out the
rumor and innuendo also. Was she, or
was she not, the mother of cloven-footed
Pan — possibly by the god Hermes, possibly by one of the suitors, possibly by all
of them?

When I was nine, I identified with
Penelope because my mind was happy to
confuse fact with fiction — and what was
she doing with my name, anyway, if she
was not some form of myself? I seized on
that story, and its furnishings, and juggled
them around to make a version that was
personally satisfying and more relevant to

my own circumstances. That nine-year-old
perception is lost, but there is the faint re-
verberation still of an early way of
thinking. And, today, an old story seems to
lend itself to other kinds of manipulation,
less solipsistic.

Paris stole Helen and took her to Troy
which was a silly thing to do because then
the Greeks came to fetch her back again
and they lit a thousand fires outside the
gates of Troy and sat there drinking their
wine to the music of flutes. Helen was fair
but actually there was someone else who
was just as fair as she was and that was
Penelope, who had to wait for Ulysses to
come back from Troy. The Greeks were all
brave and good at fighting but so were the
Trojans, so it took a long time but in the
end Troy lay in ashes. Then Ulysses set off
home to see his beautiful Penelope again
but he kept losing his way and having ad-
ventures and meanwhile Penelope was
being pestered by the princes who wanted
to marry her because everyone thought
Ulysses was dead.

So Penelope turned the princes into frogs
and you can hear them croaking still in the
reeds beside the river. And then at last
Ulysses came home and Penelope said to

him, "Thou hast been away for a very long time so I am not at all pleased with thee." She knew that he had been staying with Calypso for seven years, who was a sort of fairy. And he said that Penelope was meaner than Calypso in comeliness and stature which meant that she wasn't so pretty and that wasn't a very nice thing to say. And he had stayed with Circe too, who was a witch and turned people into pigs but Ulysses seemed to rather like her all the same. So Penelope decided that it would serve him right if she went away with Achilles, who came along at that moment.

And as soon as Achilles beheld Penelope he said, "Thou art more beautiful than rosy-fingered Dawn and I want to marry thee at once." So they were married that day and Penelope wore a dress of pink tussore silk from Cicurel and afterward they feasted on dates and ripe mangoes and persimmons and chocolate ice cream from Groppi's.

Penelope and Achilles sailed over the wide sea to Egypt and there Achilles said that it was time for him to get into a battle again so he went away into the desert with the other warriors.

There were the Eighth Hussars and the Eleventh Hussars and a great army of

Desert Rats and they had armored cars and bren guns but Achilles' tank was better than anyone else's because the gods had made it for him. Achilles chased and slew the Germans until they cried for mercy and then he challenged Rommel to single combat and he killed him. So the Germans fled to the sea and sailed away in their black ships and there was great rejoicing and the army said that Achilles must now be top general.

But Achilles had had enough fighting for the moment and after a great feast he said farewell and he returned to his beautiful wife Penelope and they settled down in a palace with rich tapestries and treasures of amber, ivory, and silver and they had a swimming pool with a high diving board in their garden. And there they lived for ever and ever.

It was a lovely funeral. I know that sounds an odd thing to say, especially coming from the widow, but it was such a wonderful send-off for him. Everyone was there, and one person who should not have been, but we won't dwell on that. All my friends, and so many of his colleagues though of course most of them I didn't know, but you just smile and smile, don't you? Someone rather high up in the government gave the address, a Sir Somebody, and he was so sweet at the reception after, making a point of coming straight up to me: "Orson was a true citizen of the world. He thought in global terms. Wherever he was, he looked and listened." Charming man. And I said, "I know. I know. And I was so proud to be beside him."

I was still devastated, of course. The whole occasion was exhausting. I was in a state of shock. Shattered. I hadn't slept. I must have looked quite fearful. I hid under my hat and hoped no one would notice.

But people were so kind. Everyone saying nice things, and not just about Orson. One felt so *valued*. Maurice Enderby was there, not seen for years, goodness had he aged, and of course he had a terrific thing for me at one time, water under the bridge entirely now but all the same it was rather good for morale to have him fussing around, with quite a look in his eye still: "Can I get you a drink, my dear? Can I find you a chair?" That is something one so much had to do without, over the years — a bit of cosseting, a bit of cherishing. Alone so much. And then when Orson *was* back, the times when he was at home, he was off to the office at some ungodly hour and gone till midnight like as not, he might as well have been still in Angola or Addis Ababa or Chad, dispensing humanitarian aid. There was just as much dispensing to be done in central London, apparently.

And anyway that sort of thing was never Orson's style. The little niceties. Flowers on the anniversary, breakfast in bed. I married a man of action and I knew it and far be it from me to complain. "Dedicated" — the number of times I've heard that word. Just that occasionally, very occasionally, I've wished a tiny bit more of the dedication came my way.

So it's hardly surprising is it if once in a while one looked elsewhere. Friendship. A bit of personal attention. Never any question of disloyalty to Orson, never never.

And it's rather a question of people in glass houses, isn't it? When Caroline showed up at the funeral I was infuriated. That she had the nerve. Looking distinctly past her sell-by date, I couldn't help noting — if you spend years and years in the sun your skin is going to tell the story. Not that I paid her any attention, just walked straight by, made sure I kept on the opposite side of the room. But it was an irritation — her having the gall to show up, *and* socializing right, left, and center, I saw, having a word with the Sir Somebody, cruising around Orson's old colleagues. A legendary hostess, apparently, that was the story. Well, maybe. Diplomatic hospitality, it's called, and possibly diplomatic in other ways too, if you ask me. She would set her sights on a man, and if he was someone else's husband, well, no matter — it was, come stay with me in my tropical paradise, plenty of aid and development to be done here, just tell the bureaucrats that you need to be gone some time, relax, enjoy. I doubt if Orson was the only one.

At least Clara hadn't appeared. I'd have gone ballistic.

And the point about a funeral is that it's supposed to be a coming together, isn't it? There shouldn't be any jarring element. You are coming together in grief and in re-membrance. Not that remembrance doesn't throw up difficulties here and there, but you don't want them thrust in your face, do you? A funeral should be tranquil, reflective, a culmination.

Orson disliked chrysanthemums. There was an acreage of them, displayed outside the church. Pink, bronze, white; sheaves, wreaths, sprays. That smell — the smell of weddings and funerals. Is that why a funeral makes you think of a wedding? Ours was register office, of course, not church. We'd had to hurry with it because Orson was going to Uganda for six months which was where I realized that that sort of place was not at all my cup of tea. The heat, the dirt. They weren't called third-world countries then; they were "underdeveloped." All underdeveloped countries were hot and insanitary; presumably they still are. Orson didn't give a damn — the more squalid the better. He liked a challenge, always has. A spot of adventure. And I found that terribly appealing, when I first met him — the buccaneer quality. And of course there was the older-man thing — he was fifteen years older than I was. Or twelve. Thereabouts.

Mummy and Daddy had invited him to lunch. Daddy had heard that he was an up-and-coming man and wanted to pick his brains, Daddy being big in the Foreign Office at that point, and I was expecting to be bored to tears, doing nice polite daughter-at-home stuff, and in the event it turned out rather different. Smoldering glances across the table and a phone call the next day. Orson never wasted time. And he could lay on the charm. Mummy thought he was delightful, though the name fazed her at first. "As in Welles," he told her, which is what he always said. "My mother was a fan." Mummy had barely heard of Orson Welles, but never mind, she was impressed by the exoticism. Daddy wondered at first if perhaps he wasn't a bit too clever by half, but after we announced our engagement he re-jigged this and said Orson was a chap who would go far. Too true. Mummy said red hair in a man was quite unusual, and I could see she was thinking about the grandchildren. As it happens, Toby is dark, like me.

We had a whirlwind honeymoon on this island, Hydra. I'd wanted Paris, but Orson wasn't having that — he had to have some action — so there was a week of scuba diving and spear fishing, at least that's what he did, I lay around and swam and drank ouzo and thought, So this is marriage — a man in goggles comes out of the sea waving a spear-gun with a fish stuck on the end.

The sex was fine, I will say that.

I was so young. Twenty-two. Fresh from art school. Totally inexperienced but so creative. Oh, I know that's not for me to say, but it's the truth. I wasn't so brilliant at painting and drawing — you did those back then — but I was really good at clothes. I could knock up some snazzy

original outfit out of a length of stuff and a
few trimmings. I always won the prize at
the college fashion show, and one thing
was already beginning to lead to another.
I'd started to hang around the Chelsea
boutiques, to suss out the latest trends,
and I made a few frocks for chums, and
people said but you're so incredibly good
at this, you should go commercial. And
then Orson swept us off to Uganda. Not
that he saw it like that. An overseas posting
is a directive, one was informed; sweeping
did not come into it.

I tried. I really did. I struggled. You'll get
used to it, I told myself. The dust and the
insects and the stomach upsets and,
frankly, the *boredom.* What was I supposed to do with myself? I dreamed of the
King's Road and London summer evenings, thin cool air not that soupy heat, a
bunch of friends drinking Pimms in a pub
garden. And oh, the relief, when at last it
was over and Orson was based at home
again and I could get on with my life. I
started running up frocks in some gor-
geous silk I'd bought in bulk in Mombasa
when we went there for a weekend —
Orson thought I'd gone crazy — just a
couple of simple styles, and I put these
witty quirky adverts in the Sunday papers

and orders came flooding in. I got another sewing machine and brought in Midge who'd been at art college with me as helper and we began a sort of assembly line. Amazing. Magic. This is what I'm for, I thought. Of course the paperwork was a complete nightmare, and the post and packaging. Soon I had to get someone else in to do that. The house was becoming a *maison de couture*.

Midge came to the funeral. Sweet of her. Of course we'd parted company long ago. She always said I should have gone into mass production: "You could have been another Laura Ashley. You would have put Laura Ashley out of business." Well, I dare say, but I preferred to develop in a different direction — something more exclusive. Just a few stunning designs, new every season, and a rather select list of clients. Much more stylish. Anyway, there was Midge, looking like a bird of paradise amid all the suits — she's a fashion editor nowadays — and we talked husbands. She's had three. I said, "I never ever wanted anyone but Orson. Despite everything. Despite being on my own so much. Orson was always first and foremost." She said, "It does you credit, darling, but you always did have such strength of mind" — though I'm not absolutely sure what she meant by that, and then she started asking who everybody was, likes to do a bit of networking, does Midge. She'd noticed Caroline — "Pretty lady. I like that outfit. Friend of Orson's . . . Oh, I see." — and she said how handsome Toby was now, which of course he is, and then she spotted Tam: "But who is the *other* glamorous young man? Oh . . . Oh, *is* he . . . I hadn't realized. . . ."

Tam does not look at all like Orson. I suppose he favors his mother, but I am not prepared to hold that against him. And I have never set eyes on Clara. She runs some sort of artists' colony on a Greek island these days, it seems.

Midge and I drifted apart after I set up in Beauchamp Place. She had her own agenda and by then I needed a professional cutter and fitter. And someone for the office — always a nightmare, the money side of it, and having to *borrow* at that stage — so humiliating. But there were people who were very kind and helpful about that. One was eternally grateful.

Of course Carlos had pots of money, he could easily spare a few bob. Banking, though actually he was rather aristocratic

— some old Spanish family. We met when his wife came in and ordered a frock, though soon after that she became his ex-wife. Nothing to do with me, I hasten to say. I was always very firm that in a sense our relationship was a business one. He was my backer, put it like that.

The sad thing is that people come to expect more than was ever intended. Carlos did become rather insistent, over time. Dear Carlos, I used to say, you were my savior in my darkest hour and I am grateful to you forever but there are other people of whom I have to think. My husband. My son. And my work. I am a slave to the calendar — two collections every year. I can never let up. My clients depend on me. No sooner is one lot off the drawing board than I need to start thinking of the next. And the hunt for fabric and trimmings . . . I am hither and thither, from one week to the next. Eventually, perhaps, I shall be able to delegate more, find myself some space, and of course you will always be among my dearest friends.

I've learned to cope with pressure — I've had to — but back at the beginning it was coming from all sides and some of it I'm sorry to say from Orson. Not 100 percent supportive. How could I possibly drop everything and go with him to some famine in Senegal or Sudan or Ethiopia or wherever when everything depended on me? And anyway by then there was Toby, always a slightly delicate child and no way could I have him dragged from continent to continent.

But Orson was Orson and he wasn't going to settle for a decent desk job in London which was the obvious solution given the way things were turning out so there was nothing for it but long periods of separation. Some people didn't even realize I was married. And I was still young and if I may say so not unattractive so inevitably there were men sniffing around. I was making a bit of a name and I met a lot of people and it would have done me no good to be unsociable, and let's face it a bit of attention from a few personable admirers didn't come amiss. But I was always circumspect. Always.

And of course when Orson was back for a while one had to make it clear that one would be less available. He was liable to turn up without warning, straight off the plane, in the most awful clothes, having come from some underdeveloped jungle somewhere, and I might be in the middle of a dinner party, the house full of people, and there's this tramplike figure: "May I introduce my husband." Not that Orson would be at all put out, not he, he'd have everyone on the run within minutes. Orson is an assertive man.

A presence. Makes himself felt. And the gift of the gab, like no one else — could talk himself in or out of any situation. I suppose that was a professional advantage, the sort of people he had to deal with, around the world. Women noticed him — oh, yes indeed. Well, we know about that.

Clara dates from way back. Toby and Tam are the same age. Not that I knew about her until later. Some kind friend always tells you: "My dear, I feel you should know . . ." She was queening it on the Seychelles — holding court at this mansion and one wonders how she came by that — and Orson fetched up there with some colleagues, stopping off after one of those so-called fact-finding tours, and why one asks were they there in the first place, but it seems that they stayed on and on until their office started sending telegrams. The story was that the island was the site of an experimental pig-breeding scheme in which Orson and his team were interested, centered on Clara's estate. The extended stay was essential for proper monitoring of the scheme. Ho, hum. Whether or not the relationship was sustained I do not know and have not inquired. Tam was sent to Bedales and has turned out a very charming young man, against all the odds.

She trapped him, of course. Women like that set their sights on a man and will stop at nothing. I don't know what she did and I don't want to but you hear a lot of rumors about black magic and voodoo and jiggery-pokery of one kind and another in places like that, don't you? Suffice it that she got him and I dare say that Orson wasn't by any means unwilling. I've been told she is remarkably seductive. Well, that's as may be, but some men go as lambs to the slaughter and I'm afraid this is where Orson's much-vaunted strength of personality seems to have failed.

I have never made an issue of it. Her name is not mentioned. Tam of course is the living testimony but I have never ever been anything but generous and fair-minded where the boy was concerned. He cannot be blamed for his mother's practices and it is to his credit that he has emerged such a very engaging young man. Of course the funeral was agony for him. He was so devastated at what had happened. Distraught.

Toby got back just in time. It took me three days to get hold of him. He was in Australia. Frankly, it was not really necessary to go to the other side of the world after that family row. When Orson said that he thought it would be a good idea if Toby went away for a bit he just meant that a cooling-off period was needed. After Orson's retirement he and Toby were never on good terms, to be honest they *fought*. Orson was too forceful and Toby had dropped out of college and he was into dope and he didn't seem to have any particular career structure in mind. And he wasn't used to having a father around as a permanent fixture. Toby has artistic tendencies though it's not clear what form these will take and of course Orson is not that way inclined. I stood aside as far as possible though I must admit I was finding Toby's lifestyle rather trying myself but basically it was a question of male egos and Orson's was dominant. And he had the checkbook. So Toby went off on what was supposed to be a sort of postponed gap year and I won't say I wasn't a tiny bit relieved, I'm much too busy still to have to endure a stressful home life and anyway his room needed redecorating.

I love children. I love to have the young

around me. But naturally there had to be nannies and suchlike for Toby because I was just not available and I will admit that I find infants and very small children somewhat wearing. A larger family would not have been a good idea which is the main reason I was so shattered when I found I was pregnant again. There was also the problem that it happened while Orson was away in Nigeria I think it was, which made things — well, a bit awkward. I suppose it was the silly fling with that photographer, he'd been knocking on the door for ages and I couldn't go on saying no forever. Though actually there was someone else around then too, now I come to think of it. I didn't realize about the pregnancy until it was rather too late to do anything so I just had to go through with it, said I was having a sabbatical and slipped off for a few months to a place Carlos had in Spain. An arrangement was made for the baby, some sweet nuns in a convent took care of everything, much the best thing for all concerned. It had something wrong with its feet, some sort of malformation. I hardly saw him so wisest not to think about it, just put it behind one.

I have needed to be resilient. Life has not been easy. An exacting occupation. A husband obsessed with earthquakes and famine relief; in my view humanitarian aid should start at home. A somewhat wayward son. And I have had to resist those whose demands became too pressing, a woman alone attracts attention, at least certain women do, and I have never been short of admirers, but people can become tiresome with their insistence on commitment. Isn't it enough that we're having such a lot of fun? I'd say. Don't spoil things. And I must think of Orson. Wherever he may be. Yes, I know that I would have every justification in taking matters into my own hands, but I'm not like that, I respect my marriage vows. One day, perhaps, I may feel differently, but not just yet. So please, my dear, don't insist. Let us just enjoy what we have.

While it lasts. Because of course love doesn't, does it? One always knew that, but it's cruel to make a point of it. To disillusion a person.

In any case, I've come to prefer rather younger men these days. Time's up for dear old Carlos, I'm afraid. Along with one or two others. Of course I have not been entertaining on the scale that I used to, since Orson came back. He was never an enthusiast for parties, preferred an evening in a pub with a few cronies. Plus he complained of the expense. But my Saturday evenings were *famous* — people just came, invited or not. I never knew who would turn up and far be it from me to be inhospitable. If Orson had thought fit to tell me he was arriving back from his final assignment, if he'd avoided the weekend, he wouldn't have found such a crowd that evening. Suddenly appearing like that, this bearded figure — for a few moments I couldn't think who this *was*. Everybody was staring and people were muttering and exchanging looks and some of the young may have been a bit offhand, but the gracious host Orson was not, I'm sorry to say. The party just kind of melted away.

Tam turned up a few months later. Toby had gone to Australia by then and the first thing Tam did was set to and redecorate the room himself which was so thoughtful. And he was a delight to have around — well-behaved, charmingly attentive, in stark contrast I'm afraid to my son. Tam is interested in a career in investment management, and I have been able to put him in touch with a few people. He was sweet with Orson, too, going on trips with him, driving him around — Orson had a back problem, arthritis triggered by an old injury, some dust-up in the past about which I have not asked questions, Orson was always combative, to put it mildly. Tam made himself thoroughly useful and what happened was in no way his fault, absolutely not, no blame attaches whatsoever and I have told him this again and again but of course he is desolated.

The brakes failed. The car started careering down a hill and Tam steered for the side and the car tipped over. Tam had cuts and bruises but Orson . . . No, I can't talk about it.

Orson would never have made old bones. I console myself with that thought. He had recurrent malaria and he had had every kind of tropical disease — there must have been any number of bugs rampaging around in his bloodstream. If it hadn't been that, something else would have got him, sooner or later.

And now he is laid to rest . . .

. . . and we must all move on. I shall pick myself up, as I have done so many times before, put on a brave face, continue. Orson is in my heart, dear man, despite all, and there are others who need me. Tam is staying here, I have said that he must feel that this is his home for as long as he likes, and he is the greatest support and comfort.

Toby took himself off again immediately after the funeral, and now there is this postcard from *Greece*. It seems he is at this artists' colony that Clara runs and I cannot feel that this is entirely appropriate but he is no longer a child and must make his own choices. Who am I to pass judgment?

I once had a letter from a reader saying that the surname of a character in one of my novels was that of an old acquaintance of hers from Chester; she wondered if my character had connections with that city, and, if so, could I please send her the character's address. I sympathize with this view of fiction; I read in this way as a child and very satisfying it was. The cast of The Iliad *and* The Odyssey *joined me under the eucalyptus trees and the casuarinas; together we defeated boredom. Everything that I read was woven into a fantasy world that merged with reality. My daily life was populated with figures from my own internal narratives, most of them lifted from my reading and tweaked about a bit to suit personal requirements: heroes, gods, mythic beasts, resourceful children messing about with boats in the Lake District — all coexisting reasonably enough with family, friends, and the teeming backdrop of the Middle East in 1942. Books were intimate and entirely relevant. Reading has never been quite the same since; it continues to fuel fiction, but differently. Penelope is no longer myself. This exercise in confabulation has been another kind of experiment, a different way of enlisting story to complement reality, at the opposite end of my life.*

About the Author

PENELOPE LIVELY is the author of numerous award-winning novels, including the Booker Prize–winning *Moon Tiger*. *The Photograph*, her most recent novel, was a *Today Show* Book Club Pick. Her writing has appeared in *Encounter*, *The Literary Review*, *Good Housekeeping*, *Vogue*, *Cosmopolitan*, *The Observer*, and *Woman's Own*, among other publications. She is a fellow of the Royal Society of Literature, a member of PEN, and former chairman of the Society of Authors. Awarded the CBE in 2000, Lively lives in London.